K. B. PELLEGRINO

BERYL KENT AND MIXED MOTIVES

A CAPTAIN BEAUREGARD MYSTERY

© 2022

Livres-Ici
PUBLISHING™

Livres-Ici Publishing™ of WMASS OPM, LLC
265 State Street
Springfield, MA 01103
1-413-788-0652
Livres-Ici Publishing is a registered trademark of WMASS OPM, LLC.
Livres-Ici Publishing books may be ordered through booksellers.

ISBN: 978-1951012212 HC
ISBN: 978-1951012229 SC
ISBN: 978-1951012236 EBook

Library of Congress Control Number: 2022

MAIN CHARACTERS

<u>West Side Major Crimes Unit Detectives</u>
Captain Rudy Beauregard
Lieutenant Mason Smith
Lieutenant Petra Aylewood-Locke
Lieutenant Ashton Lent
Sergeant Ted Torrington
Sergeant Lilly Tagliano
Sergeant Juan Flores
Sergeant Bill Border
Sergeant Bobby Barr

<u>Other Recurring Characters</u>
Chief Coyne
Attorney Norberto Cull
Sheri Cull
Mona Beauregard
Mayor Fischler
Jim Locke
Luis Vargas
Roland and Lizette Beauregard
Liam
Monique Smith
Charlotte Torrington
Martina McKay
Ian Nathan Connault
Oliver Kent

"The police are the public and the public are the police; the police being only members of the public who are paid to give full-time attention to duties which are incumbent on every citizen in the interests of community welfare and existence."

                                –ROBERT PEEL

CONTENTS

1

Notes and Explosions

Beryl Kent, notorious intrepid buttinsky, was at it again and Kay Whiterly was not having it today. As Chief Librarian of the City's main library she shuddered in annoyance, saying, "Beryl, you are always helpful and talented and a worker bee, but you have never known your place, have you?"

"Probably not, but Kay, your placement of these boring books on housekeeping up front is not the best marketing design. Put some murder and romance novels or true crime and LGBT works toward the front. I don't read most of them but others do. You've told me over and over you want more traffic here. They will get you traffic."

"Beryl, have you forgotten the rest of the members on the library board's opinions matter. They have more traditional tastes, and I know for a fact they think you are just a bit too sophisticated in your taste."

"No, they do not. They simply have heard I've been widowed three times and are curious about me. I don't respond to their curiosity making me game for further discussion. That is all. Take a risk, Kay. Try placement for a week and see what happens. The board members only visit on board meeting days. You have two more weeks. Put the new display in and then take it out in a week or ten days."

"I'm employed here, Beryl, while you are a volunteer. There is a difference you know."

"I'll tell them I insisted and they'll believe me. If there is a problem,

I'll get chastised for overstepping. Doesn't bother me. Try it once, Kay. If numbers increase, no one will say a word and your judgment will move into the top tier of library management where it should be. Now don't put the sexiest images and blunt murder images up front. I agree with you there. Find covers with better titles not needing explosive images."

Unaware of an interested listener, the two were startled to be addressed by noted and reclusive murder mystery novelist Jay Bird. "Finally, common sense prevails. Thank you, ladies. Try putting my latest book up front. It's more than a mystery. It's a thesaurus. For instance, do you think 'murderous and murdering' are synonymous? They are not, despite what dictionaries state. Have a read. Better yet, help educate your public to learn by reading fiction."

Jay Bird walked quickly away while the two women searched for his book. Beryl declared, "Quite a pitch for his book. I'd have bought it based on his pitch."

Kay insisted the two words were indeed synonymous although she thought if you used murdering as a participle, therein lay the difference. "Still, Beryl, he has piqued our interest. It is a must read."

West Side MCU Captain Rudy Beauregard sunk deep in his chair slurping double creams and sugars in his latte while questioning his detectives on two snail mails received within the past two days. Normally this morning meeting was to plan the week's investigations, close some cases, and argue over investigative situations and potential perps. Sergeant Lilly Tagliano said, "Captain, they're just words jumbled together and not connected to any case we have. We don't have time for this stuff."

Sergeant Juan Flores, Lilly's most fervent acolyte, kicked her under the table bringing a response. "What, Juan, where's the action here? Let the sender tell us what he or she means. Really this is just garbage."

A visibly annoyed Captain answered, "Do you think, Sergeant, investigating mail that has overlays of mystery is not in our purview? Do you know what the writer means? Don't you think the words sound like a warning? Who cuts out words from a magazine to send a message? Could be a nut case. Could be a true message of warning. Now let's look at it together."

Murderous is an adjective.
Does it describe intent
Murder is a noun?
Or is it always?
Murder is also a verb?
Sometimes?
Murdering is a participle or not?
Intent or action?
Past or present?
Find a body or not?
How do we know?

Sergeant Bobby Barr said, "Could be a trickster like a college kid, Captain. Someone taking an English writing course who is caught up in tense language use bullied by some professor. Thinks it's funny. He has to suffer, so should the police. Language police confounding city police. I would have liked that as a college stunt when I was younger."

Lieutenant Petra Aylewood-Locke insisted her baby Carlotta was not going to a college that encouraged this stupid reporting, explaining she was forced to rewrite a paper for using too many participles. A barrage of 'helping, hindering, playing, talking, working…' and other participles loudly prevailed in the small room inviting a glare from the Captain. He insisted, "Do we have any threat complaints made by potential victim citizens?"

None were acknowledged and they moved on to detectives' reports. Sergeant Barr reported a fire down by Turtle Pond on the twentieth of July. "It's nothing new, but the bonfire got out of control and burned down a lean-to shack the town used to store leaf waste until pick-up once a week. The police on the scene found nothing but beer cans, bottles, drug remains, some needles, and food wrappers. "None of it healthy food, just sweets to feed the pot use. Seems harmless enough with the exception of Mr. Rafferty, a neighbor reporting they were singing anti-Christian songs calling on Satan. He mentioned half the group got naked, but of course he wasn't watching. He just got a glimpse. So he says."

Beauregard questioned, "Lieutenant, have we any other complaints about Satan or witchcraft nonsense?"

She answered, "The usual from that coven church of black arts or some such name. They sell all this stuff. College kids and some ladies with nothing to do are in there. It's really just a shack with an enormous neon sign over by the river near a couple of auto garages. We've never heard of trouble except one time when a teenager's parent complained. Her daughter was only thirteen. We had a uniform visit and they promised to keep her uninterested."

Sergeant Flores shared a report on an event at the larger Hamlet Pond. "A crowd of young adults gathered and were raucous enough to cause traffic problems and families leaving the lake beach area. The complaints included evil language, nudity, drinking, drugs, etc. By the time uniforms got there they looked completely normal, but they did have some black magic symbols, witches items and Ouija boards there. Spirituality appears to be important to Millennials and Gen Xers. They don't go to church, but say they are more spiritual than us and institutions interfere with their relationship with the universe. Crap, I say."

Lieutenant Petra Aylewood-Locke agreed, adding, "Jim, my

psychologist husband, insists the revived interest in astrology and Wiccan is to reduce the stress felt from living in the modern world. Politics, he says, has not helped, but the big culprit is the 24/7 news assaults sending out all kinds of non-researched news, really opinions, which would frighten the soul of the most sophisticated in our society."

Beauregard responded with, "Enough of this. Do we have evidence of criminal activity? I don't care who is a Wiccan and sells jewelry and junk. I've been to Salem on Halloween. Everyone in the crowd looks weird, but not criminal. Let's look at the rest of...."

Millie, the Unit's admin person hustled in with a paper in hand, saying, "Captain, this just came in the mail for you to see, but, more importantly, you have to get over to Junction Road now. There's a big problem. The letter says: 'I warned you. Murderous becomes Murdering.' And it's in those words cut-out from a magazine. I called uniforms to check. They called back and said you folks have to be there and it's a mess."

Beryl was driving by Junction Road on her way to Home Depot. Today was the store's day to receive a delivery of some Bee Balm plants. She'd gotten a call earlier from one of the clerks working there and he insisted she get there before ten after which he would get really busy. Whenever she expressed her planting needs to him and if the inventory wasn't there, he'd call when it did arrive. She thought, *if you are nice to people, they do respond. He goes out of his way for me and I always put an email note to his store manager about his extra kindness. How else would they know about their special employees?*

The line of cars before her signaled a problem, but she could only see a bunch of squad cars, two fire trucks, and several ambulances signaling a possible accident. A few minutes before, Beryl had heard a loud noise. She wondered and whispered a prayer wishing only for auto body damage. As she was almost at the site, she thought, *oh, it's not an accident. Beauregard and Petra are there. Who is the tall detective who's running the show? I remember. He's Lieutenant Lent in Traffic. Petra said he was the best, but when he got his lieutenant's stripes, he was forced over to lead the traffic bureau or unit, whichever is the correct term. It was some police rule that seems silly to me, but maybe is not. I'm going to pull over into this driveway almost opposite the mess. Looks vacant, no one will mind my parking here. Funny, no one else is here; probably too lazy to cross the street. That site is run down over there. Too many police at a rundown home spells something big to me and I don't see any damaged cars, but there's smoke and fire everywhere. As **The National Enquirer** repeatedly used to say, "Inquiring Minds Want To Know."*

Beryl pulled her baseball cap down, donned her mask, pinned on her shirt what looked like a bogus temporary PRESS badge she had from a previous event and headed across the street joining several others. One guy with camera equipment accompanied a pretty woman who spoke into a microphone which Beryl figured was connected by an app to her station. There were about four ordinary, non-press folks, being pushed back by uniforms. One looked vaguely familiar despite the mask while two others were known to her. Beryl was pushed aside by the police as they shooed away the bystanders. She was not questioned by the press people or the police. Taking a pad from her oversized bag, she took notes and photos thinking, *what is there to really see? Big, big police presence! One ambulance was arriving when I got here. One the police call a bus, which looked like the Medical Examiner's wagon is loading two must be dead bodies. They're all covered. A third ambulance just pulled in. Maybe the first ambulance called for a second one.. Do they put more than one injured person in an ambulance? Don't know, but the second ambulance is empty and waiting. I'm thankful I have my roofing monocular. The cheapest and lightest*

I could find was this Roxant Grip Scope. It only weighs about seven ounces. With all his camera lenses, the photographer asked me if the bodies were dead or alive. I told him I couldn't see that well. Love this monocular and I thank my second husband. I would not have even known about carrying one with me if not for him. Of course, I didn't know then, and am not sure now, exactly what he did for a living. He certainly did not install roofs.

Beryl heard her name from a woman's voice behind her. She knew her to be Sergeant Lilly Tagliano. "Beryl, not surprised to see you here, but I must insist you move away. You are not PRESS and I'm moving them back too."

"Sergeant, I am press. I write the town's local column for the **Springfield Republican** and this certainly qualifies as news."

"Please don't make me ask for your credentials, Beryl."

Beryl pulled out a press ID from her bag to a surprised Sergeant who said, "I don't know how you do it, Beryl, but okay. This pass is dated just this year. Did you solicit it after your work in the money laundering case?"

"Sergeant, I don't solicit and you may take that any way you like. For some reason the press, and the local news for television think I'm in the know. I'm not, but they think it. Like the police, I don't have to share everything."

Beryl started to question Lilly, when an explosion resulting in a column of black smoke drove them all back. There was no visibility and Sergeant Tagliano moved forward in front of the group demanding they retreat even further to the rear. There was no need for her to give that direction. Beryl and the other two press people practically ran almost into the street. Beryl thought, *I can see we are safe but still instinctively I moved back to protect myself, while Lilly took charge to protect us. That's the difference that Nate talks about. The difference between a civilian and a professional. I want to act more professionally, but I don't have that kind of experience. Time to learn.*

The black smoke appeared to clear up allowing Beryl to get a view. She could see two injured firefighters sitting on the back of the ambulance. The police had donned a special kind of mask. She knew from past conversations with her friend Colonel Nathan Connault that black smoke indicates excess fuel. Often, it is a sign of manmade substances like engines blowing or the combustion of a fuel site. Why here? It's a commercial area but not an industrial one. The site does not service autos. It looks like a very old home with an attached 1930s style concrete warehouse. What has happened here? She thought, *I'll stay here as long as Lilly lets me. This is big and the Bee Balm will have to wait.*

2
Funny Business in Town

West Side's news travels fast and this day was like no other. Once the identity of the bodies was leaked from police at Bay State Medical's ER, conversations focused on only one subject. Political Fundraiser and business leader Art Richards died in the blaze along with his aide Corinne Thompson. Art had recently moved from his Springfield home near where he was raised to a large, lovely home over by Soule Park, West Side, named for the city's founder, Isaac Soule. The residential change was noted by all political and business commentators who felt 2021 was a recovery year, not a year for those in the know who enjoyed extra political and wealth advantages to express excess in their personal lives. Art had emerged as a woke force by his financial support choices in backing particular political candidates, and his enhanced lifestyle did not reduce criticism from both left and right, at least according to local buzz. Many were confused by this denunciation of a businessman's lifestyle, thinking moving up is the normal road for big timers with money. The commentaries against his lifestyle were generally based on his own criticism of others who were living large. The excess talk created a political side show for commentators, not the least of which was overwhelming sympathy for his thought to be, much maligned wife Darla. The mother of his several children, Darla came from a popular Irish family in another city. What folks reckoned to be a wonderful marriage of two handsome people wound down quickly.

One woman was heard to say, "Another woman interrupting a successful marriage based on too much success and too little discipline." The public insisted Art had been involved in this love triangle for over twenty years, going between Darla's and Corinne's homes.

Others hailed his supporting the success of liberal left candidates, while many criticized the limited source variety of his political donations with big dollars going to candidates who guaranteed support for insurance and financial industries. And as said at times in the Irish way about the newly demised, "Aye, there were some questions!"

One question stuck in many heads was the why of Art and his aide being there together at this strange rather rundown site. And then there were the other two seriously wounded unidentified people. Who are they? Rumor is Art and Corinne were thrown from the blast and hit by debris that killed them both. That was the rumor; whereas the other two had some burns which were thought by the public to mean they were further from the blast. But questions arose, why were they not dead? Why were they not hit by debris when they must have been near to the blast.

Beryl Kent listened to every rumor and tried to fix her brain on which idea supported her vision of what happened. She could not and thought, *well, the universe laid this on my lap. I didn't go looking for a problem to investigate today, but dead bodies in my view can't be ignored. Captain Beauregard and his detectives will be on it. I have a meeting of the library board soon. It will afford me an opportunity to speak with the Mayor's wife. Perhaps Mona, Captain Beauregard's wife, will be there. She often presents on books important to teens. For sure I will get better gossip from her, or maybe not.*

An amateur photographer uploaded the explosion photographs and video he timely took, to the distress of the police and news. Wherever he was stationed, he had captured the explosion and the upheaval with two bodies flying and then pinned down by debris and beams. Naturally, his post of his pictures was immediately taken down from social media. Still, it could be found on far-right media such as GAB and Rumble as well as You Tube. Beauregard and his detectives played it over and over in advance of getting a complete review by technical. The Captain mused, *I don't think we'll find a fatal bullet in their bodies or the scars from a beating. They appear to be moving somewhat before landing. The beams and their impact on landing did the work. Could be, this is not homicide, just a terrible accident. Doesn't mean we won't do all the work to determine just what has happened. I've already heard from every politician because Mayor Fitchett is sick of repeating himself and referred them to me. I'm not the best at public relations, but am stuck with the job.*

Lieutenant Mason Smith interrupted the Captain's reverie. "I have the names of the injured and you are in for a rough ride, Captain."

"Yeah, how could any name make it rougher, Lieutenant?"

"What about biker leader Zed Albion of the Kill2Survive Club and Minister Abu Cason from Springfield?"

"What?"

"Yup, you are in for a rollercoaster ride between criminals, drugs, and church. Not just any church, but Abu is minister of a very connected gospel church. He is into everything from education to politics and the effect of his interest is always disruption. Lots of folks would want him dead, but he, for certain, did not play a role in the explosion. He's known to be petrified of fire. He was in a fire as a child and has some facial scars. Actually, they give him a masculine air, not a deformity. His injury here makes it a toss-up for potential killers.

"Other biker leaders, some national, would want Zed out. Kill2survive Club has been making inroads in drug trafficking by violently interfering with their competition. At least sixty percent of the drive-by shootings have been linked to them, with the police in three cities unable to prove connection. Not one person arrested will open up about Zed and his group. Remember the dismembered body found in the Connecticut River by Longmeadow; it was the leader of a Crips sub-group who was tortured before the dismemberment done while he was still breathing. You don't play with Zed."

"Mason, who can shed light on a minister, a gang leader killer, an important business man and community leader and his lady friend all together in an explosion in an unlikely location in West Side? It's one hell of a story if I can even imagine a story line for this one. Let's get in the conference room. I want our uniforms at the hospital. Make the calls to Springfield police. I'll call the District Attorney. Get to the wife, if the press is not already there."

3

Misogyny, Race, and Crime

Beryl Kent found herself defending Corinne Thompson, a woman for whom she personally had little respect. Her interpersonal exchanges with Corinne centered around Beryl's hospital and charity work wherein both contributed. *I don't like Corinne. She puts people down in a most subtle manner, but they feel it. Despite that, she does good work, although she draws on the financial good work of her lover's businesses. Am I being judgmental? Yup, but I notice she tries to make me feel obligated to her. She invents scenarios for me to join her to do good work, always telling me she'll help me get to know the right people. She has charm, I'll give her that and is handsome, not in a siren's way, but more effectively. I notice she kisses up to important people but avoids any small lunches with minority women. The exception is if the woman has a husband who holds political office. Why do I bother to think about all this now; the poor woman is dead. Beryl, you are better than this. Move your thoughts to a higher plane.*

Marjorie Phipps, wife to Bishop Aaron Phipps, answered Beryl's call. "Come on, Beryl, you know Corinne was uncomfortable with me and all Latin and Black women doing good work. Her boyfriend was as well. I'm the one who's religious. I'll pray for her soul, but I don't excuse her actions. You must remember how she kissed up to Teisha Abbott, said she'd support Teisha's job application with the Mass Department of Mental Health. Later, Teisha discovered Corinne personally called the director of the specific program to say Teisha did not have the necessary skills for dealing with the public. Teisha confronted Corinne, who denied everything."

"Marjorie, I find that unusual. Corinne normally would cover her tracks better. Did Teisha have good info or was she just down about losing the position? Although I think any group would be lucky to hire Teisha. She's a worker and I like her."

"The Director's secretary was one of Teisha's students at community college. She tried to change the Director's decision, but he said that Corinne was speaking for her boyfriend who funded some of their programs. He could not go against that."

Beryl asked, "Was she the one chosen to do the dirty work for him? I thought she was just the pretty face and his lover. Corinne exudes Pollyanna type of sunshine. This behavior is at odds with her profile. Brad Surnani is his axe man. At least it's what I've been told. He's the guy with Art Richards at all news stories on his building projects, news when his businesses go public, charitable investments, etc., not Corinne."

Marjorie said, "Yes, he is the go-to guy for moving projects, but Corinne has often done little dirty jobs like the one against Teisha. The ministers did not like this particular action and their yearly recognition of citizens supporting all citizens awards (C-SACA) did not include Art Richards who has been included for the past five years. Those men knew the squash on Teisha came from Art through Corinne. I heard later Art was upset about it."

"Surnani would have been more judicious if he had taken charge of killing her chances. What was in Teisha's background to make her application for this job important enough to snuff out her candidacy? It's not the most prestigious job."

Marjorie laughingly said, "You know nuthin', dear lady. The job was administrative, required little work, but was an opportunity to meet all the bigwigs. A gal like Teisha is competition for Corinne and don't forget she's twenty years younger. Maybe Corinne wasn't told to nix Teisha's chances; maybe she did it on her own."

Beryl replied, "I don't understand this kind of thinking if it is a fact. Pulling others down does not necessarily create more chances for yourself. Get a reward for hurting others, I just don't get it."

Marjorie laughed. "No, Beryl, you wouldn't. You help the police chase murderers. Dangerous dealings with murderers don't bother you. You understand all the gory details, but you don't 'get' greed, selfishness, or unkindness in everyday life. Means you are an innocent and I am less so."

Beryl laughed. "You are an innocent, Marjorie, and you don't 'get' that."

Minister Abu Cason and biker Zed Albion's backgrounds investigation raised some eyebrows. Detective Mason Smith observed when he read the report, "You just never know, do you? Abu went to grade school with Zed. I'd never guess. One speaks the King's English with a ministerial flourish while the other sounds like an educated city sewer rat with pizzazz."

Sergeant Flores remarked, "Strange bedfellows intrigue me. What else does the report say, Lieutenant?"

Mason read some major excerpts from the men's history. Their commonality rested in juvenile delinquent pranks, drinking, and generally creating havoc in their neighborhoods which between the two kids covered ten city blocks in Springfield. Zed entered the Army after high school while Abu made his way through the University of Massachusetts. Abu had paternal relatives from Sicily who paid his tuition. He performed poorly but made it through, albeit with many discipline problems. He registered as African American on his college applications. Apparently, he had some juice through someone because he was never disciplined when others involved were. His mother is half Irish and she chose his first name. It means 'forever.' His middle name is 'Ireland.'

Sergeant Lilly Tagliano said, "That explains it. The mom is an Irish rebel. Imagine naming your kid, 'Forever Ireland' while being married to an Italian. That's tempting fate."

The Captain walked in while the detectives were laughing. His stern look quieted them and Mason continued sharing the report. The reporting continued defining a change in the two men. Abu went on to graduate school at Trinity in Hartford where he found his calling and entered the ministry.

Meanwhile, Zed received an injury while serving in Iraq. He went on to college, the community college route. He was a phenomenal student and was accepted to MIT. He graduated early in engineering with a minor in African Diaspora Studies.

Mason said, "I didn't know you could minor in Diaspora Studies of any kind. Maybe this minor shows his connection to the minister. Have any of you met Minister Abu?"

Beauregard answered, "I did. I sure as hell would know he was a liberal arts major. He can't shut up. He carries a Bible with him. He spoke at a Chiefs' meeting where I took Chief Coyne's place. I have to say he speaks lyrically, almost swaying you to listen. His Irish and Italian roots are ignored by his congregation. Mona has forced me to attend some famous poets' readings. If you really listen, you realize poets can have a hypnotic effect on folks. I always thought Abu could be dangerous, but also realized he was a great fundraiser for his projects. He has done some great projects. I don't, however, believe God was the center of his universe despite his success as a minister. There is talk out there that he's quite the ladies man."

More of the report was read.

Abu recited the prayers at all organizational meetings wherever our illustrious businessman Art Richards chaired a board. Some in the community thought it was because of Abu's race, but nowhere here does it say what is his race. He is dark olive skinned but not overly dark. He has more of a café au lait complexion. Unlike Zed, who is loaded with tattoos, Abu could be mistaken for a handsome gigolo. However, the two men have worked public events pushing for assistance for every charitable organization formed since the 1980s. Most had to do with advocating for lower sentences for drug possession, AIDS, protection of women on the streets, juveniles in distress, and drug related rehab issues.

Zed, although a biker who supposedly dealt drugs and could be violent, is a family man living in Longmeadow in a lovely traditional home. Interestingly, there was never any opportunity to catch Zed doing anything more nefarious than knocking some heads of difficult bikers who entered his bar. The bar itself is a neighborhood bar serving whatever menu the current chef wants, often leaving patrons uncertain of the offerings. This lack of food choice continuity did not inhibit a regular and large customer base. Surprisingly, there was great diversity in the patronage. There have been rumors about Zed. Rumors from rival biker groups inferring Zed is not what he appears to be. His gang also owns a franchise for auto demolition. This business brings in major profits.

Beauregard said, "He's supposed to be a killer and drug dealer, but also a well-to-do businessman. The two just aren't compatible. Something's off here. The big question is why this group of four was together in an explosion at a rundown building at the same time. Why was anyone there? Have the uniforms go door-to-door about activity at the site. Is this the first of any of the victims' visits? Doesn't compute. Another avenue to follow would be their personal lives. You mentioned Zed has a family, but nothing about Abu. He is a minister and I expect there would be a wife. I'd like to see Zed's tax returns. Follow up."

Sergeant Ted Torrington questioned, "Captain, what about our illustrious businessman and his girlfriend? How do we pursue investigating them. They are high profile. The press will be on us. We ask one question about their private lives suggesting someone may have wanted them dead, and we are cooked."

"Sergeant, they are no different from any person killed in an explosion with the exception of why they would be there in that place. Be nice but be forceful. We can't have citizens dying without understanding cause, whether it is from accident or murder."

Millie rang through to Beauregard's cell with news. "Captain, the DA wants to speak with you."

Moving from the conference room, the Captain took the call. The detectives watched him as he reacted. Beauregard shook his head in a 'no' and slammed his fist on the wall. On his return to the room he said, "Art Richards' wife is dead. She was found in her home hanging from the rustic beam in her kitchen. It's not our case. The DA called to ensure I won't butt in to the case. He insisted my review of the accident should not include any connection to Darla's suicide. The eldest son, Ricky, said the family is in such pain, they simply cannot listen to gossip about their mother's suicide."

Lilly was not to be put off that easily and insisted, "Captain, the death of an important businessman like Art Richards and then finding his wife a suicide, well, the District Attorney will not be able to prevent questions. And we should ask questions of the family as well. Why was their dad at this site is one question they'll have to answer."

Petra, who recently entered the room, spoke up. "You want to know about this suicide? It's questionable. Unfortunately, the Springfield police got there a minute before me. They let me wait in the living room, while they questioned family in the kitchen. The home is quite nice but on the level of a well-kept older home with good furnishings. Nothing stands out and shouts the kind of money Richards has. I talked with the youngest son Tim. He said he could not believe it. He thought his mom was thrilled that his dad was finally leaving the house. She had told Tim, "I'll have some peace. No more of his friends and their wives all trying to outdo each other. I like conversation. I don't like those wives all talking over each other about their designer jewelry and outfits."

Darla was a teacher and a good one according to Tim. He insisted she was always happy even when their dad was a jerk. When once asked about Art's goings-on, she said she was relieved."

Beauregard asked, "How reliable is he, Petra? It may be he's grieving and doesn't want it to be what it appears to be."

"Captain, one would think, but I then talked to the other two sons and the daughter. They were explicit and insisted their mother would never commit suicide. She was a devoted Catholic, and there was no history of mental health problems."

"Petra, at what time did she die?"

"The Medical Examiner said he would not give a time of death until later, but the kids insisted they were there for breakfast with their mother. It is her birthday today. Her suicide must have been in the afternoon. Tim returned to the home and discovered her at 3:00 p.m. Captain, the explosion in West Side occurred in the morning. Did she even know about her husband's death before she hung herself, if she hung herself?"

4

Political Expediency

Beryl happily answered the door ring greeting Nate Connault, her Colonel, with a big hello. He didn't reciprocate with words. Instead he pulled her into his arms and said, "You look wonderful and I damn well missed you, Ms. Buttinsky."

"Nate, I've told you before, I am not a Ms. I have lots of titles but Ms. is a title going too far back for me to feel comfortable."

"I notice you didn't quarrel with the term 'Buttinsky'."

"Unfortunately, dear, I've earned that one. Wait until I tell you what event has my interest now."

"If it's related to an explosion in West Side, help me dear God. She's under my feet again."

"I'm a seer, Nate. I knew there was something off about this. Richards and his girlfriend blown up at a very seedy location. And the other two men hurt who have an unlikely connection. Think about it. I have. It piqued my interest when I saw a minister and a tattooed biker together at political functions. Their presence together doesn't happen occasionally. I've seen them in tandem often. Is the biker involved in a drug case? Is the minister involved in the questionable side of the BLM movement? I must find out. I saw the second explosion which makes me a witness, which in my mind, allows me the duty to discover more. I must validate what I witnessed." And she laughed at the sour set of his face.

"Beryl, I'm working on something that may touch what you're doing now. I hope not, but to be on the safe side, I'll not give you information, if I have it… yet. Please understand."

Beryl's answer deflected his concern about one-way information flow, but raised another issue. *she thinks I'm never going to share my life completely with her. You are so wrong, Beryl. Be patient a while longer, just a short while longer.*

As they moved to the comfortable commercial kitchen with room-warming daisy arrangements in every nook, Nate attempted to appease Beryl. "Look, I have a little more time in this job, Beryl. Ordinarily, my work would not touch our relationship. I mean it wouldn't if you were ordinary, but you're not. I love you. I think you believe me, but I can't explain all my doings and travels. I will try not to interfere with your involvement in whatever you choose to be involved in. Does that work for you, Beryl?"

"Nate, you imply in every sentence that what I do is either not necessary, or a hobby. I don't waste my time exploring non-important events. I am a downright reality check girl. I do hate it when we can't share, or shall I say you can't share. I'll accept it for now, but not forever. Just be careful with your wording, words matter."

"Oh dear God, you're not talking 'me too,' are you?"

"No! Don't jump to conclusions about me. You know better, Nate."

"Words are important and I don't jump to conclusions about words alone. The same word can be interpreted differently. Context is everything. Beryl, I don't always have the words for you. Or you interpret my words other than my intent."

Beryl smirked but did not answer. She brewed lattes in front of them at the counter and pushed a plate full of warm beignets hoping to soften their emotions as she related her experience at the accident site. He smiled as she filled in the details with the stage presence of an actress. Beryl's hands shook when she visualized for him the horror of the moment. She left nothing out and included Teisha's story of betrayal by Corinne. She asked, "Did you know Art Richards? He was important in the business community and his reach was national."

"I've met him many times, but I did not personally know him. He must have been astute in his business dealings. If you examine his transactions and acquisitions, he rode the interplay between investments and government opportunities. I've been at parties for lobbyists where his money flowed at a greater level than from other project interested investors. That alone speaks to about fifty percent of his success. His assistant/go-to guy Brad Surnani is phenomenal in his judgments. He knows which politician with the most power is available in any opportunity. He is trusted. Trust is important and must be earned. One quality his Brad Surnani has is his ability to keep his mouth shut."

"Nate, why would Richards use Corinne to deep six Teisha? Wouldn't Brad be smoother for that type of work?"

"He would be smoother. Richards would not ask Corinne. And if Richards lost out on a good citizen award, he'd have been pissed at who was the cause. I don't know the answer."

"What about the two injured men? A minister and a biker appear to be an unlikely duo."

"Appearances aren't everything. Look at you. You're having lattes with me. Who could compute on that likelihood?"

"I don't think we are an unlikely pair – a magnetic connection between the spy and the buttinsky seems obvious."

"You're reading too much sci-fi, Beryl."

"Nate, you are evading my question. It's called redirecting so you don't have to answer. I won't be deterred. What is behind deceiving appearances?"

"Beryl, you are in my territory again and I can't give you an answer."

"But if I find out on my own, will you affirm?"

"Yes, but you won't, my dear Beryl."

Amico, Beryl's rescue dog stopped their conversation with his incessant barking. Beryl quickly answered the ringing bell only to be confused by the visitor on the doorstep. West Side MCU Captain Beauregard greeted her with a smile. He was accompanied by Sergeant Flores. The smile alone astonished her, but it was outdone by his words. Before she could say the niceties, Rudy said, "Beryl, you're looking great today. I hope I haven't interrupted a meeting. I'm pleased to see your guest Nate Connault here, and, well, I thought we should all have a conversation about the explosion before you jump in the middle of something."

"Captain, I think you're more interested in Nate's actions than mine, but won't you both come on in and enjoy a latte with us."

After they settled in Beryl's kitchen allowing Rudy and Juan to say hello to Nate, Rudy spoke first. "Beryl, has Norbie Cull connected with you yet?"

"Norberto Cull, most noted defense attorney, why would he contact me and about what? The Bleeding Man case is over and done with. It wouldn't be about your car accident case. I had no role in that."

"You are a witness in the second explosion at Junction Road. Norbie will be looking to interview you about what you saw. Two of the victims are trying to retain him. Unfortunately for me, you are a known witness. I'm here to listen to your story before you speak to the press or Mr. Cull. Beryl, this is a police matter. I don't have to remind you of protocol when dealing with an open case. Use your discretion."

Beryl did not react with a wise quip, surprising the Captain, Sergeant, and the Colonel. She pretended as if he had not made the jab, throwing Rudy off. "Now, Rudy, I'll tell you what I saw if you don't interrupt. Then, you may ask your questions for I know you will have some."

Beryl relayed her view of the site in detail. And questions were asked.

Rudy said, "You just saw the second explosion, how did you know about the bodies flying in the air in the first explosion?"

"Rudy, the same way you knew. I saw the bystander's video."

"That video also showed the explosion. Did the two explosions look the same to you?"

"Rudy, are you trying to trap me? I know the second explosion I viewed ended with a cloud of black smoke. I'd only looked at the first explosion video for seconds before it was taken down. I'd have to see it again to figure out if the smoke in both videos are the same. I can't be sure, so I can't answer you now."

Rudy questioned, "Who else did you see at the scene just before or after the explosion? Think carefully."

And she did, listing all police she knew by name, firemen she did not know, the two press members, and several bystanders. The Captain wanted descriptions of the press members and the four bystanders she mentioned. Beryl groaned. "Rudy, I didn't really look at them. I don't know if I'm good at descriptions."

This remark raised a groan equal to Beryl's. She responded, "I'll try. The photographer was not a big man. He struggled with his bags. The reporter was Stacia Kovac. You've seen her alternate with Biggs Travis on television sometimes at events like this. But you know all this. The four bystanders had one man who looked familiar, but I don't know him. Two other men there were unknown to me and were average looking but well dressed in rugged clothing. You know, with good labels. The woman I know is Teisha Abbott. She was driving by, like me."

Beryl did not tell the Captain what she had heard about Corinne and Teisha, thinking, *Teisha wouldn't have the tech knowledge for explosions. The Captain will hear about it on his own. To me this story is gossip. I have to draw a line somewhere.*

"Beryl, I know Teisha Abbott. Thanks, our film did not catch her at the scene. Can you tell us who the other man is you thought you might have seen before? Give me a description. It will help separate him from the others. We've identified two men. Take a look at this photo."

Three men were in the photo, two of whom faces could be seen. The third was the man Beryl remembered she thought she had seen before. His back was to the camera and he wore a baseball cap and mask. She promised Rudy she would think about him and hopefully later identify him, saying, "He did see me and didn't show the slightest recognition. Maybe I've never met him before, but he does look familiar. Even his body stance reminds me of someone. I just can't place it, Rudy."

"And you don't know the other men? One knew you."

"Which one and who is he?"

"John Conlon, Brad Surnani's top assistant; you do know who Brad Surnani is, Beryl?"

"I do, barely, but I don't remember meeting John Conlon. What would Brad's assistant be doing at the site of this explosion? If they weren't connected to Art Richards, I'd not be so interested. What's his story?"

Beryl felt a slight kick from Nate under the table leaving her wondering what could be wrong with her question. She found out quickly when Rudy said, "Remember the rules, Beryl. It's an open case. You tell me what you know but I can't share with you."

Nate asked, "Captain, it will get out that John Conlon was at the site before the second explosion. I am certain because he is well-known, others will offer info on his whereabouts for the whole morning. And that will get out. What interests me is how John knows Beryl, but Beryl doesn't know John."

"It interests me too, Nate. John says he has been in several groups where Beryl has spoken. He just couldn't remember what they were. Any ideas, Beryl?"

Beryl thought about her several speaking engagements, realizing most were before women's groups. She did speak on the SPEAK OUT concerning an audit of some spending of a large grant given to the city. The grant was from a national tech company with offices in the area, (DSI) Digital Storage, Inc. The grant backed up by federal monies was accepted by the City for job assistance for workers displaced by the pandemic. Within weeks of the receipt of the funds by West Side, there were rumors of moneys being disbursed to support several well-known commercial real estate investors who had lost tenants due to COVID-19. Beryl explained her conducting the Speak-Out. "Rudy, our government watch committee of the West Side Women's League picked up some gossip about the misplaced spending. Not having any entre into this world, we decided to do a forum on government. We invited all the politicians and Mayor to the speak-out. I presented what we knew which was not grounded in certainty. We had a large audience with citizens present at twice the number of politicians. We had done a freedom of information request for the grant, its requirements, and expenditures. The answer to the request was delayed with a date scheduled for after the meeting. That delay alone lit a bit of a fire. Perhaps John Conlon was there that day but I did not know him. I could get the sign-in sheet for the Speak-Out. The ladies would not let anyone in who did not sign-in. Of that I am certain."

Nate was interested and asked, "What info did you get for your efforts, Beryl?"

Slightly defensive, Beryl said, "Very little, and before you say it was a waste of time, it wasn't. Mayor Fischler had asked his grant director to speak. She didn't show, and quit her job on the next Monday. Her name is Jody Calhoun and she's now employed by one of Art Richards' companies in Virginia. It is my understanding that there will be no further investigation, but new spending will be according to the grant guidance. So, no evidence do I have."

Nate replied, "You did good. It's in my mind as good a result you could ever have achieved. You stopped the cash flow to the big wigs. Politically, the past is always the past especially if it can be buried. In this case it is buried."

Beauregard, who hated political expediency said, "Was one of Richards' companies a recipient, Beryl?"

"I don't know, but if it were one of them, could it be connected to Richards' death?"

Rudy responded, "Don't go there, Beryl. I'll speak with the Mayor and get the list of recipients. The grant would have to be one hell of a grant to be connected to the possibility of murder. Evidence, Beryl, without it, do not jump to conclusions."

Nate said, "Rudy, how many grants did DSI give out aside from the one to West Side? If there were many, there may be great importance in shutting down any investigation and publicity. And, Beryl, did your hearing get press?"

"No, and I was disappointed as were my other committee members. There was just a mention on the television news of our committee hearing and a small article in the paper on a back page. It made our public hearing look like a waste of time."

5

Obituaries and a Surprise

The citizens of western Massachusetts wallowed in the obituaries of its noted citizens. Conversations included the thought, if Netflix agents were to read the local papers or listen to the news, a new television movie would now be negotiated. Then again, discussion abounded regarding what really happened. Did Darla plan the explosion and then commit suicide? After years of Richards' living a dual life, now that he was moving into the high life, had she decided enough was enough? This type of thinking was immediately shut down by those who knew Darla. They said she was a practicing Catholic. She never sought a divorce and would have done well financially if she had. Her children were her prime focus. She didn't have a special male friend. They thought she was just a very nice lady married to a philanderer.

Another conversation heard included the minister and the biker as contract killers for Richards' business rivals. The motives related to some recent stories of Richards using political pull around the country to gain footholds into various industries such as solar and wind energy, the growing Cannabis Industry, and his current taking over large tracts of commercial buildings at basement prices resulting from the pandemic. Perhaps the minister's church success was due to this type of illegal activity. Maybe the biker resented the legalization of the use of pot which would result in major interference with street drug sales.

Corinne Thompson was chosen as a third potential culprit by those in the know. There had been some talk recently about her relationship with one of Richards' employees. Some close to Corinne said she was newly in love and not with Art Richards. They insisted the sexual relationship had dwindled which made sense since many thought sex can't carry such a stronghold after so many years. Corinne had done well financially through her connection with Richards. She was an attorney and a smart one at that. Corinne was also a principal in some local businesses. The investments had done well, but it was commonly assumed that Richards did the original financing for them. Bankers sometimes spill their secrets and, in this case, all talk relayed back to a particular banker who previously had a liaison with Corinne. The public talk referred to Corinne's motives based on her attempt to rid herself of a now annoying boyfriend, but of course she was now dead. That ended that idea.

Despite all considerations relative to motive, none looked at anything but personal motives. Art Richards was generally regarded as a 'good' businessman who was approachable by anyone needing help. Who would want to kill him and in such an insidious manner? It must have been an accident.

———

Colonel Connaught tried his best to keep up with Beryl's stream of consciousness remarks on the accident. He listened carefully, aware that Beryl might feel the call to action to investigate whenever the mood drew her. This could be dangerous right now. He knew a great deal about some of the parties involved and was tasked to do his own investigation into the explosion based on some history on the biker. He could not share that history with Beryl and felt certain she may shortly figure it out. Oh, to the good would that be, but not too soon. And he could not share. He thought, *the problem with loving Beryl is keeping her away from my work. She can't keep her nose from sniffing out problems. Her intelligence is skewed by her tendency to check out anything suspicious. And God forbid if a situation involves an injured party, she is fearsome. Related problems are not important. But, she is beautiful and so interesting.*

"Beryl, we are here together. Can't we be more romantic than trying to understand a deadly explosion and its causes."

"Nate, I'd love a little romance. What ya thinking, ex-military guy is the perp?"

"This," as he drew her into his arms and all was good for five minutes.

Her cell phone rang just as his did. They answered their calls which took seconds. "Nate, what was your call about? Was it a death report?"

"Yup. Tell me who died in your call. Maybe it is the same person."

Beryl said with some rancor, "Why can't you be the first to answer? It was Teisha Abbot who was killed when her car hit a tree over on Camp Road in town."

Nate answered, "Same."

"Do you know what time she died and why would someone be telling you about her death?"

"No, I don't. Think about it, Beryl, I wouldn't be getting the call if there were not problems related to my people. Who called you, Beryl?"

"Marjorie Phipps, the Bishop's wife. She is the only one I know who knew I would be interested in Teisha. Teisha's so young. I'll call Marjorie back. She was getting another call when we spoke. What would Teisha be doing on Camp Road? It's practically deserted at that time."

Beryl tried calling Marjorie. She was not successful. Nate gave her a hug, saying, "Let's grab some dinner. On the way I'll make a connection to a friendly reporter I know. She'll tell me the gossip on the accident."

They hit the West Side Country Diner for a light supper. Nate asked, "Have you tried eating here before? It may look common but the food is the greatest. Typical old style American but as pure as American new cuisine."

"No, I never even noticed its existence before. It must be a destination, located on this side street three streets away from Main Street and it still has a full parking lot. Can't imagine how it was allowed in given our strict zoning laws. How'd you find it, Nate?"

"I eat out often because the job requires it, and I find I search for home style cooking. I want a place with no bar so I won't encounter trouble. This place is my kitchen away from home. They serve great hamburgers, real fries, good entrees, homemade puddings and pies, and a large assortment of salads for the ladies. Breakfast is served all day. My favorite here is shepherd's pie."

"Nate, you're the same guy who gives lessons on French wines. You do surprise me."

"Honey, no one grows up in America on French wines. Mashed potatoes with roast chicken is a basic. It's all here. No grits are normally seen, that remains a Southern requisite. As to the zoning issue, there were no strict zoning requirements here when West Side was more rural. In the eighties, a building boom initiated the city fathers to take on the task and they did it in spades. The town or city whatever, now has some of the toughest residential zoning in the state. You need a three-quarter acre parcel for a simple small home and if there are more than three bedrooms in a planned home, the acreage requirement goes up. Some towns' zoning goes back to the early nineteen hundreds when no one had an automobile. Now of course there could be three or more autos to one home. Thus, the increased requirement for acreage for houses with more bedrooms. It's logical."

"Nate, the effect is an upper class move toward maintaining big property values, isn't it?"

"Maybe, but the town fathers like it. If there's less population density in an area, there is less requirements for fire, police, and educational issues to be satisfied."

She sighed. "Ah, money is always at center, isn't it? Budgets available for other categories. I suppose City Streets and Engineering can keep up with the work load. Looking around, we really do have some of the least undamaged roads in the area.

"And we have a great police force with Rudy as chief of Major Crimes. He's here because he can do the job with the least interference from politicians. The brass does try to interfere occasionally but have not been successful."

Beryl happily perused the menu and said, "It's all here, Nate. All my childhood favorites. Chicken croquettes with smashed potatoes and a small salad. I'm in heaven. What are you having?"

"Don't you listen my dear, Beryl? I'll have shepherd's pie and the Scotch broth."

They ordered and while waiting, Nate explained he may be out of the country for a few weeks and he was unable to share his destination with her. "Look, Beryl, while I'm gone, please don't get involved in the Richards and Thompson death cases or Darla Richards' supposed suicide or Teisha Abbott's accident. Like you, there are too many bad happenings in a short period of time, but I have a sixth sense telling me there's danger. Don't get too close, please. I love you. Don't get too close."

Beryl was poised to debate when her lunch was served. Her appetite took hold and between greedy bites into her mashed potatoes, she answered, "Your career and I don't sync, dear Nate. When will you have normal work or retirement?"

"Soon, Beryl, soon."

Sergeant Lilly Tagliano walked into the staff meeting and almost dropped her coffee on the table. Petra said, "Do you have the dropsies,

Lilly. It's the second time in two days you've been clumsy. That's not your forte. That's for the desk jockeys like Mason."

Mason growled, "I'm not clumsy, Petra. I'm just a big man in offices too small to accommodate his girth."

Petra laughed. "Yeah, it's the building's fault. I love your explanations for all complaints attributed to you."

Juan was watching the conversation and questioned Lilly. "You have seemed to be discombobulated lately, Lilly. Is there something bothering you?"

Sergeant Bobby Barr answered Juan, saying, "Your little fiancée is wondering when's the wedding. What's taking so long for you to build a nice house for her and start raising little Juan's?"

Lilly excused herself with, "Captain, I'm not feeling so well. And shut up, you guys. We have a couple of years before any wedding."

With Lilly absent, a long silence prevailed until the Captain entered the room. Reporting according to agenda started with Bill Border. He was in the process of highlighting irregularities in Art Richards' recent behavior, when Petra excused herself. All detectives with the exception of the Captain guessed her destination. Given not one detective made a wise remark, the Captain was now queued in and said, "What's up here? Where's Lilly and where is Petra headed?"

All eyes looked at Juan Flores who sputtered, "I don't know, guys, but I sure as heck am going to find out."

Juan left the room. The Captain hesitated but said, "Not our business, Detectives, sounds personal to me. Back to your report, Sergeant."

Border continued. "Richards has sold off some of his larger investments, mostly those in commercial real estate in large cities. Not surprising now given what COVID has done to that market. Word is he took a bath."

———

Juan stomped into the overly large ladies room. "What's up, Lilly?"

As he spoke he saw his Lilly crying her eyes out and Petra hugging her like no tomorrow. "Lilly, what's wrong? Why can't you tell me? Why tell Petra and not me? What could be so bad that my bad ass Lilly would cry?"

Petra glared and said, "Think, Juan. Think, just what would make Lilly cry her eyes out?"

Juan's eyes showed a glimmer of knowledge and he said, "Are you pregnant? Is that what this is all about? Tell me. Why tell Petra first? Why not me? I'm the father? Don't I have a right to know?"

"There you go, Juan. It's all about you. Yes, you're the father, but I'm the one whose life will change. I'm the one who'll leave the force. I'm the one who'll get fat and dumpy. I'm the one who won't have the big Mexican/Italian wedding. Our parents will hate me or us. It's all ruined…all our plans. That damn COVID did this."

And she cried and cried while pushing Juan away when he tried to comfort her. Petra could almost feel Juan's confusion. Then, in a surprise change, Juan started laughing. Since both women thought this was not a laughing matter, they practically sputtered together, "What's wrong with you, Juan?"

"Not a damn thing is wrong. Life is wonderful. Lilly, my parents were married in a little chapel with just the best man and maid of honor. Look how happy they are. You want to stay on the force, you stay. I'll move out of MCU. I'd be great in crime prevention. Mamita and Papi will be thrilled with a new baby coming. It's all good, Lilly, don't make it a problem. It's not a problem. I'll talk to your family. They'll be happy, I just know it. It's fate telling us we were taking too long."

And she did not look up. She kept crying. Petra signaled Juan to shut up and let her be. What they deemed an endless amount of time transpired before Lilly reacted and said, "I'm too old to have an accidental pregnancy. Who is going to believe that and if they do, they'll think I'm stupid."

Looking a bit goofy but happy, Juan said, "I like stupid, Baby. Not to worry."

"Now, don't you go telling anyone, Juan."

"Sorry, Baby, but I'm telling the world, only after you agree to marry. Next Sunday will be a good day. What do you think?"

"I want a church wedding, Juan. That can't be arranged that quickly."

"Lilly, I'll get a church wedding for a week from Sunday. You get a dress and start inviting family. You'll have to do email and phone calls. No time exists for snail mail. You better ask the Captain for a few days off. Petra, can we pull it off?"

Petra said, "You bet we can. I'll help you with the priest over at St. Agatha's in town. He'll figure an available time for your wedding on Sunday afternoon. It'll cut into his golf game, but he'll do it."

Lilly through more tears asked Petra, "Will you stand up for me, Petra?"

"I can't believe you'd ask. Just assume, Lilly. I feel privileged. Yup, and I need a special dress. What's your favorite color? I'll get a dress in that color. And I know a great florist…."

And the discussion took a turn keeping the three of them busy until Millie entered the room and said, "Juan Flores, get out of the ladies room. I need some privacy."

Naturally, Millie was informed on the upcoming nuptials and joined the wedding planning.

6

Library Speaker

The West Side Library Community Room was abuzz with a crowd large enough to require extra folding chairs. This was a big event. A local mystery author, normally a curmudgeon who rarely invited conversation, had agreed to speak. His topic was, "Community Libraries Must Reach Out Beyond the Ordinary." Jay Bird was central to the Library Board's last meeting discussion. Kay Whiterly gave an impressive talk on display marketing for the library. There was resistance to her current display featuring mystery, murder, and reality crime. One man questioned, "Don't we have enough crime in West Side what with Beauregard solving all these serial murders. Do we want to home grow new ones to keep him in business."

There was laughter amongst the members, but Beryl saved the day with some stats on selection tools libraries use. She insisted readership is a major guideline for libraries. Since this library did a great business in mystery, sci-fi, real crime, and LGBT genres, why wouldn't the library give display to what readers wanted. One board member headed a large marketing firm and he joined her band wagon. This helped quiet the naysayers. The member insisted, "Why don't we invite that Jay Bird, the famous mystery writer who lives in town to speak. Kay, you said he wanted his latest book displayed. Let him tell us and our community why."

Following the command, Kay Whiterly sent our several formal

'requests to present' to Jay Bird, followed up with emails, but he did not call. Beryl, who often appeared to have the dumbest luck, quite fortuitously met Jay at a local coffee shop, and dared to question him. "Mr. Bird, you placed the chief librarian Kay Whiterly in a great deal of trouble with her board of trustees. She went out on a limb to display your book as you requested and now you won't give a little book signing talk to the community. I think you are ungrateful, not reclusive, and I'm embarrassed for you."

Jay Bird flushed a brilliant pink, stammering, "I don't do book signings anymore. Everyone knows I avoid the public eye. Why should I feel guilty? I asked you both to do something reasonable which would help the library. I didn't say I would pay for my suggestion. I think you should be embarrassed, Ms. Kent."

If Beryl was frustrated with Jay's answer, her actions did not reveal it. Instead, she replied, "Nice return, Jay, but I've read your latest book. Anyone who can create a whole novel around the meaning of a few words surely understands layers of social obligations. I can see you are not overly shy when you can bounce back with an attack on me for questioning you. You may truly desire to be reclusive, but you are not afraid of an audience. Why can't you be appreciative of Kay, who went out on a limb with your idea? By the way, we've never been introduced. How did you know my name?"

Jay Bird slowly formed a big grin. "Well, Ms. Kent, you were all over the papers wearing blood from the bleeding man on the ground. I was mesmerized by the possibilities behind the accident. Even I could not have formed a plot equal to the reality behind that story and that's if I'm truly privy to all the facts. I'm pretty certain I'm not, despite my close relationship with the West Side Police Department. So, you think I'm not appreciative. I'll tell you what, I'll speak if you come to the signing and have dinner with me afterwards. How's that for an accommodation?"

"It'll be a late dinner. You'll have to find a restaurant serving after nine p.m. Not an easy task in this area. The library functions are all at 6:30 in the evening and generally last until 8:30."

"That's my worry, Ms. Kent, not yours. May I call you Beryl?"

"Of course, now that we're friends and you are willing to step up and help our library."

Beryl smiled as she remembered the previous exchange. Nate would say she didn't have the personality to be embarrassed or ashamed. How wrong he was, but she knew, that observation of her was true for the previous Beryl, the one before who lost three husbands through no fault of her own.

The crowd in the library grew to fill all the seats with nine latecomers standing in the back of the room. She knew quite a few of the attendees. She thought, *it's still COVID but only half of the people are wearing masks and the chairs are not six feet apart, more likely three feet in distance. Why am I worrying about it when I am vaccinated and most of these people are? No one's kissing each other. I hated getting the vaccination when it has so little history, but I just threw my hands up and reminded myself of the many risky things I had done in my life. Guess these folks are dying for in-person entertainment. OOPS! Shouldn't use that word dying.*

Jay Bird entered the room and his resemblance to the archetypical serious author from his dress in a corduroy jacket with patches on the elbows and a rugged blued denim shirt was striking. Jay brought out a few murmurs of, "He is so good looking in person" from some of the younger gals. Beryl noticed two West Side detectives in the audience. She remembered them from the 'Bleeding Man' case. They appeared not to be on duty, dressed casually and clearly enjoying the few refreshments served.

Jay spoke for close to forty-five minutes sharing the plotting process and his style of choosing characters. He brought up the recent explosion that killed and maimed without naming names. He explained that events such as the questionable deaths of two people made writing a story almost an urgency in his mind. Jay said he wrote fiction and rarely dabbled in reality crime, but felt most plots include real life happenings in some fashion. He ended his talk with, "Look to fiction writers' works and you'll almost always see in mystery fiction a connection to some real-life horror."

When he opened the forum to questions, Beryl and Kay felt some discomfort. The questions centered on how Jay Bird would approach solving a case such as the one so recently in the news. Did he believe it was an accident? Wasn't the association of the two injured people bizarre, and did it point to a conspiracy? After a half hour of these types of questions Kay interrupted and said, "Jay, your latest book defines words and uses definitions to discover the murderer. As a librarian, I am thrilled to see an author paying attention to words and their multiple meanings. Could you elaborate on your inspiration for this novel?"

Jay Bird gave a thank-you grin stating, "Kay, you and your library did. I am often in the carrells working because of the silence it offers. I must turn off my phone. I find that difficult to do at home. For my breaks, I watch your public. I listen to them and am often shocked when I hear one of your librarians answer a basic question which I thought shouldn't need an answer. And in one case, the questioner could not understand why a word on a book cover could have a secondary meaning from how she used the word. Naturally, I think about murder on a daily basis for my plots. This time I thought of murder and related words in a different way."

The discussion trailed into all kinds of words and their uses in different situations. Beryl thought, *this discussion is now out of hand. All the English teachers present are layering all the 'onomies' and mixing polysemy with etymology. Ugh, I've had enough of this.*

She held her watch out to Kay motioning her to close shop for the evening. It was early, but Kay welcomed the push from her. They both had the common idea the audience would leave upon Kay's generous thanks to the audience amidst groans, applause, and some gripes. They didn't take end, as end. It took Jay's slowly receding out the door to complete the end signal to the attendees.

As Beryl and Kay said their good-byes, Kay thanked Beryl. "There was so much excitement and interest tonight, I noticed our most difficult board members fascinated by Jay and the audience's discussion. Thank you, Beryl, without you I could not have achieved this."

Beryl left as quickly as she could. Jay had said he would meet her at the new Turkish restaurant in town which was close by. The owner had agreed to keep the kitchen open for them. Beryl had never been there and was surprised when she entered the main door to see a vision of business at the bar and at the tables. The food smelled wonderful and reminded her of her travels to Turkey with her second husband. They were good times for her and she had to keep the tears back from the memory thinking, *can't I ever close a door completely?*

The owner was at the door waiting for her. He said, "Ms. Kent, I'll escort you to your table. Mr. Bird is waiting."

Jay sat in the last corner booth at the far end of the restaurant. She thought as she approached the table, *he really does avoid the spotlight, even when dining out in a public place. No one would notice him back here.*

Good manners were not lost on the author. He stood and graciously asked if she minded sliding to the inside of the booth saying it had the best view of the comings and goings. Beryl laughed, retorting, "Am I supposed to be looking at what's going on here when I'm dining with you?"

The back and forth began between the two referencing the outlaw Jesse James who supposedly always sat with his back to the wall so he could see if someone was coming into a place with the idea to shoot him. Jay pointed out it was a good practice to be aware of one's surroundings at all times. His further explanation centered on his writing career as a murder mystery novelist and his military service. "Not unlike you, Beryl, life has shaped me. I am not as they tag me, a curmudgeon, but I am slightly reclusive. As a native New Englander, I'm almost steeped in cynicism and suspicion, but I truly like people. I don't necessarily want to distance myself from others. I want to assess them before I get close. I know you think I don't like people, but I do. I also do like my privacy. The only folks I don't like are backstabbers, and the world seemingly abounds with them."

"How do you think life has shaped me, Jay?"

"You are hyper-aware of your surroundings which I think is a great balance for your deep feelings of empathy. I see a reticence when folks try to get too close to you. You then quickly pull back. You have suffered but it does not show. That kind of empathy, which may be natural for you, has been honed by experience. I'll wait for you to tell me about your life. It would do no good to push you."

The waiter interrupted and drinks were ordered. Jay did not try to order for her nor did he make suggestions. She thought it was odd, *most men have a favorite drink and I am always assured I would love their particularly favorite cocktail. It's nice not to have to say 'no' in the first instance.*

Scrutinizing the menu, they made quick decisions. Jay asked, "What have you decided for your entrée and are you up for appetizers?"

She mentioned the lateness of the hour and said, "I'll have two appetizers for my entrée."

She explained that the adana kebap, dolma, and potatoes and onions in olive oil with a name she'd never seen before and could not pronounce and a rich honey kind of layered lough for dessert looked awesome. Jay was impressed with her choices. Then he went on to insist she was a constant planner and now understood she had planned her confrontation with him about his appearing at the book signing. "You are quite devious, Beryl. For all my plotting, I normally don't deal in subterfuge, where you clearly are a master."

She took mild offense and said, "No way am I alone at planning reactions to possible affronts. I've read two of your novels. Jay, your mind is all over the place. You place red herrings everywhere. You lead the reader on a merry path. I did however solve your mysteries but only toward the end, and I am a natural at investigation and putting two and two together. Don't you tell me for a minute you're not devious."

Orders were placed and the couple discussed the book signing event. Jay was surprised he could not keep the audience focused on his book, saying, "You cold heartedly convinced me to do my civic duty and the audience was more interested in the potential for real crime. After all, we don't know yet if Art and Corinne's deaths were an accident or not. I don't get it, but what I do get is my appearance was not as important as you made me think."

"Jay, just how disconnected from people's emotions are you? Your appearance set off a discussion on an important event. The audience knows that two of their own neighbors were killed in an unlikely blast while two others were injured. The other two's presence at the blast site together and with Art and Corinne would be enough to make the casual observer notice.

"Further, because you are a mystery novelist, they think you may have insight. They were totally silent for forty minutes while you discussed plotting and character choices. Get your head out of your ivory tower and think for a minute."

"Beryl, I thought for a minute we might have a lovely dinner. You make it difficult when I feel I have to constantly defend myself. Do you dislike me? And if so, why?"

Beryl laughed and her gaiety was interrupted by dinner being served. Dinner appeared to subdue the two when halfway through, Beryl said, "I must have been really hungry to have gone after you that way. Please forget my inconsiderateness."

Jay was already halfway through a Turkish sub of some kind which was a masterpiece of enormity from Beryl's perspective. He did answer, "All's forgiven and you made a valid point. I do not mix easily and I guess it has made me a trifle insensitive. My military experience forced me to sit back and keep quiet. You know I've read about you. You are not the only one with research skills."

"Well, you are a writer and I'd expect nothing less from you. Now just what have you discovered from my past? I'm comfortable because there's no blue sheet on me nor do I have a criminal record. Tell me what you've heard."

He laughed. "No one would dare get a blue sheet on you and take charge of your life. However, I didn't check on a criminal record because I never even imagined such a thing. As to what I've heard, you are a take charge lady with friends everywhere. Beauregard regards you as the best of the pain-in-the-ass citizens who interfere with his work. Says you're smart. Norbie Cull says you have good instincts and would like you on all his juries. Mona Beauregard, the Captain's wife, says you are good for the force; you keep them thinking. And on and on and on! What else do you need to know?"

"Jay, you're a writer, protagonists need to have flaws. How do you know Norbie Cull?"

"Beryl, what makes you think you're not a minor character instead of being a protagonist? Your self-esteem shows brilliantly here. You have flaws. You flout danger. You are nosy way beyond the norm. And you have led a most interesting life. How's that?"

"And I want to know how you are in the inner circle of Beauregard, his wife, and Cull."

"I'm not. I figured it out from reading the news and listening to the ladies at the library and I happen to know Norbie Cull personally. I still try to stay out of the public's eye, but have big ears for stories."

"What about the explosion case? Accident or murder?"

"Or something in between, Beryl!"

"What do you mean something in between? What about the unlikely company of the four present at the scene?"

"May not be so unlikely if there was a business reason for them all to be there. That site is up for a private sale and the price requested is, I heard, quite high. I asked myself, just out of curiosity, why so expensive and had no answer. Then I asked Jonah Cronin, the commercial real estate guy. He said there are actually over ten acres going back on the site, phenomenal frontage on one of the busiest main drags in town, and until recently, no one thought it was for sale. It's an old shabby concrete small building zoned both commercial and industrial. It is a gem. Maybe the four wanted to buy it. Cronin's now the broker for the property, but it's not being advertised. It's a private sale."

Beryl had not known about the land and thought, *for the first time, there is a potential motive. What motive is it, greed or land use questions? Maybe it has nothing to do with the personalities of the victims.*

"What an interesting possibility. Jay, you haven't answered the direct question, is it murder or an accident? And what about Art Richards' wife's suicide?"

"I am not the fountain of wisdom on the subject, Beryl. My instinct tells me there is a real problem with it being an accident. I saw the explosion for just a minute on YouTube. I have a serious problem calling it an accident. Did you see the video?"

"Yes. What did you see leading you away from an accident as cause?"

"The bodies had some movement as they flew in the air and landed, but it wasn't a free and frightened looking movement. Their moves looked slight. I want to know what they were doing before the explosion and where the bomb or igniter was in relation to their location on the site. Were Art and Corinne under the influence? That could explain the lack of great movement. As to Art's wife, I knew her and she would never commit suicide. It was totally against her moral code. She was quite a lady. That death is questionable and terribly sad."

7

Real Estate

Attorney Norberto Cull clicked off his cell, signally his assistant Sheila with a scowl, saying the real estate deal had gone south. She thought, *there goes my extra big bonus this year. Norbie loved this deal, but I did remind him that his role was questionable. He did the work for the current owner of the building based on his own old-time relationship with Barney McAuliffe. What now? I can't wait to see if this deal is involved with the deaths of Richards and Thompson. I don't know who I liked less. Probably Richards. You know who he is, at your first meeting with him. He can't hide his ugly side behind his handsome face. Corinne Thompson is a snake and she fooled many because she looked good. I'm sorry anyone died there, but those two are not a moral loss.*

He said, "Sheila, you're thinking too much. What's up?"

"Why did you waste all your efforts for no fee? I don't understand, Norbie; another client would have to give you upfront money or property. Why not Barney? And I never heard you talk about Barney before. Is he someone from your past, someone you feel some obligation?"

Cull smiled and said, "Some debts, Sheila, can't be repaid. This is one of them. Although I am in for a lot of billable hours on this deal and I doubt it will end well."

"You did all the development for this sale. Normally the seller would have their accountant do pro forma expense related statements. And the title was a bit knotty leading to increased cost. Also, you researched

46

Barney's rights when he inherited the land and buildings. What a nightmare! His siblings were awful before they died. He wanted to sell ten years ago, but he held back because of their vitriolic attacks on him."

"Barney's dad was a drinker, but a good guy. He knew Barney was the only decent one of his three children. The other two are now dead and don't have heirs. I think that fact and Barney's age pushed him to make a sale. He had no idea how valuable his inheritance was until after I got the appraisal. I was damned surprised myself. Richards and Thompson were one of the potential buyers who contacted me in addition to the minister and biker. I was told there were others interested. Barney wanted me to do a private auction, but now there is just too much notoriety. It would bring a carnival style atmosphere to the sale. I couldn't reach him but left him an email about waiting until the situation is resolved. He'll call when he's ready."

"Norbie, how will a year resolve anything?"

"Well, if it is a murder, I'm certain Barney wouldn't want to sell his dad's estate to a murderer. Let Beauregard do his job first."

"Do you really think the minister and the biker would get themselves so damaged by killing Corinne and Art. They'd have to be stupid and they are not. Outrageous are those two, but not stupid."

"Sheila, I said there were other interested buyers. I just don't know who."

Rudy Beauregard found the overwhelming influence of Lilly and Juan's impending nuptials on his team's focus annoying, thinking, *I can't say anything. My broken femur disrupted the unit. Even Mason is carrying on without his usual cynicism. And Juan is the happiest man in town expecting a baby and finally capturing the elusive Lilly.*

Clearing his throat as a signal to duty, the Captain said, "Settle down and congratulations, but our job is to determine what happened here. Ted, what is going on at that property to have gathered such a host of distinguished citizens on a weekday morning? There was no for sale sign and the place is rundown. Who owns it?"

Ted said, "Rundown it may be, Captain, but it's worth a minimum of a cool five million, probably more given a particular use. The owner is the fourth generation in his family to own the property. I don't think real estate agents knew its size and what I think is also important, its frontage on Junction Road, the most easily accessed area in West Side. I called my friend who deals in commercial real estate and he said the property is hot and our good friend, the illustrious defense attorney Cull, represents the seller. He is not acting as broker, but has done all the work related to the title and the appraisal. I think we should get him in here. He'll know all about potential buyers."

The Captain nodded, snarling, "Cull and that Kent woman again must be my penance for missing mass last week."

In unison, he heard a general agreement. He looked at his agenda for the meeting. Next was a report from Mason on the medical results. Mason said, "The ME, even after reviewing the tape, thinks something was wrong with the bodies when they rose up in the explosion. They may have looked like they were moving but the state's fire investigator thought if they were alive at the time, they were impaired. They found no obvious signs of assault or knife or bullet wounds. They're waiting for the toxicology report. I spoke to the doctor who did the autopsy. He did not smell alcohol, but the charring on the bodies would have prevented a good smell test for alcohol or pot, which are both legal."

"How are they doing? Who's on watch at the hospital?"

"A uniform, Linehan, you know Jesus Linehan, Captain. He's got a Latino/Jewish mother and Irish father who are the fodder for his comedy routines. He plays all the Western Mass comedy circuits, but really wants to be a detective. We're the only MCU group without an assigned uniform in all major cities or towns in Western Massachusetts. He'd be a good addition and we need the help, just saying."

"Petra, do we really need more comedy in here?"

"Yes, Captain, it would be helpful to fight your known devotion to the job. Got to lighten it up."

He thought, *am I really that serious? Mona says thank God for our middle son who lightens my fugue. Linehan's a good guy. I might, with a little politics, get him over here."*

Beauregard questioned Sergeant Bobby Barr. "Do you have the explosives report?"

"It's not complete, Captain. The front dilapidated building was used for storage of gas cylinders. Most were argon, nitrogen, and oxygen. They don't have dates on them, but the first blast came from those cylinders. What caused the ignition is still unknown. Contact with the owner wasn't made but neighbors say he would never have authorized storage for anything. That same neighbor saw a truck there two weeks ago unloading what looked like cylinders. Something had to ignite them to explode.

"The second explosion was from fuel. They think fire from the first explosion got into the rear building and set off the storage of some chlorine tri-fluorine gas. There used to be a small production of parts for the electric industry. It's been there for years. The business was small and shut down twenty years ago. The business owner left everything behind. Surprising it didn't blow before."

Beauregard repeated some facts. "Recent storage of gas cylinders in the front of the house, storage of one chemical in back of the house indicates cause, but what's the motive. Who has keys to these buildings?"

No one answered. Beauregard answered, "Get on it. And I want the owner in here for questioning. Have you contacted him?"

Petra speculated, "I don't think it would have been too difficult to get into the first building without keys. Whoever stored gas cylinders had access to the building. The owner could have given access. The firing device for the primary explosion could have been done remotely. Who's the owner?"

Sergeant Barr responded, "His name is Barney McAuliffe. Neighbors haven't seen him for a while. Can we do a wellness check, Captain?"

"How old is he?"

Barr said, "Ninety or more, Captain."

"Yes, go ahead."

———

Barney McAuliffe lived in a modest three-bedroom standard ranch with a two-car attached garage on two acres of wooded land. Sergeant Border agreed the land was the more valuable resource. Sergeant Barr knocked loudly, announcing, "Police, here for a wellness check."

There was no answer. The two detectives were about to encircle the premises to glance in the windows, when Barr turned the door handle and opened the door. Agreeably surprised, Barr again yelled the wellness check. When no answer came, they walked around the first floor. There was that smell so well known to the two men. They looked into the tiny den and saw the man settled in his lounge chair in an unhappy appearance of decomposition. Bill Border called the Captain, an ambulance, and the medical examiner. They waited outside.

Later the ME phone conferenced with Beauregard. Dr. Simpson, called by everyone who knew him, Gerard, said, "Rudy, I just happened to be in the office when your guys called. I know Barney and recognized his address. I'm saddened at his death, but I suppose it's time. Still, the scene is funny. Don't you think?"

Rudy and the two detectives had already discussed the scene, simply because another death related to the property on Junction Road seemed one death too many. Rudy replied, "I didn't see his body but my detectives took a photo and detailed what they saw. I don't know, Gerard, but unless he was asleep and had a heart attack or stroke immediately immobilizing him, I don't understand why he was in the flattest level that chair will go. I have that same model chair and if I even jerk a little releasing some of my top weight the chair jumps back to a forty-five-degree angle not a seventy-five-degree angle which is the level the guys found him sitting. They didn't get close to the body. That's your work when they smell that bad. I couldn't see anything more from the photo other than the body's a mess. I think three or four days old."

"I agree, but I did get close. There looks to be some damage to his neck. Hard to tell because of the state of the body, but the autopsy will inform. I'll call you, but as far as I'm concerned, cause of death at this time is unknown."

Rudy thought, *when does Simpson find it easy to say cause of death is unknown. He saw something. Is there something here? Barney's the seller and he's dead, but he's old by most standards.*

"Gerard, what was he like? You said you knew him or of him. Was he in good health?"

"Spry as a fifty-year-old, Rudy. Kept this house pretty well for a guy who's lived alone for thirty years after his wife of many years passed. I'll check with his doctor. I liked Barney, Rudy. I liked him. Too bad he had to die alone, but I guess it happens to a lot of the elderly who don't live in complexes."

Bill Border was quiet, too quiet for the loquacious detective. After Simpson's call ended, Bobby Barr quietly asked the Captain if he knew if Border had some problem. Beauregard approached Bill Border, asking, "Something up, Sergeant? You are unusually quiet."

Border looked uncomfortable but answered, "That's me, Captain, all alone, found dead some day in my condo disintegrating to dust. I don't want to be alone."

"Sergeant, you have the beautiful Dr. Jessica Taylor as your significant other. Why haven't you popped the question. Are you afraid of marriage?"

"She won't marry me. That's what she said a year ago. She said I need to learn to listen. She's not my significant other. We have in her terms a 'friends with benefits' relationship."

Rudy was surprised. Jessica always acted as a loving lady friend. He remembered her at Lieutenant Ashton Lent's wedding and she had tears in her eyes. He said, "Do what you have to do, Sergeant, she's a keeper. Learn to listen, but personally I've seen you change in the last two years. Try again. The lady won't pop the question to you."

8

Police Question

Lilly Tagliano was feted by Petra Aylewood-Locke, Mona Beauregard, and Charlotte Torrington to a wedding shower at the Delaney House in Holyoke. Lilly had wondered if she was the only bride ever showered two days before the wedding, but circumstances pushed the celebration. Beryl Kent helped Mona make the arrangements and her magic touch for design showed. She gifted the flowers placed everywhere along with a gift certificate for five days at the Mohonk Mountain House in New York with additional SPA reservations for the couple. Lilly, a New Yorker, who had always wanted a weekend there was thrilled. Juan and Lilly's relatives created a happy and noisy afternoon affair, prompting Mona to tell Beryl, "Best shower I've attended and Lilly is loving it. The families get along. It's all good. Thanks, Beryl."

Two days later Lilly and Juan were married at Saint Agatha's Church. It was a small wedding with parents, grandparents, and siblings of the couple attending. A reception at the groom's home greeted a much larger crowd to a fifteen-piece mariachi band and a buffet of Mexican and Italian entrees leaving Lilly's mother questioning her lost Irish heritage. "Juan, where is my shepherd's pie. Don't you forget, this baby is 25% me."

The cultures blended beautifully and the bride's mother was quieted when the Mexican band played an Irish ballad following an ancient

Irish war song. Lilly and Juan danced, cut the cake, greeted all their guests with kisses despite COVID and the crowd was pleased to see the cynical bride in love with her so-called shy groom. Charlotte Torrington commented, "Juan's not shy; when it's time to move, he does. He's like my Ted. Never underestimate the quiet do-gooders."

The biggest problem for Rudy as he viewed the happy crowd was the disappearance of two of his detectives leaving for a week's honeymoon. He knew he was short staff to begin with and now there was possibly some connected deaths and only two-thirds of his manpower available. He said not in a whisper, "Why don't they marry when it's convenient."

Beryl Kent approached Rudy. "Be happy. You'll solve your cases, Rudy. This little break is such a stress reliever. I need the highs of beautiful living and you do too. You are not immune to happiness. You couldn't be. Mona wouldn't let you. As to your temporary reduction in work force, use me."

Rudy could not hide his astonishment. "Beryl, out of the question. You know to stay out of police business."

As he moved towards Mona, Beryl followed. "I understand protocol, but I cannot, as you know, be prevented from being a good citizen."

———

Captain Beauregard received a call from Springfield's MCU Lieutenant Joe Stellato. "Rudy, the Richards woman did not commit suicide. It's a murder. Given you are looking at the husband's death, I'd like to review what we have on Darla Richards with you."

Rudy was surprised. Much as he liked Stellato, they were often at logger-heads in other cases. Professional competitiveness is what his Mona called it. Still, he wanted in and said, "Got time to come over the river? It's much quieter than in your place, plus you have the nosiest of interferers over there."

"Just what I was hoping. Be there in twenty."

The two detectives examined the autopsy report leaving Rudy to exclaim, "What the hell! Does the murderer think we are amateurs? Even I would have been immediately suspicious. Look, Joe, the bruising from the rope is superimposed over a smaller cord used in the original strangulation. Any fool pathologist would pick up on this."

"Rudy, I don't agree. Think of Art Richards' national importance and his legacy of contributions to successful politicians. Locally he had his hands on all of them. He could smell which ones would be successful. They would not wish to raise his ire, but now he's dead. No one cares if he killed his wife. But why would he kill her?"

Rudy said, "Sometimes a good woman is difficult to divorce. If she had expressed her desire for more than or even half of his money, well that alone is a motive for murder. But I don't think she was interested in money. Why would she have stayed in such a publicly humiliating situation for so many years if money were important? Even Richards would not have deigned to kill his wife in this manner; why not just a fall down the stairs. It would be less suspicious. They lived on a street with houses close by. How did the murderer get in there in broad daylight? Have you questioned all the neighbors and delivery personnel, Joe?"

"Not yet, I just got this report. I'm here to force your brain cells to help. I know you're thinking what I'm thinking. Is there a common murderer? And what about this Barney guy dying the way he did? Are you sitting on information helpful to me?"

"Joe, you are in the know. I shouldn't be surprised, but tell me how you heard about Barney."

"Rudy, he did all this volunteer work with every organization dealing with alcoholics. Even lately, you'd see him doling out dinners for the walking wounded. Low key, he was, but noticeable for his kindness, his attitude. You know his father had a drinking problem, not to that level, but an uncle died on the streets. All our cops knew Barney from his good work. Is his death normal? I mean, he's in his nineties and dying then is normal."

"I'll call when I get the autopsy report, okay?"

"Thanks, Rudy. Are the minister and the biker in good enough shape to be interviewed yet? I want to talk to them about Darla Richards. What do you know about their involvement. It's the land deal. That's what Di Felice says. You know him. He's our resident cop in the know about real estate. Money's always a motivator for murder. I just can't fit Darla's death into that picture. Keep me in the loop, Rudy."

Stellato's visit was the prompt to act that Rudy needed. A short time later, the Captain and Sergeant Barr were speaking with Minister Abu Cason who was the first of the two injured in the blast to be allowed a visit by police. Abu appeared wide-awake despite some bulky bandaging on his legs, arms and chest. His face was not damaged other than some fading small scars reminiscent of a childhood fire experience. Sergeant Barr's questions were met with some initial resentment. Abu said, "Why would you ask me what my business was at the site. Does my race prevent me from looking at real estate property for sale?"

Abu smirked as he presented his question with arrogance. His attitude did not rile the Sergeant, who said, "Minister Cason, the question as to why is important. It will help detail for us who might not want you there. Were you there to examine the property to make a potential offer? Was Zed Albion your partner? Were you to join Art Richards in an offer? How did you know Barney had finally relented and was selling his land? Answers to these questions help the police in discovering motive for these actions."

"My business decisions are always in flux. I may have a potential partner one day who is discarded the next day if my possibilities allow me no partner. I would have taken on a partner to anyone speaking to

Barney who had an edge. As of today, I have no partners."

Beauregard intervened. "Is that because Art Richards is now dead? Was he a partner before his death?"

"You don't give up on this, Captain, do you? He was a potential. I only heard of his interest in the property the night before the explosion when his associate attempted to talk me out of being a contender. Once someone does that, I just become more interested in the deal. It's not like I was offered something big to remove myself from the competition. Richards thought I should just bow to his elite business acumen. Stupid idea for him to have considering his recent business blunders."

"Was it Corinne Thompson who approached you to get out of the deal?"

"You think I'd do business with her? She is a weasel. No."

"Who approached you, Abu?"

"Brad Surnani, who is, or I guess now, was, his velvet glove hatchet man. The guy is cool. I often wondered why Surnani wouldn't break out on his own. He has class, skills, intelligence, and training. Why would he work with Richards who is nasty? I could see his doing it fifteen years ago, but he's outclassed Richards. It's time to move on."

"Were you to meet Barney at the site that day?"

"Yeah, I was, and his broker as well. I was pissed when I saw Art Richards there. It meant Barney was going to see us both at the same time. That's a no-no in private real estate sales. You work one potential at a time. It was not a public bid where the bidders are often shown the property at the same time and everyone has the bidder list. Not this time or this sale!"

""Why would you be upset at seeing Art at the site? Brad's approach was a warning Richards was interested. He was, after all, Richards' man."

"Captain, you are not as they say 'in the know'. Brad is and has always been his own man. I wasn't sure if he was representing himself or

Richards on this deal."

"Abu, you just told me Brad should go out on his own as if he never would."

Abu smiled. "I am a seer, Captain. Quite often, the Lord helps me see things in advance."

Sergeant Barr said, "Is the Lord helping you with financing on this purchase, Minister Cason? Barney was going for the gold."

"Yeah, the price he wanted was outrageous. If that lawyer wasn't in the game, I could have swept Barney off his feet with cash for one hundredth what his lawyer advised him he should get. It took the whole situation to a new level."

Beauregard asked, "Who's the attorney handling the sale."

"You know, the guy with all the advertising, Norberto Cull. He looks like a Catholic school angel, but has a mind like a computer, and to give him credit, is well-liked even by his competitors. I'd use him if I didn't get free legal work already."

Sergeant Barr asked, "If you're worried about paying for legal work, how could you finance this property? You and the biker were together in the explosion. Is he your partner? You do have history with him."

"There you go again. A Black man can't finance his own projects. You wouldn't say that to a white man. And you think I need the biker. We have history as kids, but we don't travel in the same circles; just like you, Sergeant, I don't see you around in my district."

Barr responded, "Not true, I've been to the Heavenly Gospel Church when you were the guest preacher. You did a good job. Almost made me think you didn't care about worldly possessions."

"You don't say. I got lots of praise and publicity from that sermon. You caught a good one, Sergeant. Your being there doesn't mean you're not racist. Would you ask Richards, if he were alive, where he was getting his funding?"

"Sure would. Ask Captain Beauregard. I'm always interested in where the money comes from today; family money, savings, good credit which can be checked, black money and I don't mean race, etc. So where is your money coming from?"

"Not my job to tell you my financial secrets. You want to know more, call my lawyer."

"And who is your attorney?"

"Attorney Tobias Nigella. Great guy. You'll love speaking with him. He's a man of few words. Now let me sleep."

The detectives checked in with the nurse's station on the biker's health condition. To their surprise, he was wheeled into a room across from where they were standing. They waited for all the settling in and spoke with the nurse, who said, "Captain, go grab some lunch. We have to do some work to make him comfortable and also feed him. He'll be available for you within an hour or so. I'll tell him to expect you."

Barr quickly said, "Please say nothing until we rejoin you."

Over great pizza ordered from Sal's Pizzeria, the detectives munched away. The day was an autumn beauty in New England kind of day supplying visual delight as they ate the forbidden, for Beauregard, pizza sitting in the car. They agreed the previous interview was not as helpful as they expected. Beauregard said, "Bobby, our biker Zed Albion will not give us much more. If he admits to a potential partnership with either the minister or Richards, I'd be surprised. I do believe Abu in his declaring it was every man for himself, but the resources needed to purchase and develop this land are huge. No bank will lend easily, whether there be some federal or state bonds available for those kind of dollars or not, without good collateral. Richards is known for having business problems, the minister is a lot of hype, and the biker is looking as the more fruitful financing source possibility if it's true he is into dealing drugs.

"We did hear from the grapevine Richards may have had leanings to a partnership with Abu, if what Abu says about Brad trying to talk him out of the deal is true. The big news is Norbie Cull is Barney's lawyer. Let's pull him in for an interview. His client is now dead and he may be quite interested in speaking with us. I want the autopsy report on Barney when we get back, before Norbie joins us. Get a preliminary summary if the final is not ready. Gerrelson is there today. He'll do it. If Barney was murdered, Gerrelson will know or at the very least suspect."

They entered Zed's room to find the biker sitting up and looking quite well. The Captain introduced himself and Sergeant Barr. Zed's answer was, "We've met before, Captain. You may not recall. I was partying in your town when I was a kid. You brought me all the way home instead of arresting me. First and only time I got a favor from the police and I wasn't from West Side. So, go ahead and ask your questions. I'll try to answer them unless I feel the need for my attorney."

Sergeant Barr asked, "Why were you on the Junction Road property and on that particular day?"

"Sergeant, you can do better than that. I've been in here long enough for you to have done your homework. Barney's property is for sale. I am interested in it."

"Do you have a use for it, Zed, and if so, what is the use?"

"Not really your business, Sergeant, and frankly I am uncertain whether I want it for business or personal use."

"Zed, it would be a hell of a costly personal use."

"Not a problem, Sergeant."

Beauregard spoke. "Are you partnering with Abu on this project? I ask you, because you were found injured together."

"Captain, Abu and I are old friends, but I am not his partner. I registered for the showing that day, arrived early, and was waiting for Barney when I spied Abu. Then we both saw Richards and Corinne at the street side of the property. I'd gotten there early to walk the property, or at least, to walk what I could. The property is large. Then I saw Abu who had walked in from the street."

"Zed, was it Barney you were to meet? Did you get a letter from his attorney or real estate broker?"

"Got a voicemail from a lady asking me what days I was available. I gave her some days. Got a typed note from Barney a day later by snail mail agreeing to a date and time. Barney had a real estate broker, probably didn't need one. He had Attorney Cull watching out for his interests. Big money being asked for this property, therefore, big fee for Cull. He doesn't work for nothing unless he feels sorry for someone who's been wronged. Cull has a little missionary side to him sometimes."

"Zed, walk me through the first explosion. What did you see?"

"I didn't see anything at first. I was teed off that Barney had Richards there. I have never liked the man and as to Corinne, she's uptown trash, if you know what I mean. I heard the explosion, went for the ground as did Abu. Military does that for you. You grab for the earth first and then look. It's what I did. I saw their bodies crash. That's it. We moved back near a rear storage building to get away from the fumes. Captain, it was a hot fire. The place was abandoned. Barney would not store chemicals or oils. He was old time. You know, he would clean everything out. It was set."

Beauregard questioned, "And then what happened? How long before the second explosion?"

"Long enough for Abu and I to get off the ground, capture our wits, and listen to fire and police noises. I saw a couple of ambulances, but the visibility wasn't good and the fire and fumes prevented us from leaving the lot. Don't know how long it was before the second explosion. We thought we were safe, when I saw fire leap to what looked like a twisted cord and I knew we were in trouble. I told Abu to get down and we did, but the blast gave some little fires that hit us. I thought I was going to burn up. Abu was hysterical. I don't remember the rest, but I'm lucky I was wearing a bulletproof jean jacket and heavy woolen pants. It was chilly in the morning."

"And why were you wearing a bulletproof jean jacket? I didn't know they had them. Must be heavy to wear every day."

"I appear to have many enemies from the liberal establishment. Seems prudent to me to be careful. Now, I feel tired and it's time for my meds. I hurt. Captain, you are noted for your persistence. Don't give up on finding this bastard. Abu and I will have pain for a long time from this experience. I don't like pain. Discover who wanted Richards dead."

"What makes you think Richards was the target? What time were you supposed to arrive?"

"10:15 was my time. I didn't ask Abu what time he was scheduled. I got there at 9:35. Are you saying the explosion was set for a certain time?"

"I'm not saying anything about who was the target, if there was a target. Just getting some facts. Zed, it's important for you to go over it all again in your mind. If some new detail occurs to you, call me. Here's my card."

Zed gave the detectives a strange look and said, "I don't want to die. I have a family. They are what's important to me. No matter what you've ever heard about me, I'm a family man."

9

Beryl Gets Nosy

Beryl called Cull and invited him to lunch. He said he was too busy, but could make breakfast at the Crepe House in West Springfield at nine the next morning. He asked what they would be discussing and whether she needed legal help, which in that case would be better handled in his office. She waffled with her answer and he said, "Okay, tomorrow."

Pleasant as Beryl was, she couldn't hide her inquisitiveness from the astute Attorney Cull. "Norbie, I count five deaths and two injuries all connected to a piece of land. A cluster of evil if you ask me."

"Where do you get five deaths, Beryl?"

"Richards, Corinne, Barney, Darla, and Teisha in my count."

"Who's Teisha, Beryl?"

Beryl reviewed for Cull the details of Teisha and Corinne's difficulties. She also said, Corinne's involvement cost Richards one of his regular civic awards, and he was upset. "That is the rumor, Norbie. Teisha was creating havoc with her friends in the minority community. They blamed Richards more than Corinne. I think it's cultural. Corinne was not the boss. Richards is and should have known Corinne's banning Teisha's shoe-in for the job would mean he was the one who ordered it. Even if he didn't."

"Teisha died in an accident. It wouldn't be connected."

"Did she? I want you to find out. Will you? Don't say 'no' until you consider how unlikely or overly coincidental are these five deaths. Think the timeline, Norbie. Too much for me to swallow."

"Beryl, I know from your history with the 'Bleeding Man' you infer connections, but I remind you they are not always there. How important is Teisha, not to say that her death is not a terrible thing. Do you have any reason to think her death is other than accidental?"

"I'd like you to look into it. If you say it's accidental, I'd believe you."

"Look, Beryl, I'll ask around, more than that, don't ask."

"Norbie, Teisha, according to Marjorie Phipps the minister's wife, was a real go-getter. She only wanted this position because it would give her access to a lot of important people. She, herself, was licensed as an investment counselor. She was financially independent, didn't need to work, and had some interesting male acquaintances. There may be several reasons to kill her if she were killed. She was a player, at least two of her male friends had to be called off by the police."

Cull asked, "You were at the scene of the explosions. Who was there other than police and fire that you can identify?"

"You mean aside from Teisha? I did tell you Teisha was there, didn't I? There was a man who was familiar to me, but I can't recall where or how I met him. He was wearing a mask."

"Who else was at the scene in addition to those two?"

"Two were completely unknown to me. I wonder if the photographer got a scan of the bystanders. Could you get a look? I mean, fire starters love to be at the scene of their incendiary accomplishments, maybe bombers like to be there too."

"My thoughts and I'll get a look at your familiar man."

"Does this mean you'll help me?"

"It means I have a billable client, Barney's estate, which allows me to ask questions."

***

Sergeant Border had reviewed the video retrieved from the pretty news anchor Stacia Kovac. She was most helpful when Barr suggested they view the video over coffee. He paid the coffee bill thinking, *she's interesting and pretty pleasant for press. Maybe it's all a put on. It takes a little time to see what's behind a good-looking woman. I have a little time; hell, I have a lot of time.*

Stacia said a thank you for her double espresso latte, and pulled some still photos from her giant bag, saying, "You can have a copy of the video, but I had stills printed of all the non-police, fire, and press for you. I count four people and one woman who said she was press, but I didn't believe her. She's that Beryl Kent from the Bleeding Man murders. She is cool. She got the cops to leave her alone with some hokum about being a reporter. The other four I don't know. They were wearing masks. I doubt if they were local."

"Why's that, Stacia?"

"Two of the three men wore suits while driving on Junction Road. It is a highly trafficked road for West Side, but used by trucks, locals, people going to the dump, mall crawlers, but not business type folks. It wouldn't be their choice of travel through the area. The third one was dressed like a college professor in expensive corduroys and vest. The photos are good. One of the suits took his mask off to scratch his nose and I caught him. The woman was dynamite looking. I think her figure and top of her face would identify her. Another suit didn't move much so you have the best I could get. The professor type is a stud. Try the gyms unless he has home equipment."

"Stacia, are you a detective? Nice work."

"You don't watch local news, do you? I'm the anchor. It's not New York City but I like it. I have to stay local to care for my parents who are not doing well. They were old when they had me. I'm an only child and no, I wasn't spoiled. I had to look out for myself and I think it makes me observant."

They talked for another forty-five minutes. Stacia said she had to leave. He asked if he could call her. He recalled her quickly retrieving a card from her case, saying, "Please do, Bobby. I would like to know you better."

No wise-ass or flirty remarks, all quite straight forward, and Bobby thought, *I want to know her better too.*

———

Border asked, "Bobby, what you dreaming of, some lady or vacationing in Aruba?"

"No, maybe, but right now I'm looking at these photos of bystanders at the explosion scene. You take a look, see if anyone looks familiar."

"John Conlon, Brad Surnani's assistant, is this one. The second one in the casual up-country look clothes is unknown. The third one I met him when he worked for the Secretary of State and not in his father's businesses. His name is James Richards, Art's son. He was quite personable and not like his father. He always showed respect and was interested in other people. I can't believe it's him and he watched his father die. He showed no emotion in his face. The other suit is not familiar to me, but he appears to be talking to Conlon in this photo. Maybe they came together. I can't see enough of the masked man to identify."

Beauregard showed great interest in the photos. "Call Conlon in for a chat and don't take a negative. He is now a witness and the photo is evidence. Does he look upset? Nope, nor does the kid. The lady is Teisha Abbott who is now dead in an accident. When's Richards' funeral and are they doing a double with his wife?"

Sergeant Border handed Beauregard three obituaries. "Captain, they're being waked in two different funeral homes but services together in one church. Guess who's being waked in the same funeral home as Richards? Yup, Corinne Thompson is the answer. Talk about setting up a public relations situation. From my point of view, it is a disaster for the kids. What do they do, go back and forth between funeral homes? We have another week before the events. The bodies are just being released tomorrow."

Beauregard growled and said, "I want detectives split between the two funeral homes and video. How did Bobby get these photos? Normally, I have to press the press to get stills."

"Captain, he got them from the pretty blonde anchor on the local news, Stacia Kovac. Bobby is a stud and nature took its course. Ask him to request she share any video of the wakes and funerals."

Beauregard called a conference of the four detectives available. Mason, Ted, Petra and Bill made reports on details from the explosions, preliminary forensics, and interviews. The Captain switched to Teisha's accident. "Has Barr gone over the early reports? He was the best when he was in Traffic Enforcement and knows what facts accident re-constructionists need to make a determination. What do we know about her?"

Mason had the scoop on Teisha. He explained she was hot and ambitious. "The whole community was rising up against Surnani, because he killed Teisha's chance for a position promised to her. Corinne Thompson did the behind the scenes dirty work. Teisha had a motive to kill the two of them, but she was not one to put herself in jeopardy. If she had lived she would have made them both suffer. Of that, I'm sure."

Petra read important details from Teisha's accident report. Noted for her ability to spin words in her direction, Beauregard advised her to report straight, "With none of your personal lens clouding the facts. I want to know about a Jodi Calhoun, who was a former grants manager for the city."

Petra, annoyed at Beauregard's criticism continued. "There is a story out there about Teisha at odds with Corinne Thompson over a job she was assured she would get. Turns out Corinne didn't help her, she killed the job. Teisha and her community were angry with Richards, who denied he had anything to do with it. I, personally don't think a job loss is big enough to murder two people."

The Captain interrupted. "Facts, Petra, not opinion."

"Troubling there, Captain, there aren't many facts. The car had no engine problems. She was not using her cell phone at the time of her accident. Point of fact is we can't find her cell phone but know her number. Her usage for the last three days shows just four numbers. She phoned Art Richards several times before the accident and get this, Minister Abu Cason twice."

"Women today don't leave their cells behind, well maybe accidentally. Have you checked her home?"

"Yes. She lives with her mother and daughter. The daughter's about four years old and cute as a button. They thought it was strange Teisha's phone wasn't found because she never, ever left it behind. They said the never ever, twice."

"What has Lieutenant Lent said? If it's supposed to be a problem, why didn't he tell me?"

The two heard the long strides of Ashton Lent, leaving Petra to say, "Do you have a crystal ball? We were just about to call you."

"Captain, you called after badmouthing my timeliness or lack thereof."

"Yeah, I want your thoughts. This dead lady may be connected to the explosion case. What does it look like to you? Does it smell as an accident?"

"Sure smells, Captain. This Teisha had to work to hit that tree. Could easily be suicide or falling asleep, or texting except we found no phone.

Strange for a mother with a little kid not to have her phone nearby. I don't have all the toxicology reports yet, but a preliminary exam including the smell test and her temperature says she was inebriated. Her beautiful new Lexus told us where she was before the accident. She'd been at McCafferty's Tavern in town. The bartender remembered her. Said she was a looker and several men approached her before the main guy came in. He didn't know him. We went through the footage and the guy is unknown to them or to us. The description is typical for a fairly young handsome dude. Helpful if we know more about her male relationships. The mother said she had no steady boyfriends, but recently she met a man she said was worth the wait. The mother never met him. I've got the name and I'll check on him. The child's father is dead."

The Captain asked, "What name do you have for the boyfriend?"

"Jonathan Witner who is a commercial real estate agent in Springfield. He's supposed to be reputable. I'll tell you more after I meet with him. Was she drunk and maybe also high? I don't see her as a boozer or druggie. Makes me think it's not accidental.

"Her home was immaculate with no evidence of depression. The kid was crazy over her mommy as was Teisha's mother. Took it hard. Teisha was an ambitious go-getter who was smart and beautiful. Nothing stinks of depression. A new boyfriend was in her life. I smell something's up, Captain. When I get toxicology, I'll call you."

Beauregard harrumphed, saying, "You sound like Beryl with your insights. I need something more. Get outta here."

Petra said, "Captain, there is a boyfriend to investigate. I'll get on it. I'll talk to her work pals. Ashton has good instincts."

The wake for Darla Richards was packed with good people. The religious connection was obvious. James Richards stood next to one of the funeral directors and acted as guard at the entrance. There was no pretense. Any business person or politician not liked by Darla was turned away. Some of the visitors denied entrance got excitable. He or she in some cases was almost forcibly removed. It was helpful that Darla's body was not on display. She had asked for cremation. Stacia on Bobby's bidding got photos of all altercations. Sergeant Barr wondered, *if they know Darla didn't like them, why come to the wake?*

Half hour later Sergeant Border was joined by Sergeant Barr and the press team for Art and Corinne's wake. The team took a ton of pictures, particularly of those people shying away from the camera. Barr asked Stacia, "Isn't that the Kent woman sitting over there with some of the family? The Captain won't like her being here."

Stacia answered, "She was at the explosion site pretending she was press. I take that back, she had a current press pass from the newspaper. Bobby, she was at the other wake. Didn't you see her there?"

"No, I didn't. Did you get a photo of her? Her being at both wakes says she's butting in again. Bill, you tell the Captain, I'm not in the mood to listen to him rant about the Lady Kent."

Border said, "It's a carnival in here. Not just because Kent is here. Probably twenty deals are being made while the ashes sit quietly in a container. Brad Surnani is over there holding court. Bobby, I'm going for a listen."

Surnani was speaking quietly to his aide and James Richards. Sergeant Border smiled. He took out a VR 16 voice activated recorder and switched it, thinking, *not supposed to tape a conversation unless I'm a party, but these three have no claim to privacy. There are a hundred people in this room alone. I don't have to get too close. If the conversation is useful, then and only then will I worry about legal implications.*

The conversation was controlled by Surnani. His voice was angry but whispered. Even with the VR some words escaped him, but the subject was the land deal. Surnani said, "What the hell was going on with the real estate agent seeing all of us at the site at the same time? Well, not all of us got there in time. I saw that Colonel who lives in West Side driving by just before the explosion. Is he involved with this? Have you reached Jonah Cronin? What kind of game is he playing? Cull put the deal together for Barney, but Cronin is the agent. He hasn't answered my calls and Barney is dead. I'll get nothing out of Cull. I don't want to lose this deal do you hear me?"

John Conlon did not look disturbed by the questions. He answered, "What colonel? Lots of bidders but not all could go the distance. It is now a shit show and you can expect many more offers for the land now the press is all over the explosion story. Just because you were one of the first to show interest, it's not going to matter now. First could be last."

James Richards said, "Stop trying to rile Brad, John. The land sale is a legitimate deal and you, Brad, well it looks to me as if you're the only one left with enough bread to bid it out. Maybe you didn't want a bidding war, but that's where we are now so stop the bitching."

Brad answered, "Don't give me all that PR claptrap. Deals are made in back rooms, not outside for the world. As to the Colonel, he's government. Pretends he's a businessman, and maybe is, but don't be surprised if he was going to be at the site, but was late."

"No back room deals with Cull involved. He may negotiate in back rooms, but the deals he handles are always legit. We have to involve government in this for use purposes. Be cool and don't look worried. We all want this deal."

"What are those wounded two outliers doing? What profitable use could they have? Churches don't pay taxes and this is a white community."

"Cut the racist talk. The biker is loaded and according to my banker could raise the funds. They may be together in this."

Sergeant Barr was taken aback, thinking, *I thought the Richards kid didn't do any work with his dad. Can't be true if he's working with Surnani and Conlon. Were separate offers to be made by Art Richards and Surnani? How is James involved?*

10
Enough of Words

Beryl had listened to multiple conversations as she attended both wakes. Surprising to her was the lack of vitriolic statements made by the Darla wake attendees. Any mention of Art Richards appeared to be verboten. The memorial display did not include Art in any of the family pictures. There were many crying and the kids were clearly distraught including James. Despite his loss, however, he spent some time in a conversation with Surnani and Conlon. Beryl could now identify them both. *Surnani, Art's aide is here, no mention of the father Art, what gives? James trusts Brad Surnani and John Conlon. A business deal, the land deal, is the draw. Why aren't the other kids angry at Surnani and Conlon? There is more to this. Darla must have liked these two men, while she excised Art from her life. Darla in one of these picture looks vaguely familiar, but I don't think I've ever met her.*

Art and Corinne's wake was analogous to a business conference. I heard five different deals being closed. I wanted to hear more but Stacia was always around with her partner doing video. I think I stayed out of her way, but she was being directed by Sergeant Barr. There is too much of what my hippy mother would call astral presence. I thought Mom was nuts, but I felt some presence, maybe just negativity and anger.

Beryl left the last wake, and as she did, she noticed a familiar car pulling away. The Colonel had been at the wake and he didn't approach her. He did not want to be seen by her or maybe not be seen with her.

Just as she was walking to her car, she heard, "Beryl, wait."

Jay Bird rushed over and said, "I'm so glad you are here. Shall we grab a coffee. I saw you at the other wake too, but you were sitting with the family and I didn't want to intrude. It's just a short drive to the Italian Pastry Shop and Coffee Bar. Do you have time?"

They settled in with two espressos and split a large gooey piece of fluff filled with cream and jam. Jay said, "I knew you'd be there. What I didn't know is how close to the family you were. Want to talk about it?"

"No, because I don't know the family. I know one of Darla's closest friends and I sat with her. I'm ashamed to say I was trying to grasp how this woman could commit suicide which was at odds with all my friend Patty ever said about her. Darla had many friends as you saw and I found astonishment everywhere about the suicide."

Jay said, "You were at Corinne and Art's wake also. You're involved in this with Captain Beauregard, aren't you?"

"God, no, Jay. The Captain will be annoyed when he hears I'm even at these wakes. He'd say it was police business and not the business of nosy citizens getting in his way. Why were you at both wakes?"

"I told you. Real crime following in my lap, in my city, calls to me. I simply can't ignore the possibility of a good novel. I've already set the scene and characters. Now I'm just chasing facts. Of course, my novel will be fiction. If I mention you it will not be by name."

"Jay, I don't think I want to discuss this case or any cases any further with you. I don't want to find my words in your book. I can't do much about what has already been said, but I can cut you off now."

"I wouldn't write about you without your permissions, but I can't say I won't write about a lady who has her wits about her and follows evidence in crime. Fiction writers, Beryl, use life experiences to make up characters and plots. You can't tie my hands too tightly."

"I know you are a professional, words, words, words, and their meanings are interpreted differently by others. When I write, and mostly non-fiction, Jay, I write carefully using words which I hope will be understood to describe a feeling, a thought, a connection."

"You're kidding yourself, Beryl. Take a typical word I use such as 'murder.' Or take 'murdering' or 'murderous' all of which can mean many things. Use, as a noun, verb, or adjective is important. He has murdered clearly means he has done away with some person or thing or idea, but without specifics, we don't know. He could have murdered the English language. To say he is murderous tells you how he is inclined. Still we don't know if he is inclined to murder dogs, or cats, or people. As to murdering, he could be in the act of murder or he could have a personal trait of being a murdering bastard. In that case, he could have murdered or be inclined to murder. Beryl, we can always fight over the meaning of words. I think in a work of fiction, the whole decides the meaning of the particular. I could never write about the whole of you. You are too complicated. So, rest easy."

"Cripes, Jay, your years of sitting in English classes and writing as a basis for conversation exhaust me."

"I will stop if you promise to relax. I won't ask you for more information about the explosion. I have other sources."

Beryl did not pursue his other sources, thinking, *if he answers my questions, he'll want answers to his questions. Writers always stay on point. I'll try to enjoy this coffee break and maybe he'll let some words slip out. He is quite an attractive man. I can always grab a word he uses and discuss word usage.*

Beryl sipped her espresso, while Jay excused himself to use the restroom. On his return, he was masked and his movements told her a story. Although she was not overly interested and she knew the answer, she said, "There was a man at the explosion site who looked vaguely familiar to me. I'm trying to remember just who he was."

Jay's face clouded before he responded. She expected him to question her about the man's appearance. He didn't. Jay said, "Cut the nonsense, Beryl. You know it was me. Why didn't you just ask? I would have told you. No need for this Nancy Drew subterfuge. It's beneath you."

Beryl whose friends knew her as absolutely incapable of being embarrassed, replied, "I wasn't certain it was you. How could I state what I didn't know for sure. Let's get on with what's important here. Why were you there? Are you a bidder for the property?"

"Now, you cut to the chase - I was considering bidding. I'd spoken with Barney, but he referred me to his real estate broker, who said the property was being shown on that day, the day of the explosion. He said to put in my request for a showing in writing. I did, but decided to crash the showing on the day of the explosion. I was a bit late, thank God."

"Do the police know you were to attend the showing?"

"They'll figure it out and will visit me. I'm not encouraging them to seek me out. If I'm stuck, I'm stuck. Don't be telling them, Beryl."

"I don't have to tell them. Stacia Kovac was taking video of the crowd. She has me there, she'll have you. It's just a matter of time. Who else was bidding? Do you know?"

"Aren't there enough already? How many people have the funds to pay the asking price? I did ask Jonah Cronin, the agent, and he wouldn't tell me who was interested but he said there were four to six who'd called as of that date. I would be added as a seventh. You can't go by that number, Beryl."

"Why not?"

"Because to bid at this private auction, a cashier's check of one hundred thousand dollars is required as a token of serious interest. Not every developer can muster that amount."

"It is refundable, Jay. I suppose the average nosy person wouldn't be allowed but others could be there."

"Beryl, I've been straight with you. We seem to have been at logger heads from the start. I'd like to change directions. I'm interested in you, but scuttlebutt says you are in a relationship. Are you?"

"I don't answer invasive questions, Jay. I would not lead you on if I were part of a couple."

"What about Colonel Connault? The police say he was at your house last Christmas."

"I have friends, Jay. I have family. I spend Christmas with friends and family. Enough of the personal questions."

To onlookers, the handsome couple quietly finished their coffees and left, leaving viewers surprised to see the two not kiss, but shake hands before getting in their respective cars.

Nate Connault spotted Beryl's car in the coffee shop. He parked and waited for her to exit. Beryl emerged with Jay, shook his hand, and got in her car to leave. Nate called her cell and said, "Don't leave, Beryl. I'm parked on the other side of the lot. I saw your car and wanted to say 'hi'."

Beryl answered, "Well I've had coffee and dessert. What about lunch. By the time we get to a restaurant I'll want something light. Name it."

They headed for Panera's in West Springfield and both ordered soups and salads. Nate also ordered a crusty pastry filled with jam. Settled in, Nate asked, "You were having a meeting with Jay Bird, the author. What's that all about?"

Immediately he regretted asking, thinking, *if I just waited, Beryl would have told me about her day. Dumb, so stupid of me and so unlike me to rush a conversation. Am I jealous?*

Beryl hesitated before saying, "You know Jay Bird. How do you know him?"

"There you go again, Beryl. I ask you a question and you return the question to me. I'll answer. Jay was in the military many years ago. We served together."

"And…Tell me more about him. Two of West Side's detectives know him from military service. I wonder if that is his source for information from the police."

"Why are you interested in him, Beryl. I'm not certain I want to help you in your quest for info about Jay Bird, the elusive mystery novelist."

"Nate, now you make him sound exotic. I'll tell you my interest. He was at the site of the explosion. I wanted to know why."

"Do you now know?"

"He was considering bidding on the land."

"Beryl, it's a big number buying the land. I know he's made a bundle with three of his books bought for movies. What would he do with the land? Did he say?"

"No, and I wonder the same."

———

Captain Beauregard considered the new info reported by his detectives who attended the two wakes. The morning conference enjoyed the presence of all his detectives, which pleased the Captain. It was re-focus time. "What have we so far? Beryl Kent was at both wakes. Who did she speak with, aside from sitting with Darla Richards' family? Pull her in for an interview later. She will have learned something we may have missed."

Mason said, "She'll get more info from us than we'll get from her."

Petra did not agree. "Mason, she'll be up front with us. She will tell us what she knows."

Beauregard said, "Just get her in here. I'm hoping she's figured out who was the fourth bystander at the explosion. Now let's settle down. Do we have a list of interested parties invited to view the property on the day of the explosion? I want the times they were scheduled to appear. I know Barney's dead but what about Jonah Cronin?"

Sergeant Barr said, "Captain, we've not been able to find Jonah Cronin. His wife said he left a few days ago for a trip to Canada. He has a hunting lodge there and cell activity is hit or miss. He's expected back whenever. That was her answer."

"Sergeant, doesn't he have a secretary? He's an important agent in the area."

"I visited his office. Janice, the manager for the agency, said Jonah kept information on his clients close to the vest and Barney's land was a big project. Jonah knew Barney and his father and was trusted by Barney. So, no-go from her."

"What about the toxicology report on Teisha?"

"It's a good thing advanced testing was done quickly. The lab found traces of GHB (gamma-hydroxybutyrate) in her. That combined with alcohol could have knocked her out if the dose were large enough. The trouble is GHB leaves the system quickly. I think we have to talk to the bartender again and get the video for that night. Lieutenant Lent didn't take it. I'm hoping they still have it."

Beauregard posed a question. "Just who would gain from Teisha's death? Richards and Thompson are dead. Teisha may have roused her culture against them, but it has no value once they are dead. How is she connected to the land deal? She has no great wealth. I suppose she could have some info about the deal, but I don't buy her being a part of it. I think Teisha's murder, and I agree it is murder, is personal. I want family, friends, work colleagues, and whomever interviewed. Get the video. I don't know why Ash didn't take it."

Beryl's invitation to visit the station was a surprise. She wondered, *what is the Captain expecting from me? He normally doesn't want me near his cases. Oh God, how could I be so damn dumb. I went to both funerals. He must be wild thinking I'm asking questions on his cases. Time to go tame the tiger.*

The Desk Sergeant greeted her and directed her to go right up. Apparently warmed by his warmth, Beryl's walk bounced as she headed towards his office. He greeted her at the door and did not direct her to a conference room. She said, "I'm pleased with your personal invite today, Captain, but it is surprising. You're normally rushing me out the door, not inviting me in."

"I don't think that's a fair assessment, Beryl. You and I have worked well together. I have no reason to caution you about interfering in police investigations, but I do wonder about your attending the Thompson and Richards wake along with Darla Richards' wake. I heard you sat with family at Darla's wake. Perhaps you can tell me the why you were there and what you observed."

"Captain, I am uncomfortable with explaining my actions all the time. I am a citizen with the right to go to any public gathering. Why did I sit with Darla's family? I know a close friend of the family and sat with her because I knew her. What did I learn? Probably not quite as much as your detectives learned. I am certain Darla would not commit suicide. She involved herself in every Christian charity. Her family adored her. James, her eldest, left some questions for me. He is known by all her friends as Darla's protector, and yet he's pretty friendly with his father's friends. I saw that at her funeral. James was the gatekeeper stopping unwelcome cronies of Art but allowing Surnani and John Conlon entrance. Knowing how Art treated Darla, I was surprised. At Corinne's and Art's funeral, there was a dearth of Corinne's friends. I concluded her life was Art. Although I heard several people say she was tired of Art and was looking out for herself. I found that confusing since they moved together to West Side. Interesting to me is the fact no one, and I mean on one, cried at Corinne's and Art's wakes. The wake appeared to offer the opportunity for some business deals. Sad."

"Anything else strike you as odd?"

Beryl paused before saying, "I remembered who the fourth bystander at the explosion site was."

"Who?"

"He is Jay Bird, the mystery author. He did not identify himself to me that day, despite his knowing me."

"What made you able to identify him now? He was wearing a mask."

"It was the way he walks and carries himself. I asked him and he acknowledged he was there."

Beauregard said, "Where did you see him to speak with him? Surprising."

"He was at both wakes. He's thinking of using the explosion in his next novel."

"Beryl, how do you know him?"

"The same way two of your detectives know him. He spoke at the Library Speakers Forum."

Beauregard questioned Beryl about the business deals discussed at the wakes. His instincts were good. There really was only one deal discussed and it was Barney's land deal. Beryl had one request. Would the Captain, when he interviewed Jay Bird, which she said she knew he would, please say they identified Jay from the photographer's photos at the explosion site. "Please, Captain, there is no reason to bring me into this. He won't lie that he was there. You don't need me as a witness."

"Beryl, why? When have you ever been shy about your involvement in investigations?"

"That's not the issue. I don't want him to think I'm too close to the police. And I must point out, Captain, you don't want him to know. Am I right?"

Beauregard grunted in some form of acquiescence. "So, I'm to say to my detectives identify him from where again, a library forum? Do you know which detectives?"

"Ask them. I think your newer detectives who are quite good looking and easily converse. I know them by Bobby and Bill."

"A hell of a description, Beryl. Some investigator you are!"

"I'm not always great with names. Generally, I need to have a tidbit of personal history to remember names."

"Beryl, is there any other fact or idea you have gleaned from your associations you think I should know?"

Beryl answered with a precise 'no.'

Captain Beauregard walked the lady Beryl from the station to her car. Beryl said, "Why such courtesy, Captain. I do appreciate the kindness and thank God your broken leg is healed enough now to allow you to walk and do stairs easily. You have recovered quite well."

"I am not known to be overly solicitous of visitors to the station, but you have been straight forward with what you know. This is my way of apologizing for distrusting an honest, but clearly nosy citizen. Thanks, Beryl. Keep in touch."

Driving home, Beryl laughed, thinking, *I don't know about you, Captain Rudy Beauregard. You trust me today, but if I step out of line, I will hear from you and it won't be a positive thing. I do want to be your friend.*

11

Where's The Agent?

The overheard conversation of Surnani and the others at the wakes renewed Beauregard's push for bringing in the real estate agent, Jonah Cronin. With Barney, the land's owner murdered, there were two remaining possible witnesses in the know. Cronin and Norbie Cull. If possible, Rudy wanted Cronin in first, thinking *you get nothing from an attorney except a few basic facts already known. Although in this case, it's a land deal, not Cull defending some criminal.*

Sergeant Barr told the Captain, "Cronin's office personnel could give us nothing but his location. His hunting lodge is not in Canada, Captain. It's in Pembroke, Maine, near the Canadian border. Area hunting offers hunters whitetail deer, black bear, or wild turkey and upland game birds. Of course, all hunters in the area are looking for the legendary moose. I've been up there. Beautiful country, god darn beautiful country. Town has less than nine hundred residents. It's located a few miles from Cobscook Bay. Beautiful."

"Skip the travelogue, Sergeant. Call the police chief up there. He'll know where to find Cronin. If he won't talk to you put him through to me. Those guys up there were born suspicious. He'll want to check us out before we get anything from them."

An hour later Beauregard received a call from the police chief who once he determined the legitimacy of the source said he would have an officer reach out to Jonah Cronin. Later in the day the Chief called.

"Captain Beauregard, no one has seen Jonah for at least a month."

Rudy pushed his inquiry. He was assured Jonah was not in hiding. His lodge was not occupied and there were no footprints or truck tire imprints around his area. Beauregard was now concerned. Why would he hide out? Did Cronin think he was at risk after Barney's death? Why would a land deal cause these problems?

Sergeants Barr and Border paid visits to Cronin's wife and office. They spoke with neighbors. Cronin was a gregarious guy. One neighbor said, "Just wait, Sergeant. Jonah has to be with people. It's why he's successful. He can talk and talk and talk. He can't be quiet for long. Wherever he is, he'll surface. He's a good family man and his wife is a good cook. He'll come home for her cooking. You think I'm kidding. I'm not. Good guy. He wouldn't hide from anyone."

Rudy had no other choice but to bring in his friend and a co-conspirator with whom he was often at legal odds.

Cull was busy with a client scheduled for a deposition the next day. He was willing to come to the station after five. Rudy agreed but thought, *Cull makes my life damn inconvenient. We're having the parents over tonight for dinner. I'd better call them before Mona. Calling ahead will help smooth things with her. She thinks I make up situations to allow me late entry so I don't have to help. I don't, but the thought has occurred to me from time to time. I'm just not that devious. Well, not that devious when dealing with Mona.*

Norbie and Rudy talked family and weather for a minute or two before Cull cut to the chase. "Must be important for you to call in an attorney for info. What's up, Rudy?'

Rudy asked about Jonah Cronin's whereabouts. Cull reacted quickly. "You've searched unsuccessfully or you wouldn't have me in here. Jonah doesn't hide from anyone. He has a hunting lodge in Maine. I've been up there. I know a couple of guys with places near his. I'll call up."

Cull arrived a few minutes earlier than planned. He said, "Nada, Rudy, no one has seen Jonah up at the camps. They would know if he was in the area. I think he has a sister, but his wife would have told you if he were visiting the sister. I don't like his not being available. It is not Jonah's style to be incommunicado. The spotty cell phone service up in Maine drives him crazy. He's that wedded to his phone."

The two men discussed the implications related to Cronin being missing. Neither could see any connection to the explosion murders. Rudy asked Cull, "What could Jonah know about the land deal and the potential bidders to put him at risk? I mean you know everything about the deal and you're not missing."

"Rudy, you sound as if you'd rather it be me than Jonah, but don't worry, I understand the deflated value you sometimes put on attorneys. I don't take it personally."

"Cut the crap, Norbie, I'm serious. What would he know and you not know?"

Norbie went through the basic history of the land deal and Barney's difficulty in handling his family, which was solved when the last family member dies. Other than the family problem and the land appraisal, the deal was not overly complicated. Jonah was chosen as the real estate agent for a couple of reasons including Barney's comfort level with Jonah who was an old friend and Jonah's reputation for closing deals with clean private auctions. Cull concluded, "Rudy, the only aspect of this commercial transaction I was not privy to is the list of bidders. I would have gotten them from Barney in the normal course of events. What is particularly strange is Barney did not tell me he was showing the property. I knew he would be in the next few weeks but it was not his practice to keep me out of the loop. Another question I have is why he would show the property to all the bidders on the same morning. Normally he'd tour with each of them separately. He'd get their development plans and report back to me and Barney. That way we could assess who had plans of interest to Barney and those with economic potential for success. If Barney didn't like a potential development, he would have put off a bidding. It's a question bothering me. Doesn't make sense given Barney's sensibilities."

"Who were the bidders? Do you have any knowledge of the amount of bidders?"

"I only know from business gossip. The four people at the site were said to be interested. I did hear Art Richards' son James may have a group of investors interested in an athletic complex. The need for one in the area has been floating around for years. The land is in my mind too costly to use for that purpose unless there's free grant money. I suppose if it's set up as a non-profit there would be that tax incentive. Aside from James, Barney didn't tell me about other interested parties and neither did Jonah. Did Abu or Zed tell you who contacted them. I imagine Jonah's assistant did the calling."

"Nope. She says Jonah was very private about this transaction. She said he kept most of his business in his head. Zed says he got a voicemail from a lady asking him what days he was available. He told her his availability and then got a typed note from Barney a day later by snail mail agreeing to a date and time."

"The note is not from Barney. I can tell you that. He has no typewriter. He handwrites all correspondence. If a lady called it would have to be Jonah's administrator. Something is fishy. Ask Abu how he was contacted. Pull James Richards and Surnani in and ask how they were contacted. Surnani would have taken the letter for Art Richards and scheduled the appointment. What has he said?"

"Surnani's up for an interview as is James Richards. If what you say is true, and I don't doubt you, Norbie, someone set these bidders up. If James Richards didn't get a call and note, then he wasn't considered a serious bidder. And I was told there were more bidders interested in the property."

"Barney and Jonah both said there was a great deal of potential action. Have your guys called a couple of other brokers? They would have tried to talk Barney into using them. Barney may have spoken to them if for no other reason than to support my judgment. In the end he trusted my judgment. Shake the bushes, Rudy. These murders were planned."

The Captain appeared thoughtful after Norbie left the station. Surnani and James Richards had separate interviews scheduled later in the day. He thought, *it's strange. Who set these men up? I'll send Petra to see Abu. He may be more forthcoming with a woman. If he was contacted in the same way, then Art and Corinne were also. I don't understand why Surnani was not with Art Richards at the showing.*

Petra's visit with Abu the next morning was fruitful. She thought during the meeting, Abu *is a cagey character, but he is in some pain and on meds. Patients get talkative when on meds. Either that or they sleep. His story on the invite to view the property is the same as Zed's. He's fuming at almost losing his life to some weirdo. I didn't tell him that Barney was not the one who sent the note or made the call, but he knew it. This guy has his ear close to the ground even from his hospital bed. He was aggressive in attacking me and the police for not knowing more. I made some small talk, but he attacked.*

"Lieutenant, it is murder. Just who was their mark, I don't know. My time slot was listed at 10:15. I got there somewhere around 9:30. The blast was about thirty minutes later, long enough for me to get to the back of the lot and see Zed."

Petra asked, "Do you know what time Zed's invite was?"

"Yeah, the same time as mine which we both thought was weird."

"Abu, are you sure about the explosion time close to 10:00? It's important."

"Lieutenant, just check with first calls to 911 and you'll find them clocked at a couple of minutes later. You can check on my memory."

Petra headed over to the Witner Real Estate office in Springfield. She was exiting her auto when she caught sight of Beryl Kent leaving the building. She made a quick decision to call out to her, surprising the lady. Petra said, "Fancy meeting you here. Are you buying some commercial properties, Beryl?"

Appearing not the least bit perturbed, Beryl replied, "Petra, good to see you and no, I'm visiting a friend."

"Is it a condolence call, Beryl?"

Surprised, Beryl answered, "Yes, do you know Jonathan? His friend died in a single car auto accident. He is quite broken up."

"You do know who his girlfriend is, don't you?"

Beryl said, "Yes I do know his friend, Teisha Abbott. Why are you interested, Petra?"

"Aren't you the one who doesn't like coincidences, Beryl? Was Teisha's death accidental?'

"No, I don't believe for a minute it was."

"Beryl, are you here to give your condolences or to ask questions? Do you know him well?"

Her answer surprised Petra. "I know him quite well. He went to university with my son Oliver. He is quite broken up at Teisha's death. Theirs was a long-term friendship. He may have liked it to be more, but it wasn't. I didn't ask him too much about Teisha. I just listened. Please be careful in your questions, Petra. Jonathan is fragile now."

The two women said their goodbyes.

Petra liked Jonathan. He was open about his Teisha and said he counseled her to put the Corinne and Art thing behind her. The job to him was not important enough to cause her so much stress. Petra asked, "Was the position important because Teisha is short of money?"

The answer was an absolute no. Her husband left a large insurance policy leaving her financially comfortable. Teisha was not stupid about money. She invested the policy in a financial instrument payable over her lifetime. She lived with her mother because her mom helped with her little girl. Teisha supported her mom. He said, "Look, Lieutenant, I'm having a difficult time with this investigation. I hear Teisha was drunk and on drugs. Can't be. She was not a big drinker and she'd never commit suicide. She loved Gracia, her little girl and would never leave her."

Petra asked, "Jonathan, did you meet her at McCaffrey's Tavern shortly before her accident?"

"No. I was at a fundraiser for the mayor. She was to meet me later that evening to talk. She wanted to discuss a financial investment with me related to real estate. She said she trusted my judgement."

"You don't know who met with her at McCaffrey's?"

"No, and I am surprised she went to the tavern alone. It must be about business. Lieutenant, Teisha is from a different culture. Her going to that tavern is surprising. I can only imagine her meeting was with a business associate. Teisha was into politics, business, and public relations."

"Would you know most of her associates if I were able to get a sketch of the man she met with at the Tavern?"

"I know some of her friends but not all of them. I'm not the social animal Teisha was. I liked that about her. She brought me many clients. I'll give it a try. Bring the sketch and I'll try."

"Jonathan, do you think Teisha's fiery temper would allow her to make an error in judgment about whom to trust?"

"Teisha was not raised in the hood. Her upbringing was typical middle class, but she aligned herself with the Black and Hispanic Communities. She did fundraising for anyone in those groups who needed public relations or marketing for their events; all on her own time. She felt obligated to help. It's why they were enraged by Art Richards and Corinne Thompson's deceitful actions. Teisha would have understood if they had not encouraged her application. Teisha was not going to let the falsity of their actions go unnoticed. She told me she would carry the story publicly as far as possible. I explained she was not the only one harmed by those two and nobody got the best of Art. He is or was too powerful."

"Somebody did, Jonathan. Given her strong reaction to their lies, do you think Teisha played a role in the explosion?"

"Never, don't you see, she used words as weapons, not violence. She was the sweetest person I ever met."

"Jonathan, you're in real estate, what do you know about the Barney Land Deal?"

"Only what scuttlebutt tells me. I'm not a commercial broker. I specialize in residential real estate. I have worked in partnership with developers on residential housing tracts, but the Barney deal, from the dollar quotes I've heard, is out of my league."

"Do you know the agent for Barney's land?"

"Everyone does including me. Joshua Cronin is a great guy. The thing about commercial real estate is you often have to sit on a project a long time before the right party gets interested. Cronin is financially able to do that. Most of us need regular turnover to keep afloat. Residential is popping now. The pandemic has crippled the commercial market. Businesses are leaving big rents. This property is commercial, but is valuable for the right party. Apparently, Barney felt this was the right time to sell and he wouldn't have done that if attorney Cull had not agreed. Makes me wonder just who was interested besides Richards. Richards has been selling off commercial properties from what I've heard. Yet he's going into this large deal. He has a use. I just haven't heard what."

Beryl Kent found herself alone in her kitchen for the first time in a long time. And it felt good. The stillness grounded her, leaving her to rambling aloud, "There must be a motive to kill the first two. That's if the right people were killed. Maybe the victims were supposed to be the biker and the minister. Requires a different analysis if true. Look at subsequent to the murder crimes. Teisha dies and Darla dies and Barney dies. What is the connector? Barney would know who was to visit and at what time. He also knew all those interested in the property. With Barney dead, some of those questions can't be answered. Maybe the agent can fill in some. I can't wrap my head around killing Teisha. Richards would figure a way to punish her. He didn't have to plan her death. What did Teisha know that caused her death? So much coincidence, but I can't find the common thread."

Beryl reviewed the explosion as she remembered, thinking, *if I weren't going to Home Depot, I wouldn't have been on the scene. I was there early right after the first explosion but before the second. Fire and ambulance were there but the station is in view of the explosion area. Wait a minute, the men who were interested in the property probably had appointments for viewing and I suppose Jay Bird could be included in the group. He said he was told to show up but also said he was just thinking about bidding. But how…. how did the press get there so early? It's ten miles from their station. Even if fire called them, they wouldn't be there before me. I have to ask Beauregard to check this out. Something's fishy.*

Beryl heard from the desk sergeant at the station the whereabouts of the Captain. Her relationship with the day sergeant was one of trust which left most folks in the department questioning how this trust came about. The rumor of Beryl's charms prevailed as the answer. Not understood by the sergeant's peers was the fact both Beryl and the sergeant belonged to a very small club of New York Times Crossword Puzzle solvers who used ink.

Beryl showed up at the local coffee shop and, not surprisingly, saw the Captain and two of his detectives, Barr and Border lunching on hero sandwiches. Without invitation Beryl joined the group causing the Captain to belatedly say, "Please join us. You must have something important to tell me. How did you know I would be here?"

"Serendipitous, Captain, I was driving by and saw your car and thought I'd catch a moment with you and a salad."

The waitress quickly took her order while Beauregard slowly processed his luncheon companion had a mission which he would not have been able to stop, thinking, *now witnesses take the license to join me. Nothing's sacred anymore. Bobby and Bill are suppressing big smiles. This had better be good. Although I did tell her she could interrupt me at any time if she had a thought.*

"Captain, do you realize the photographer and news reporter were at the explosion site before I got there. I wonder about the timing. I was two minutes down the road when I heard the first explosion, arrived no more than three minutes later, parked and crossed the street. They were already set up. Now the others who were there already may have had a reason to be there since I expect they were potential bidders for the property. I've thought the fire department was right on the scene but they're only a mile away. If someone there informed the news immediately, the news team still couldn't have arrived that fast unless they were in the area for another reason. I think you should question their timeliness. Did they get a phone call and from whom?"

Beauregard was interested and for the next fifteen minutes he appreciated Beryl's presence as a witness at the explosion site, saying, "Beryl, witnesses always know more than what they think they know at first."

Sergeant Barr said, "I can call Stacia. She'll tell me who directed them to the site."

Beauregard cautioned, "Don't call. Buy her a coffee. Be a little indirect at first. She's a news person and will quickly figure out its importance. Just let her think we're looking at all those present and their timing to put together their views on the explosion. Mention you have just come from interviewing Beryl. I want her thinking this is just police filling in blanks."

Barr replied, "I'll be happy to spend some extra time with the lady. Thanks, Captain."

Barr left the remaining three at the table with the check. Beryl tried to cover it but Beauregard was faster. He said, "Lunch on us. You're the witness."

12
Missing Pieces

Stacia Kovac smiled as she drank her double espresso latte, saying, "Sergeant, how nice to see you again and during your work day. It must mean you're about police business."

"Yup, but Stacia, that's not all. I happily chose you as one of the witnesses to the explosion I wanted to interview. They gave me some guff about my extra wiliness. We're interested in the exact timing each witness arrived, just to put together a fuller picture of what was seen and heard. I've just finished interviewing Beryl Kent. You know her?"

"Yes, and I don't know how she got her press pass. She arrived shortly after we got there."

"How did she knew about this? Beryl seems to always be where there's trouble."

"Probably just was driving by, Bobby. I think the men were there on business and were too late to get blown up."

"How'd you know about the explosion, Stacia? Were you just driving by?"

"No, Robbie and I were out looking for something for the news. Lots of church activities such as craft sales during this season. We needed a human-interest story. Normally someone calls in with a story but nothing that morning. Robbie gets a call and said there was something going on over on Junction Road. We thought it might be an accident. Instead, just as we pulled up, there was the first explosion. We were parking on the same side of the street as the explosion. We got a lot of dust and debris on our car. We got great pictures. It was a scoop."

"This Robbie, have you worked with him for a long time?"

"Only about a year. He has a knack of being at the right place and time for a scoop. I love partnering with him. He doesn't talk too much and knows the shortest routes. He has a list of about forty people who give him heads up in each neighborhood. When we have nothing, after an hour of trying, he'll start making his calls from his list."

"Were you there before the fire department which is only a mile away?"

"Yes, I didn't think about the timing, Bobby. His fire department connection must have called him as they were leaving. Wait, we were there just a second before the first explosion. Who could have called Robbie…..it must have been someone who suspected something. I never thought about the timing. I'll call him now."

"Please don't, Stacia. We'll interview him. It's best he doesn't have a heads-up. We want a fresh interview. Please don't make that call. It could be interpreted as interfering with a police investigation now that you've been requested to refrain. What's his surname?"

"Layden." Then she added, "And you would arrest me, Bobby?"

"No, maybe just house arrest at my condo. But don't call Robbie. Promise."

"I won't. About that house arrest. You will let me know so I can pack a few things."

"I will let you know. It's a given but the timing will be after this investigation."

"Just don't forget, Bobby. I won't."

Beauregard, when told by Sergeant Barr about the timing issue, requested Bobby find Robbie and invite him to the station for a witness report, saying, "Tell him we want him to view our video to see if there's something we can't see but he can. Mention nothing about the timing and I hope your gal Stacia doesn't warn him."

"She won't, Captain."

"Oh, to be young enough to be fooled by a pretty face! She works with him every day. Don't think loyalties aren't developed between colleagues, Sergeant."

Just in time to interrupt Beauregard's lunch, Sergeant Barr walked in with Robbie Layden. Robbie appeared fascinated with the goings on at the station and had peppered Barr with a thousand questions. Barr settled him in an interview room and Robbie asked, "Is that a one-way mirror?"

"Yes, but no one's on the other side. We save personnel for when we have a serial murderer in here."

They both laughed. Robbie asked if his interview would be taped and the answer was, "We tape everything said here for both your and our protection, but the Captain will tell you that before he starts questioning."

"I guess you'd have to tape it. I imagine it's on video as well. Right?"

"Yeah, of course. If there are ever questions about behavior, it's back-up to support our actions. We're used to being audited and judged. Don't you watch television crime shows?"

Robbie nodded affirmatively just as the Captain and Lieutenant Aylewood-Locke entered the room. Beauregard thanked Robbie for his assistance. Robbie said, "Do all the witnesses have to appear at the station? I thought it was only for material witnesses."

The Lieutenant answered, "Robbie, we have video to show you. Didn't Sergeant Barr tell you?"

Robbie said, "Just checking to see if your stories are the same. You guys do it all the time, you know, make up different stories to make witnesses tell the truth."

Petra ignored the remark and started questioning him about when he got to the scene. His answer was consistent with Stacia's story. Petra said, "You have a remarkable reputation for being 'Johnny on the Spot' Robbie. You must have friends everywhere. I know from policing how important it is to develop connections for information. Who called you that morning to tell you to get over there?"

And the cat and mouse game played out. Robbie insisted the fire department called him. When faced with the realization that he got there before the fire department and that the fire department was only a mile away, he said, "We must have been closer when I got the call."

Sergeant Barr explained the fire brigade was caught off guard, and a representative there reported no one had time to call anyone.

Robbie's demeanor clearly showed his distaste for being questioned. He insisted he was called by Fire. Barr insisted he was not. Robbie changed his story to, "Well, I assumed it was from the Fire Department, but might have been one of my many connections calling. I don't know all their voices."

Petra said, "Robbie, how could you get a call to go to an event and get there before the explosion event? You see, don't you, how important is the timing."

"Who said we got there before the event? I think it was right afterwards."

"You said it. Others have said you were there just as the explosion occurred. How could anyone know when it would occur before the explosion happened?"

His answer was unexpected. "I want my attorney. You're trying to rope me into something. I'm well known for my connections. For all I know, it was the guy who rigged the explosion. I don't know him."

"What were his exact words and are you certain it was a man's voice?"

He said it was definitely a man who said, "Robbie, don't ask. And don't play word games with me. Go to Junction Road for a story."

Robbie then shut down all conversation when Petra asked for his cell phone, saying, "Talk to my attorney."

The Captain and Lieutenant left the room while Robbie called his attorney. Beauregard relayed his thoughts. "Petra, I'm not sure what's going on here. The guy is a wanna-be cop, plays games, and I don't believe him. But, and this bothers me, how could he know about an event in the future if he is not involved or hasn't talked with one who is involved. To me he looks like a weak sister, not smart enough to get his story straight. I want a history on all his famous scoops. He is known within press circles, but again, the anchor gets the publicity. I'm certain he wants to be more important. I don't like the report 'Don't play word games with me.'"

Petra said, "You don't think it has to do with those pasted messages, do you, Captain?"

"I don't know, but we have to figure it out."

<hr>

Lieutenant Mason Smith, the department's computer guru and researcher, was pleased with his morning's work. His focus was twofold and it appeared he had accomplished what he set out to do. Mason was famous for his smug look and his celebratory attitude when he felt victorious. He walked into the Lion's Den and loudly exclaimed, "Research beats feet on the street every time."

Bill Border laughed, answering, "And what does our Wizard have for us today?"

"You all have given me a shit load of requests. Not being a linear thinker as my brothers in blue, I choose what I want to pursue, unless you label a request as urgent. Given that, I chose what was of interest to me to chase down. Lo, I know the current location of the real estate agent. And, I have some gossip from the in the know folks about Jay Bird, James Richards, and Minister Abu."

Beauregard said, "Cut to the chase, Lieutenant. Where is Jonah Cronin and how did you find him?"

"Logic, Captain. I used plain old logic. Cronin is missing. He lies to everyone about his destination. I couldn't find credit card use. What's left? When do folks hide their destination? He's having an affair which doesn't work because even if he was secreted in the lady's place, they would have sent out for meals and there'd be charges and use of his phone. Nada! I couldn't get his credit charges or bank statements without a warrant and he wasn't reported by family as missing. Where would he not use his phone or even have it? Somewhere that doesn't allow the use of phones. I eliminated a high-end health resort because he is supposedly in great shape. I made some calls. Some of his friends said he was a regular bar fly at the local country clubs. Voila, I chased down famous drying out spots. I'm not talking about the low-cost ones. I'm talking about the pricey ones. Getting info on his placement took me a bit, but I went by his recent trips and found he went several times to a Vermont town famous for its cushy personal help for big players. A month stay is fifty grand. I took a chance and had a friend in the area chase down his car in the parking lot and it was there. He'd shut off the location settings before he went. Smart dude. Now how you reach him, Captain, is the question."

"Not to worry. Give me the info for the police chief in the town. I'll find a way. Now get to the next bit of info, Mason, with no dramatics please."

"Abu Cason has history with Jay Bird. An unlikely duo if you ask me. Bird is famous for speaking about science vs religion. He is a known agnostic with little respect for ministers, priests or rabbis. Cason and Bird are both major players in a new cannabis delivery business in the area. To get an in with the company's investment group required a great deal of up-front cash. They joined the group as an LLC called "Health Investments, LLC. How's that for an unlikely pair of partners."

Beauregard said, "Not so unlikely. Finance brings about strange relationships. It's for money. How much was their investment?"

"Total is one and a half million. They'll make that back in the first year, but meanwhile, where are they getting funds to invest in the property on Junction Road? Chase down their banking connections with your friends. You can get a heads up on how either one of them has that kind of credit. What's backing it up? We need to do the same for James Richards. I question how a man in his early thirties could be in such a great financial position; unless his dad gave him a substantial amount. I don't see a strong relationship between he and his dad, plus Art Richards wants to control everything. If he were to have given James assets, there'd be a string attached."

Beauregard smiled, saying, "Good work, Lieutenant."

Petra said, "Captain, we've never had a case or cases with so many moving parts and such a question about motivation. The contact by Barney to the bidders smells. Cronin's not here to answer questions about why he called all the bidders for the same morning and how he contacted them. I don't think Barney and Cronin knew about the bidding. It was a setup for murder, but did the right people get murdered? If it's not these victims who were the chosen ones then we are further behind on figuring out a motive for murder."

"Petra, we know nothing right now. Look at your murder boards and make sure all info is attached. I know some of you use other programs for inter-connected murders. If your programs allow you to reshuffle data, then do regrouping of murders leaving one murder at a time out of the connections. There may be two murderers or more in this mess."

"Captain, I don't think we should make this too complicated. We should do what you tell us; find a commonality. Maybe it's not the land deal. Could be it's something else. Killing all four people over a land deal is not normal. Greed is normal. Passion is normal. Jealousy is normal. Anger is normal."

"Lieutenant, thanks for the reminder. We may be too focused too soon. Not like me. Thank you."

The search for Jonah Cronin presented Beauregard with problems. Drying-out high-end establishments had heightened security ensuring complete privacy for their patients. The Captain connected with the local police captain. When he explained the importance of Jonah Cronin as a material witness, he was gives some assistance. Still, there was a two day wait. The rehab had rules. Jonah could not see anyone outside until a certain date. If the interview with Beauregard was too stressful, the staff would stop it. Beauregard thought, *it's no different than in the damn hospitals where doctors and nurses control. I never thought of the stress on the patient who is there for alcohol or drug cleansing. I guess they are just as fragile. Two days will work. It has to because I can't move them to break their rules.*

When interviewed, Jonah Cronin appeared subdued. Sergeant Border and Beauregard both expected to see the jolly happy-go-lucky real estate agent known for his sociability. This man was calm and quiet and at first terse in his answers. He said he was willing to speak with them but wished to speak with Attorney Norberto Cull first, saying, "Norbie brought me into this along with Barney. I can't believe Barney was murdered. He was the best of the best. For years, I'd kid him about selling his land. I knew it was valuable, but was surprised with the appraiser's big number. I don't want to get into legal difficulties by speaking out of turn. Just let me check with Norbie. If he thinks it's okay, I'll tell you everything I know. Please, if I am a witness, do you have to say where you interviewed me? It's my business and I'm seeing into myself and my jolly nature's cover for my demons for the first time in my life. Please don't expose my situation. I'll tell my wife when I get home, but not now. I'm not quite ready to take on the stress of explaining."

The Captain responded, "I can't promise it won't come out, your situation, I mean, but I'll try to keep it under wraps. You've invoked your need for an attorney. I can't deny you. Make the call. We'll go into that little sitting room and wait for you."

The wait was not long. And as expected, Cull told him to tell them all. "Captain, I am astonished to hear the potential bidders were notified of a walk-thru. I had planned for one in two weeks. It was too early for one. I hadn't gone through the property for safety. I'd not made up sign-in sheets, nor have I received info from their banks. They would not have needed their cashier check, but certainly would present bank letters as to their financing capability. And if you think I would be having all the parties on a walk-thru at the same time, you are mistaken. This is not a public bid. I use showing the property as my chance to question their motives and their truthfulness about their business plan. Barney chose me as agent because he knew I would look out for buyers who would put in businesses he didn't want. A big one was the rumor the land would be for production and sales of marijuana and related products. It may be legal, but not what Barney thought was appropriate for this area of town. He did not approve, but more than that, he thought the traffic would change the direction of the whole area. Another thing I'm shocked at is the idea anyone would think I am not in the modern era. Imagine sending out invitations to attend by snail mail in a typed letter. My office is completely computerized. The killer must have notified these people. This was pre-meditated, Captain. I did not send out invitations. It was too early. I hadn't even composed the letter I would send, nor determined to whom I would send it. It is only after composition I would have Jesse send letters out."

"Jonah, Jesse said you keep all big deal details close to your vest and it's why she couldn't help us."

"Captain, Jesse would tell you nothing. No matter what you would ask, she's smart enough to play dumb. In this case, it was the truth. She knew nothing. Once I give her the letter, anyone in the office could see it and see the list of names; not until then. I wouldn't send out anything until I spoke with Norbie. He was in control of everything Barney wanted done and you know better than me, Norbie is loyal and honest."

"Can you give me the list of known bidders to you. The list is important in investigating these murders."

"Captain, I think I'm able to give you the list. Just let me call Norbie again. It's a private sale, but the potential bidders won't be happy to be interviewed."

"Call Norbie, Jonah, but don't worry about the bidders. I have multiple murders and I'll interview anyone I think has information. You cover your tail with Cull. I'm interviewing every person mentioned to date who even talked about an interest. It'd be better if you helped, but if you don't, I'll be speaking to every commercial developer in the area. They'll blame you even if they've never been your client."

"Captain, I don't want to be on your bad side. I'll have Jesse send over my list. I'll call Cull and if there is a serious legal problem, you deal with him on the list."

13
Potential Bidders

The day at the station began with breakfast bagels and cream cheese from Alex's Bagels in Longmeadow in celebration of the return of the newlyweds. The razzing of the couple required Juan to speak out. Surprised it was not Lilly, Petra asked, "What happened to your voice, Lilly? Lost it on the honeymoon?"

Instead of back talking, Lilly answered, "Nope, I'm back in holiday mood. Must be my hormones because you all look lovely."

Silence reigned until the Captain insisted they get to work as they noshed. The list of potential bidders had been delivered by Sheila from Cull's office. He did not want anyone at his office other than Sheila seeing the list as long as it was an investigatory priority for the police. The list was surprising. It included James Richards and Jay Bird. Beauregard asked, "Bird and Richards were at the site. How the hell can they explain being there if they had not been in contact with Jonah?"

Lilly, who had spent an hour memorizing the murder board detail, said, "They'll say something like they were driving by or they joined a group interested and knew about the showing. I saw the connection between Abu and Bird. Abu could have told Bird about it and Abu said he got there earlier than his time. Bird is a writer, probably never gets anywhere on time. As to Richards, he most likely heard his father was coming and was to meet him but was too late. Our detectives' reports from Darla's funeral support his having great interest in the parcel of land. The assumption we held concerned Richards and his aides working the deal. We don't know yet if they were both trying to bid."

Petra asked, "Who's on the list, Captain?"

Beauregard shared the list. It included nine names: Richards, Thompson, Bird, Cason, Albion, Surnani, Connault, Conlon, and Abbot. The Captain said, "Three of the names are dead and two are injured. And yet, we still don't know who was marked for death with the exception of Teisha Abbot. Teisha was not on our radar as a bidder. She didn't have that kind of financial backing. Her death must be related to her holding some dangerous information on the deal or is not related. We have no way of knowing who was marked for death unless the timing of the device is determined and can match one or two or three of the bidders invited presence. Talk to each bidder and get their invitation letter from them. I'm quite interested in Nathan Connault as a bidder. We've known him as a government man, whose work appears to be undercover. Must be setting up a retirement package for himself. Leave him alone for now."

"We now know the land deal is central or why else would Teisha be killed. Who knew she was a bidder? Get that out of your interviews."

Lilly said, "We have Zed the biker's scheduled time of 10:15 a.m. He got there early at 9:35 a.m. The video on the explosion times it at 9:50 a.m. I'll work on getting their scheduled times, Captain."

"Schedule an interview here for each one and ask for the letter received supposedly from Barney and Jonah. Do it today, Sergeant, please. I'll sit in on all interviews. Let me know their schedules. One of these bidders knows more and knows or is the murderer."

The meeting was interrupted before it closed by Millie. "Captain, Darla Richards' father insists he speak with you now. He is an older man, but quite unstoppable. He insists you are the only honest detective in the area. He goes on and on. What should I do?"

Beauregard answered by accompanying her to the conference room and introducing himself to George Courtin, Darla's father, saying, "May I offer my condolences, Mr. Courtin. From all I've heard Darla was an exceptional woman. Now how can I help you? You understand this is a Springfield case and whatever you tell me will be relayed to the Springfield Major Crime Unit's detectives as they are conducting the investigation."

George huffed while almost yelling, "I don't care who the hell you tell. Nothing I'm telling you has not already been said, but they don't listen. I heard good things about you, Captain. Don't blow it. I spent twenty years in the Marine Corps. I know a fluff job when I hear it and that's all I've been getting."

Rudy tried the soft approach, saying, "I cannot speak to an open police case even if it is not my department's case, but I will listen to you. If I think your thinking is off the walls, I'll tell you. A marine will listen to an outsider telling the truth. Even if I believe you have something, I'll be quite circumspect in response. I can't promise more but can say if it were my daughter instead of Darla, I'd want to know all the facts around her death."

"Damn right! My grandson found Darla. How do you like that? Boy shouldn't find his mother hanging. By the time I got there the medical examiner was having the body removed. I insisted upon seeing her. She did not do this to herself. I know that. She had a birthday breakfast with three of her kids. James was not there. He's the second oldest and has a great business head. I asked Ricky, Tim, and Colleen where he was. They said he was at some real estate deal. Later, I find out he was on the site where his father was killed. Art Richards was my son-in-law for thirty-eight years and I've never known a shrewder and more uncaring guy. How James could go to a deal with his father and miss his mother's birthday, I don't know. It's not like him. He was the closest to Darla.

They had similar mindsets. James was the one insisting his mother divorce Art. Not like him. Something's up, I tell you. Can I get another autopsy done if I don't like what I hear. If it's suicide, I won't believe it."

And tears rolled down George Courtin's cheeks which he quickly brushed away with his large calloused hand causing Rudy to ask, "What did you do for work, George, aside from being a marine? I do know once a marine, then always a marine, but after your service."

"I've been a large equipment operator for construction. Did well. Made a bundle to leave to my grandkids. I told Darla, I could support her. She didn't need Art's money, but she believed in marriage. This piece of dung-heap only believed in himself. He only thinks or thought about himself. Not even the kids mattered except as a photo-op or for bragging rights. I think Darla was murdered and if that SOB were alive, I'd blame him. He hated her in the end. She was a mirror to all his faults. Darla was a generous and kind person. The kids are depressed and you know what the stigma of a parent's suicide does to the kids. There's a tendency for repetition in the family. Finally, Darla was reaching out as if she got a new lease on life."

The Captain in a few carefully chosen words questioned how George knew. He said, "She was getting a divorce, not just a separation and I think she was seeing someone. She wasn't reachable from four to eight on Tuesdays and Thursdays. I thought it was a man, but was afraid to ask."

The Captain inferred he believed there may be something more to Darla's death than suicide and ended with, "If I believe it's suicide, George, then you'll have to live with it."

George, holding back tears but with a fierce expression on his face agreed to accept Rudy's statement. "I trust you to give me the truth behind her death. I'll leave it at that."

Beauregard questioned, "George, I wondered about your grandson

James. He's the second oldest of Darla's children."

After an affirmative nod, George said, "He is and was very close to his mother, which is why it's strange he wasn't at Darla's birthday party. I haven't said anything to him. I don't want to stir the waters. He's already so depressed. James was the business heir apparent to Art's empire until several months ago. They had a falling out. Neither one would explain why. I thought when I heard James was at the explosion site, it meant they were reconciled. Much as I hated Art, I didn't want a division between father and son."

"Does James have a lady friend, someone he trusts?"

"Yeah, he did but she turned him away. She already had a little girl. I thought he needed to marry and start a family, not get one ready-made, but it seems to be the fashion today. He seemed lost at first. He's probably over it now."

"Do you know her name, George?"

"Never met her. One of the kids will know her name. Try Colleen, she'll know."

The Captain made a call to Beryl Kent thinking, *I'll probably regret this, but this lady may be able to get done what I can't get done. I just have this feeling and I don't want to ask Colleen Richards for the info.*

Not even an hour later, Beryl welcomed Beauregard to her kitchen, saying, "I would have come to the station."

The twinkle in her eye suggested she understood his motivation. He was forced to say, "Eyes are everywhere. I don't need the world to know we collaborate."

Beryl said, "It might be a good thing if they knew, Captain. You hold all your public with respect. What would be wrong with planting that thought?"

Rudy took the professionally prepared cup of Beryl's latte, sipped, and explained his visit. "There are questions I have, Beryl, which must be asked in a more delicate manner than would be typical for my detectives. And you, Beryl, can manipulate better than anyone I know."

"I'm not flattered by your remarks, but don't worry, I'm not particularly insulted. Did you ever wonder why manipulation is used. It's used when a person has power to be in the room when decisions are made but no status to contribute. It's used when straight forward conversation would not garner information needed. Manipulation is also used as a power play by sociopaths and narcissists to control others. I approve of its use in the first two instances, but not in the third. Think, Captain, what you are asking me."

Rudy laughed. He then detailed his request. "I understand Colleen Richards is quite close to her brother James. James was recently dumped. I think that's the word used. The girl's name is unknown. You know people close to the family. Could you reach Colleen and ask her without telling her it's police business. And while you are at it, ask her whether James' split with his dad was reconciled. Do you know James' financial resources? If not, see what you can discover from the family. I cannot be successful if I or one of my detectives try to extract info."

"Rudy, you have an idea about James' former girlfriend, don't you? If it were just any girl, there'd be no reason not to have your detectives interview her. You want her name, but think you know her name. You think she's connected to the deaths. Are you speaking about Teisha? You can't interview a dead woman. She had a boyfriend? You're not speaking about Jonathan Witner. He was just her friend, not her boyfriend."

"Can't you just do what I asked?"

"Yes, I can and now I am interested, very interested to see if Teisha was James' girlfriend. All kinds of implications if so."

"Beryl, why did you so quickly hit on Teisha as the one who dumped him?"

"Easy, Rudy, she's the only one related to the case who qualifies in beauty and smarts for James."

———

Contrary to Rudy's thoughts about the direction Beryl would head to for info, she called her friend Marjorie Phipps and scheduled lunch at the Puerto Rican Bakery and Restaurant on Walnut Street where they could dine in. Beryl searched the menu for a small dish and was having trouble when Marjorie suggested they split an order. When the order arrived, the women discussed their wisdom in sharing. Marjorie said, "Enough food for a week. I like small plates but the food is good."

Beryl waited patiently until Marjorie moved the conversation from the sadness of Teisha's loss to Teisha's daughter Gracia. Beryl was able to steer the conversation to Teisha's love life, saying, "She was bright and beautiful, Marjorie. Did she have some significant person in her life? I would think men would be hanging all over her."

"They were. Beryl, Teisha lived the active life of a quasi-community supporter. She was educated in public relations, but from her perspective, it meant doing good. She did not give her body away easily. Lately there was some talk of a special guy. I never heard of her being out with one. I know Jay Bird the mystery author took her out for dinner a few times, but Teisha said he had no religion. Do you know him? Maybe writing murder mysteries took away his soul, but she was not impressed. She didn't like him rushing her. He showed up at a few public events she was working and tried to monopolize her. She told me he was too controlling for her. He kept showing up."

"Was Jay the only guy trying to shall we say court her?"

"He wasn't the special one. The only other man I witnessed her talking to for longer than ten minutes was James Richards. She was probably giving him hell for his father and Corinne's actions. I don't know of any other men. You need to speak with a younger person or her mother."

Beryl left her luncheon with Marjorie convinced that James was the man. She deliberated, *I need to connect with Colleen Richards before I speak with James. Did I see Teisha at Darla's wake? She died a couple of days later. Beauregard has video of the wakes. If she were there, she'd have spoken to James at length somehow. The way of romance if it were a romance.*

Beryl phoned her friend of the Richards's family, asking, "Erica, how is Colleen doing?"

"I don't know what to say, Beryl. She's quite disturbed and very angry with her father which we all understand. Colleen insists her mother would never be a suicide. She thinks someone murdered her. She wonders if her father arranged a murder before he died."

"How do James, Richard, and Tim feel?"

"They agree with Colleen but are more closed mouth. James is suffering. His girlfriend died in an accident. I don't know who she was but Tim says his brother was about to buy an engagement ring. None of the family had met his lady. Tim thought maybe it was because she was of another race. His dad was totally against mixed marriages and Tim thought maybe James was uncertain about how the rest of the family felt, because he asked Tim not to say anything yet."

Unlike Beauregard, Beryl did not need more data to form her own conclusion. "It must be Teisha was the girlfriend, thinking, *I wonder how Jay Bird liked being thrown over by Richards' son.*

Aloud to no one, Beryl said, "Time to call the Captain and Cull."

14
Personal or Business?

Beauregard was surprised to receive Beryl's news by cell phone. He wondered, *damn woman, I can never get ahead of her. Now, she doesn't even come in for a conference knowing I'd ask more questions. She phones with her news and assumptions. They're pretty good. I know she'd not have called me if she thought there was a chance she could speak with James Richards. My call, now, and if she's on point that James was Teisha's special friend, then it is necessary to ask questions about whether motives for these murders are personal or land project related. And then there's Jay Bird, big important writer who gets thrown over for James Richards. Must be galling when fame doesn't give you an edge. A younger man wants the woman he wants. To make the story better, Teisha, James, and Jay are listed bidders. Personal or business, either could be the motivation, or maybe both.*

Within an hour, Sergeant Juan Flores presented James Richards in Conference Room 1. Millie was instructed to bring in lattes from the Unit's very expensive espresso machine funded by the detectives themselves. Beauregard often expressed his thoughts to his crew they had expensive tastes in food and drink. In this case, the investment was worthwhile. James said, "It's nice to see quality coffee in the station, Captain. Shows your guys do more than eat bad donuts."

He laughed lightly at his own joke, pleased the Captain did not take offense. Beauregard answered, "Donuts have lots of cholesterol. Although with some of the add-ins for lattes, they may not be much better. Thanks for coming in, Mr. Richards."

"Please call me James, Captain. I've gone throughout my life with my father called 'Mr. Richards.' It's not for me."

"Sergeant Flores will be asking you some questions along with Lieutenant Smith. We have multiple murder inquiries relative to West Side. Before we start, please accept our condolences on the death of your parents. The losses must be overwhelming. I understand that Teisha Abbot's death was a heavy loss to you. I am sorry. We are investigating that accident as well."

James Richards' eyes welled up, but he was successful in holding back the tears. Sergeant Flores said, "I do have questions about Ms. Abbot's death, James."

Before the Sergeant could explore further, James said, "Good, because Teisha would never commit suicide. She was in love with life, and she wasn't a drinker."

Flores said, "The rumor is you and Teisha were a couple. Is that true?"

"I bought her a ring to give to her that night. She didn't show up and didn't answer her phone. I learned about the accident the next day. That night, I went to her home, but it was too late to wake her mom and Gracia. Besides, I've never met her mom. I waited, but she didn't come home. The papers said she was with a man at a bar she would never enter. It all smells. I know she loved me. She wanted to be careful because she knew my father was racist as hell. In fact, we were considering eloping. My mom met her and liked her, and now they're both gone."

James asked for a minute. "I'm sorry for the emotion, but my world has gone upside down."

Juan took his time before the next question. "Did you know, James, that Teisha was a listed bidder along with you."

James grimaced. "How did you know? I heard the letters didn't come from Barney or Cronin. I never spoke with Cull. Only Barney or Cronin could have told you, but one is dead and the other has disappeared."

"I can assume from your answer you knew Teisha was a bidder?"

"I didn't know she got a letter. She wasn't there that day."

Flores corrected James. "She was one of the bystanders like yourself. Didn't you wonder why?"

"She knew I received a letter. She didn't say she received one. I thought she was there to support me."

"I don't understand, James. You said you knew she was a bidder. Why wouldn't she have gotten a letter?"

"Because I thought at first I would be the only bidder to be shown the property. I came early for my time but arrived after the explosion. She was horrified by the spectacle and we didn't discuss letters after that. And then my mother died and I saw Teisha at Mom's funeral, but we couldn't talk. We were to meet the night she died and I already had the ring burning a hole in my pocket. I couldn't wait to ask her to marry me. Frankly, I needed her to say yes."

"Weren't you also at your dad's funeral on the same day as your mom's?"

"Yes. He was my father. Are you finding fault with my attending my father's funeral?"

"No, of course not, but Teisha didn't go to your father's funeral. If you were that close, why not?"

Beauregard appeared worried at this line of questioning, but did not interfere. James answered, "Teisha hated my father and Corinne, and for good reason. My father prevented her from getting a position he coaxed her to apply for, saying he would support her. It was a gimme, we thought. I argued with him about it. He said she was getting too self-important. I think he knew she was a bidder and was pissed. He did not know I was a bidder."

Beauregard asked the next question. "Why would you bid against your father? He has far more resources than you."

"My use for the property was for a sports complex. It is very much needed in the area. Our plan is quite robust and financially sound because we have some important investors behind us. Teisha brought in churches and social agencies from all over to invest smaller amounts but whose support would have been important to Barney. He was a good man. Whereas, my father wanted a Cannabis Dispensary and Production Facility, which would be fabulously successful. Barney would have to be talked into that use. Captain, with Barney dead, the decisions will be made by lawyers and businessmen and my use will be thrown under the bus."

"James, do you think Teisha's participation in your joint venture could have been a motive for her murder?"

"I've thought about it. My father had no scruples, but Teisha died after he died. Kind of removes him from doing it, right? Captain, I feel enormous guilt for bringing Teisha into this project if it was a cause of her death. She was gung-ho on our partnership in this venture. And her public relations side was awesome. The connections she made relative to the buildout, financial partners, athletic public figures, well they were a home run. I do think now our project is in jeopardy."

"Our information said you were recently dumped by Teisha?"

"Hell, no, but I did float that rumor to my father so he would leave Teisha alone. His inability to support my love could have been, in my mind, dangerous. Art Richards expected everyone to back off if he didn't like what they were doing. It's one of the reasons Corinne was getting rid of him. He was a control freak. She'd put up with it for years, but now had a new guy."

"Do you know who he was?"

"I am not certain, but she and John were spotted at some events unrelated to my father's work. People were talking."

Juan said, "Did your father know Corinne Thompson and Teisha were bidders?"

"He did not know about Corinne. She was there with him at the site. If he knew she was a bidder, he'd never have gone with her. I guess she must have gotten a letter or she didn't get one and went with him as his aide which was normal for her. We'll never know. Could the killer have wanted both of them dead or just my father?"

The Captain spoke. "What was your father's use for the land?"

"Cannabis, Captain, all the other bidders were about cannabis. At least that's what I've heard."

"Do you think your father and Corinne were bidding together? I wonder if she was bidding as his shill. Maybe a woman would have a better chance in winning a bid based on her gender. It would be important in getting funds from financial institutions."

"My father would never trust anyone in a bidding process bidding who was close to him. He trusted a known enemy more than his friends. He didn't want anyone close to him who was not relying on his power to survive. It worked for him. Look how he treated my mother."

Beauregard answered, "James, you don't paint a pretty picture of your dad. Did you kill him?"

"My dad was not pretty, he was one mean and selfish man. I would not kill him or anyone. I'm built like my mom emotionally. I'm kind of like she was, with one difference, I was getting out from under his control. If he hadn't died, Teisha and I would have made the bid together and Barney would have taken our bid. No one understood. Barney had values and would have seen our project as the best."

Juan said, "James, I'm confused. Just who do you think killed your dad and was he or Corinne the chosen victim?"

"I don't have a clue. If I knew who the bidders were, I could take a guess, but I don't know them all, only Surnani, Conlon, Teisha, me, that writer I saw there, Abu, and Zed."

Beauregard asked, "Are you referring to Jay Bird, the writer? Wasn't he Teisha's boyfriend? How could he come up with the funds?"

"Bird is a birddog. He went after Teisha when he knew I was interested in her. She said he was stalking her. Teisha was about to report him, because he wouldn't leave her alone. I stopped her. She was a quasi-public figure and it would have made a great but useless public story. So, I spoke to him and I can tell you, he is scary when he's confronted. She said he was loaded, not just from his writings, but was born wealthy. He has a great deal of family money and she believed it was why he acted so entitled. Teisha was sensitive to class issues."

Juan asked, "How did the conversation go when you spoke to Jay?"

"Not well, he accused me of using my father's power and money to interest Teisha. Jay said he could bury me if he had a mind to it. What was she anyway; just another single woman of color with a kid looking to break the cycle? I blew up. He got right in my face and then realized I was not afraid of him. It ended when he walked away muttering, 'You'll learn a lesson soon and so will she.'"

"Do you think he is involved in your father and Teisha's deaths? Or, did he think you were going to be there at the time of the explosion?"

"I hope not. I would then be to blame for exciting him to hurt Teisha."

Jay Bird appeared to take up the whole conference room. Sergeant Flores felt dwarfed by the writer and overwhelmed by his ego, thinking, *how do these guys do it? They act superior and are able to make you feel lesser if you let them. Seven inches in height does not make him a better man.*

Beauregard entered the room with Officer Shaughnessy. The usual acknowledgements were conducted. Jay said, "I don't understand why my statement taken on the day of the explosion is not enough information. What do you want? I will not change anything I said then and I have not gathered any new thoughts on the event."

The Sergeant in his best public relations manner reminded him he had not given a witness statement at the explosion site and assured the writer that all witnesses to the event were being re-interviewed and further, he was also interested in Mr. Bird's relationship with Teisha Abbot. Jay Bird quickly responded, "I barely knew Teisha. Had coffee with her a couple of times. Why would you be asking me about Teisha. Ask that minister and James Richards. It's too late to ask Art and Corinne, who could tell you a whole lot about Teisha."

Juan backed off the Teisha conversation, returning to the explosion. Jay said, "Take my statement. That's it. Nothing more I have to say."

"It's a problem for us. I just said you never gave a statement at the scene. My officers said you moved away too quickly before they could connect. Was there a reason you didn't want to be seen there, Mr. Bird?"

"No, I was just driving by and stopped to see what happened."

"At what time was your appointment to scope the property? Did you get there later or earlier than your appointment?"

"Why would I want to see the property? I had nothing to do with this property."

"Mr. Bird, we know you were on the bidder list. What time did your letter state for access for a view of the land?"

"Where'd you get that info? James Richards is just trying to ruin me with lies."

"You have a problem with Mr. Richards? How so?"

"He thinks I'm a bidder. It could only come from him."

Juan pushed. "Mr. Bird, you are on the list of bidders. You could not be there if you hadn't met the financial qualifications. Why deny it now?"

"You're trying to ruin my good name. I'm a mystery writer, not a businessman. So, I had a thought about the land. I don't have it now."

"The letter, did your letter state a time? You may have been the target for all we know. What time was stated?"

"You think I could have been the target? What time was the blast?"

"You first, Mr. Bird."

"The time stated for me was 9:45. Now what time was the explosion?"

"Close to that time but not on the button. We need that letter. Do you have it with you?"

"Well, I did prepare for this meeting."

Bird took the letter from his pocket, prompting Juan to say, "Why all the baloney about not being a bidder? Did you think we wouldn't learn about you in our investigation?"

"Frankly, no, I don't have a lot of respect for police. You're always pushing confessions from the wrong person. I didn't want to be one of your hack jobs. I know nothing about the explosion, but now I think I could be the victim. I was late. I'm often late. You better find out who was behind this soon."

Juan said, "There was a financial requirement to be a listed bidder. Where is your money coming from for this endeavor, not just the land but the development as well? Are you a partner with one of the other bidders?"

Bird answered, "I'm a wealthy man. I don't have to partner with anyone. I'll tell you what, after Art and Corinne's deaths, I don't want this deal. I'm out. The killer is getting rid of bidders and I don't want to be his next victim."

Juan pursued the discussion but he was met with denial. Bird also insisted that Teisha really liked him until James Richards interfered in the relationship. He said he had words with James who from his perspective was trying to get out from his father's yoke. He continued relaying his thoughts that James may have felt some freedom with Teisha with

Corinne and Art's deaths. Nevertheless, it was James' father who killed Teisha's chances for a high-profile job, saying, "Art and Corinne got their comeuppance when Art lost an award he had become accustomed to receiving. I don't know how James wormed his way back into Teisha's good graces. He must have done something. Maybe he promised Teisha the job, now that his father was dead. James is well known in political circles and well liked."

Sergeant Flores asked, "Do you think James had something to do with his father's death?"

"I didn't say that, Sergeant. Don't put words in my mouth. Just because I know James didn't trust or like his father, it's not an inference he is a killer."

Juan said, "How was James' relationship with Teisha before she died? Do you know?"

"It couldn't have been too great. She was at a bar drinking the night she died and not the kind of bar Teisha would normally frequent. I heard she took pills and it caused the accident. It's all on James. She wouldn't have done any of that before he was in her head. She had recently dumped him, so I heard."

15

The Loyal Wanna-bes

Lieutenant Aylewood-Locke, seated across from Brad Surnani, smiled pleasantly as she introduced him to Captain Beauregard and Sergeant Flores. She explained in her most charming manner the reasons why he was there for an interview. Before she could finish her intro, Surnani interrupted. "Look, I know the process. I was there at the explosion site and despite your charm, Lieutenant, let's call it for what it is; you're looking for motive. I had no motive to harm either Art or Corinne. Art was my bread and butter and Corinne and I were good friends. I was devastated at their loss."

Petra said, "Mr. Surnani, you were there as a bidder. What time was your appointment?"

"Who told you that, Lieutenant? And please call me Brad."

"Who - doesn't matter, just know the information comes from a reputable source. Please answer the question."

"I was a bidder. Don't know now if I will continue to be one given bidders are being killed left and right."

"Do you know who all the bidders are? I mean you are inferring in your wording bidders are dying left and right."

"How can you deny it, Lieutenant? Corinne, Art, Keisha are dead; and add the two seriously injured bidders meant to die. Even for your Captain Beauregard, it's a lot of murders."

Captain Beauregard answered Brad. "I can't disagree, Mr. Surnani, but why murder bidders? Why not wait until some bidders left the project or were removed for not having the appropriate land use?"

"Barney was an old man with old-fashioned ideas. His idea of a good land use could be naïve or even fiscally stupid. I suppose Cull would have added some balance, but you don't screw around with these old guys. They think it's the second world war and the marines will take the next hill. They don't understand subtlety."

Beauregard asked, "Did you have conversations with Barney or just with his agent?"

"I spoke with him at length several times. He would ramble on about how Cull put the land on the map and before Cull, he thought the land was worth a couple of hundred thousand dollars. Besides, it didn't really matter what it was worth, he wanted to sell it to someone whose bid use was socially important to people and the city and not for 'happy stuff.' He couldn't tell me what use he envisioned. He kept saying something about doing good for the City."

Beauregard nodded and asked, "How did you know Teisha was a bidder?"

"Teisha, a bidder, I laughed when I heard it. She didn't have the financing ability. I figured she was going to Boogey-back on the mystery writer or James Richards. Both were hot for her. She could sweet talk just about anyone including Barney. She dated both guys and one of them won the prize with her. Could be the loser killed her."

The Captain said, "You're saying each bidder may not be a sole bidder but have a partnership with another bidder. Why wouldn't they team up early? Seems to me it would make them look more formidable."

"Think of it this way, Captain, if Teisha won the bid, every other bidder would be courting her as a partner. Other than Art and Corinne, no one had the political connections. Maybe Abu could move some, but I don't know if he had broad power. Teisha worked both sides of the aisle, not just the minority side."

"What about you, Brad? Weren't you Art and Corinne's go-to person? You can't tell me you didn't develop connections."

"It doesn't work like that, Captain. I'm not the man; without him there are no connections."

Beauregard countered, "There is a rumor out there you were going out on your own. Is it true?"

"It's true now."

"The question is not now; before, were you about to go on your own?"

"Why would I leave the golden goose? It's just a rumor."

The Captain said, "Why would you bid against your boss if you were not going to go on your own? It doesn't add up, Brad."

"It does in one sense. Barney would find me more acceptable as a bidder than either Art or Corinne. He personally despised the two of them. Art caused some problems for Barney's siblings years ago. Granted, Barney's siblings were nothing but trouble, but Barney is a loyal guy. He wouldn't sell the property while his kids were alive and to anyone who caused troubles for his brothers. Sat on millions of dollars for years to avoid their disappointment. The sole purpose of my being a bidder before was my value as a more likable bidder."

"Brad, are you telling me you were not looking independently for financing?"

"My financing projects are my business. I'm always looking independently for financing. I have some of my own projects going now. Art was aware of them. Any financing you may have heard about is related to existing projects."

The Lieutenant added a question. "Talk about rumors, Mr. Surnani, what is your relationship with Corinne Thompson, beyond being a colleague?"

"I'm not listening to this. I've lost two friends. I've had enough of your invasive tracking of gossip."

And Brad exited the conference room.

———

Petra was adamant. "Brad is a liar and a player and there was something between him and Corinne. He walked out when we questioned the gossip about Corinne."

Beauregard answered, "We don't have enough on these players' backgrounds. And we need John Conlon in here. He is Brad's aide. Isn't he to be in here today? I want him here before Brad gets to him."

Lilly Tagliano entered the room announcing, "John Conlon is in the next room. He saw Brad as he entered and there was a harsh whisper from Brad. John whispered back, 'Don't f..k with me, Brad. It's all over.'"

The next hour spent with John Conlon was more of a confirmation of what was previously known or suspected. John appeared open and cool under pressure. His take on Corinne and Art was consistent with others. He stated they were decent enough but ruthless in business. "You didn't get in their way on a deal or you suffered some consequences. Corinne was particularly skillful in finding any opposition's Achilles' heel and acting on it."

He was blasé about his being a bidder, insisting it was at Corinne's bequest to flesh out a group of bidders. The group's interest would keep other bidders out. He was surprised when he heard Jay Bird and Teisha were bidders. He asked, "Was Beryl Kent a bidder? Barney would have liked her."

When asked how he knew Ms. Kent, he laughed. "The Bleeding Man story made her infamous. I've been following, shall we say, her close relationship with MCU. She caused quite a stir when she ran some women's public audit of grant funds public meeting. I was there to watch. She was also there at the explosion site. I assumed then she was a bidder. The Colonel drove by the site. I saw him. When he saw Ms. Kent, he looked away. They could be working together on the bid. Barney would have liked the Colonel. He was fond of all military and the American flag."

There was an easy flow of questions and answers. Beauregard thought, *this guy is irrepressibly friendly. If he's an aide to Brad Surnani who was Art Richards' aide, John beats them both in happy talk. Good looking, non-evasive, charming, and probably liked by every person he ever met. Doesn't like Jay Bird. Seems to be directing us to group Jay with Teisha. Wants us to believe Beryl was conspiring with the Colonel. Tells me he doesn't know all the bidders. Maybe the killer doesn't have to know all the bidders. Maybe all he or she has to know is who may be big competition for the bid.*

Beauregard continued. "I find it strange that you, Brad, Corinne, and Art would all be listed bidders which from my understanding required a large bond for each bidder placed before the bid was made. Did you place a bond to insure the seriousness of your interest and was it from the same financial resources as Brad's and Art's bonds?"

For the first time in the interview, John looked riled. He quickly recovered and said he had no idea which financial resources Brand and Art used. The Captain explored his previously stated rationale for being a bidder, saying, "John, you inferred your bidding status was part of a plan to frighten away other less affluent or goal directed bidders. Are we to assume Art Richards paid for your bonds? You are aware, we will be able to trace the bond sources used?"

Conlon said, "It's not that easy. Corinne was leaving Art, only Art didn't know it. Brad was leaving Art, and again Art didn't know it yet. The real estate agent promised me he would not tell any of the other bidders who their competition was until the day of the auction. I just assumed Art was a bidder. I didn't find out until much later that Corinne and Brad were both leaving Art. I then assumed they might bid, but never knew it for certainty. I don't know if Art ever discovered my or the others' bidding. I was confounded at the explosion site to see Brad there. He asked what I was doing there? I said I was driving by. I think we both realized the other was a bidder. At first, we didn't know Corinne and Art were in the fire, but we saw both their cars there. Normally they would drive together. It hit me then Corinne was also a bidder. She had good credit resources but I don't think she had enough to support purchase and development of the property. I assume now, she was partners with Brad. There had been some talk about Corinne and Brad getting cozy."

"Tell me, John, were you leaving Art too?"

"If I got the bid, yeah, I'd drop him in a heartbeat."

"You'd still need a partner, who would it be?"

"I don't have all the public relations connections Brad, Corinne, and Teisha had, but I have a lot. I would need money. I know Zed well enough. He lives near me and we get along. Brad would be my downfall, although he has made many enemies doing Art's dirty work. I'm the nice face in the group."

"How powerful is Minister Abu? Could he get the bid?"

"Captain, are you telling me he is a bidder?"

"No, I'm not, John, but you mentioned Zed who was injured in the blast as was Abu. I then wondered what they were doing there."

John said, "I did too, but now after thinking out loud with you, they both must have been bidders. Surprise, surprise, I am surprised."

Beauregard said, "I'm surprised too. John, you were heard at Richards' wake talking about the bid with Brad and James Richards. You knew you all were bidding. What gives? You wouldn't answer the question about the source of funds for your bond. When you were asked if Art was the source, you played games with your answer. Did Art know about your individual bids?"

"Not mine, but I knew about Brad's separate bid and Art was not behind it. I don't know about Corinne's bid. There was a separation there. Art moved to West Side and they said they were moving in together, but she kept delaying the move, saying something about staying in her condo until she could find a home for her cat. Art was allergic to cats. That condo is a showpiece and could have been sold in a week. Corinne and Brad were tight."

"And…what do you mean by 'tight.' Were they romantically involved, John? If so, how do you know?"

"Captain, I can't fathom Brad and Corinne having a romantic bone in their bodies. They are corporate entities striking deals; it is their life. I've never seen a real expression of empathy from either of them. They could put on a show of empathy but it was never real. When they gave large donations to charities or individuals, you can be certain the tax break was available and they got lots of publicity. Were they in love? Brad wasn't in tears at Corinne's wake and funeral. He did not pretend. He showed no real emotion, but said all the right things."

Beauregard questioned, "What were you going to do when Art and Brad discovered you were bidding independently? Do you have independent income other than from Brad who probably got reimbursed for your compensation from Art Richards?"

"I was ready to leave. Art paid the bills but I had to earn my draw and was guaranteed ten-percent of all projects revenue I brought in. I have made a lot of money under this arrangement. I was making more than Brad. I knew it was the end of the road. Captain, you can't be a bigger fish than your boss. I am considered more trustworthy than Brad or Corinne or Art. People would rather deal with me. I have spent and saved wisely. I was ready."

The Captain moved his upper body closer to the table and asked, "Who knew Art's empire was crashing besides you?"

"Art hasn't closed a deal in two years. It's been Brad or me. Art has not been focused. His moving to West Side at first surprised me, but then James said his mother didn't want him in the house. I think Art wanted things to stay the same. He was not happy with the move. The architect and builders had to keep calling him. He wasn't into it. In another guy, I would have thought he was ill."

"Do you think Art was angry with Darla?"

"Captain, I see where you're going, but if Art had any feelings they were for his history with Darla. I don't think Art would have had Darla killed."

"Why do you think Darla was killed and not a suicide?"

"Easy - Darla would never, never commit suicide and leave her family. She was a very balanced lady."

"Who then, John, would have a motive to kill Darla?"

"Captain, I've wracked my brain since her death and I don't have an answer. Darla had no enemies, so unless she met up with a pervert I don't know about, there is nobody who would want to hurt her. It has to be related to Art and the land deal, but Art was already dead before she died."

John Conlon left the interview room and the detectives were disappointed in the conversation's result thinking he offered more questions than gave answers. Juan, who was often noted for his interest in small detail, a trait shared with the Captain, said, "This guy sounds true-blue, Captain, but I don't know about him. He knows too much, is too savvy, and tried to direct us to others. Perps often do that. I'm looking at his history. He went to local colleges, AIC for graduate school and Springfield College for undergraduate. He is an achiever. Did well at both colleges and received too many honors to detail. His first jobs were in social working and counselling in several non-profit social do-gooding agencies. He then picked up an online MBA at SNHU. He must have had some dough cause SNHU tuition would be a major portion of his salary at that time. His father could have paid for the best, but the gossip is his dad wanted the kids to appreciate money. His parents retired to Vegas of all places and his sister is married to an FBI agent. His father had some sort of a fastener business and did well. I'll check into his profits before he sold the business. I know it had five hundred employees and is still a going a concern under new owners."

"Juan, who are the new owners and does John have a role in the business?"

"Malcolm Owens is the new owner. Don't know anything about him. I'll check, Captain."

"Do a financial rundown on Malcolm. I personally know him. I've met him at the country club. I'll call Cull, who plays golf with him."

Cull answered his phone, saying, "Who have you arrested, Rudy? I hope you have someone in your sights."

"Norbie, justice is slow as you know. I'm looking for info on Malcolm Owens and his fastener business. I think it's called AFI. John Conlon, one of the bidders' fathers was the previous owner; actually, he was the business founder."

"What do you need to know, Rudy? I have to be careful here because I handled the sale for John's father. Be specific with your questions and I'll try to help you."

"Norbie, was the sale covered by the press at that time? It must have been when the company has five hundred employees. There, I've answered my own question. There's no need to compromise you, but what do you think of him, as a person?"

"It was a seamless transition between buyer and seller. I think one of the reasons is that Conlon's son John is still on the board. Malcolm values his advice. John is a minority stockholder, but has never made problems for Malcolm. I don't think you'll find any dirt on Malcolm, Rudy."

"Norbie, is the company profitable? What does John take out of the company?"

"Look, Rudy, public records will show John owns thirty percent and his father owns ten percent. Malcolm bought a sixty percent interest. I think Malcom pays out dividends regularly. More importantly, the company probably pays lots of personal costs for the owners if they participate in the company. I don't know for sure, but I suspect. Phone, internet, gas, cars, resort corporate meetings, and admin services are worth over thirty thousand a year. Add in dividends, could be a lot of money for John."

"You're saying Malcolm thinks John is a good businessman and worth the money. John's being paid to keep him out of Malcolm's hair?"

"Nope, I'd say John is a business and political star."

"Thanks, Norbie, he sounds like a winner. What I don't get is how he played second fiddle for eight years to Brad Surnani."

"He didn't. Brad is cutthroat and smooth, but his manner can't compare to the nice guy image. He's not in John's league. John gets a percentage of what projects he developed for Art, and I heard Art gave John a bigger percentage than he gave Brad. There was some rancor there. At least the business rumor mill said."

"Was Art Richards ill?"

"Why do you ask? I've never heard he was. You have the autopsy report. Don't you know?"

"Cull, they were burned to a crisp. So far nothing has been said. I'm going to ask for more testing for illness. If he was chronically sick, it could explain why he was unhappy with being forced out of the house."

16

Oliver Comes Home

Oliver was home; not for a week or month as before, but permanently. Beryl loved her son Oliver, and could easily live with him despite his occasional tendency to over protect, but forever? She thought on the subject often; *he needs a wife. I introduced him to a beautiful lady but as often happens she returned to her music in Austin and her old boyfriend. I doubt she would have if he was ready to move to Austin. He was not. It couldn't be real love. I would have crossed the ocean for any of my husbands. But to live with your mother. He makes tons of money. I blame COVID for this. As an engineer, Oliver can work from home with an occasional trip to Boston. He's clipped my wings. He asks me where I'm going and who I'll be with and what time is he to expect me home. When I argue, he says, "you ask the same of me, Mom." And now he has coffee with the Colonel when I'm not there. I'm surrounded and feel hounded. My friends think it's wonderful to have someone to cook for and to have a son who wants to come home.*

The doorbell rang and Oliver, faster than Beryl, got to the door first. A man named Jay Bird introduced himself. The diligent reader Oliver responded, "You're the writer. I heard all the ladies in town just loved your talk at the Library forum. Maybe they just loved you. I can't remember which. Come on in. I expect you're looking for Beryl. She's in the kitchen."

Before he moved to follow Oliver, Jay said, "And who are you? Do you live here? Beryl never said she had a boarder."

Oliver smiled and said, "I wouldn't call me that."

Jay did not smile back. Beryl greeted Jay with, "I didn't expect you, Jay, but do have a latte with us. I see you've met my son Oliver."

A more relaxed Jay sipped his latte when it was quickly delivered and said, "I hope you don't mind my intruding but there is a rumor flying around. Actually, there are two rumors. I thought you could help me assess their veracity."

"Spoken like a writer, Jay. Anyone else would ask if the gossip had any truth. I assume you're talking about the explosion. What have you heard?"

"One rumor says I'm a bidder and partner with Abu. The other rumor is that I was to be a bidder with Teisha, but killed her when I heard she and James were together."

"Jay, I've not heard either rumor. Are you looking for a sub-plot for your book? Don't use me as writing fodder. I've told you that before."

"I only asked if you heard these rumors. They are out there. There is one that says Colonel Connault is a bidder. I suppose you don't know about that one, do you?"

"Jay, I have not heard that rumor and I don't know if it is true, just as I don't know if the other rumors are true. I think you are fishing for information and I don't like it. If we are to be friends, then be honest. Ask your question."

"It's okay for you to fish for info but not for me. What have you heard? Is that question straight forward enough for you?"

"Yes, but it is an invasive question and too general. What do you want to know?"

"I want to know what Cull and the Colonel are up to. Did you know they were both military, that Cull knew the Colonel?"

"Weren't you military also and knew them?"

"See, Beryl, you answer a question with a question, but with no answers."

Beryl seemed quite tired of the direction of the conversation and in an attempt to put an end to it said, "Jay, what difference does it make if you all knew each other in the military unless some action brought out some bad feelings in one or all of you? Why do you care if the Colonel is a bidder? I know you are a bidder and tried to mislead me into thinking you were not. Why is this important? Do you believe a bidder caused the explosion and you are trying to point fingers away from yourself?"

His answer was abrupt as he stood to leave. "I've had enough of your insincerity. I expected more from you, Beryl."

Oliver, the witness to the exchange, thought, *Mom and Jay look like two cats hissing at each other but holding back from attack. I put my money on Mom. For a writer, he's not at all subtle and he doesn't have a clue for handling Mom. Sugar, sugar, sugar is what I would use with her. He looks to me like one of those professors who dates their students. Mom is probably outside his age range. Good if true – I won't have to worry about her. Yet, he has the gall to visit her at her home without an invite. Not cool, Mr. Jay Bird.*

Jay left rather quickly. Oliver asked, "What's up with this guy? You were overly direct but he was difficult."

"I don't know about him. I've had dealings with him before. Don't you remember? I told you about his speaking at the Library Forum and the ladies thought a mystery novelist could solve the explosion case. He was charming, can be charming, but certainly wasn't charming today. He has a problem with our Colonel, Nate."

Oliver answered, "What I got out of the conversation is, he wanted to know if the Colonel is a bidder and was certain you knew. Do you?"

"Yes, I heard the Colonel is a bidder and he never told me. I never directly asked him while I did ask Jay and he lied at first. Why is who is a bidder important?"

Oliver said, "Could be one of the bidders is the murderer or he's trying to figure out who is the main competitor. I wish I knew a little more about hacking without leaving a trace. I know a lot, but since this is a police investigation, I better not get in the middle."

Beryl sighed. "No, Oliver, stay out of it."

Oliver nodded in agreement, and left the kitchen to finish some work. Beryl thought, *I can't always trust his word. If he meddles and Beauregard discovers his actions, we'll both be sorry. How much does Oliver even know to cause trouble? There are the news stories and what he heard today and whatever I may have said before. He'll be back questioning me. I'll read the riot act to him then. Why didn't Nate tell me he was a bidder? What on earth would he do with the land and why keep it a secret from me?*

Oliver was smiling. He thought, *I got Nate's banking information before when I checked him out in the 'Bleeding Man' situation. I know he's undercover for the Feds. Mom knows it also. He's smart and from Mom's description of his home when she first met him, he is a computer hack himself. You don't need three large screens and tons of peripherals if you're an ordinary joe. Plus, he told me he didn't know a lot about computers. Mom's not nuts. I believe her descriptions, so he's a liar or a fibber. Dear Beryl would say it that way. He knows I've checked up on him before and said nothing, he won't say anything this time, I hope.*

Oliver was painstaking in reviewing funds going in and out of Nate's account. He found the inflows challenging. There was retirement income from his military, from three separate companies Oliver never heard of before, and many deposits of nine thousand dollars. The expenditures showed a purchase of a $500,000 bond. He only knew it was a bond because he had used the same vendor for a project. He thought, *Nate's a legitimate bidder, bond and all, but the multiple deposits of nine grand each are just below the amount banks must report timely to the government. Is he a criminal or is this part of government money movement? What do the Feds want with this property?*

He logged out of the account and reviewed Nate's history he had previously uploaded. He had never found Nate's earlier history, only later years. He tried to remember what Nate had disclosed to himself and Beryl in normal conversations. He remembered his mother's surprise at being brought to Van Horn Park. She said then it was not on any tourist book she ever saw. He explained to her he lived in the area for two years when he was a kid. Oliver checked Springfield's map researching the park which was located in an area called Hungry Hill, a formerly Irish section of the city. Currently the area had developed into a diverse area of Latino, Black, Asian, and Arab with Irish still clinging to their 20th century experience. He noted the Lady of Hope Church and remembered one of his roommate's from college referring to his grade school with the same name. He pulled up a photo of the church and could see a school next to it but it was a city school. He thought, *it must have been the church's school and like many Catholic schools was shut down. It's a shame, but I have a starting point. Beryl said Nate was raised Catholic. I'll go to the Catholic Chancery and seek help finding my own friend. Mom said his full name is Ian Nathan Connault. Someone will know him. I know from his behavior he was churched as a kid. If I have no luck then I'll check the Springfield Boys and Girls Club which is practically next door to the church. Too convenient not to be taken advantage of by parents. I'll hit the nearby Irish bars. I have his age. There's always someone who knows.*

Beauregard, noted for his repetitive attention to detail examined the murder boards. They were a mess. He thought, *I don't care how much is computerized, when there are multiple murders, confusion reigns. Too much information hides important details and we miss them.*

Mason interrupted the Captain's thoughts. "I've gone over all the detail asked about and I think is worthwhile; so, have Juan, Petra, and Bill. The problem is we see possibilities for motives but haven't been able to connect one motive for all the crimes. The Richards woman screws everything up, but taking her death out of the equation has not helped us. Bill did a review on all the interviews. We've interviewed all living bidders except for this Colonel Connault. Why not interview him, Captain. You've stopped us and we don't understand why. I know he's with the Feds in some capacity, but this is murder and he is a listed bidder."

"That he is, but if he either has a personal interest in the property and I tell you, if that's so, he is not a murderer or he has a government role here. I don't want to interview him and have a hold up on it. It could be he was following Richards' money and the explosion coincided with his investigation and his personal interest. He is not the murderer. I've known of him for years. We've almost collided professionally a couple of times but he is legitimate."

Juan asked, "Where from here, Captain? I don't like Surnani and Bird's attitudes. Conlon comes off as clean but is a touch evasive. As to James Richards, he is likable and seems straight forward but where's his money coming from and his mom and girlfriend being murdered – just too close to him. I always suspect those closely connected to victims. Albion and Cason just invite analysis. Mason, what about all the financial detail?"

Mason responded, "I've checked all bonds with associated payments from personal and financial institutions. It's interesting. All but Cason and James Richards paid for the bond from their own checking accounts. Cason and James' payments for their bonds were from checks from Teisha Abbott's checking account. I get why she'd pay for James

Richards bond, but why Cason?"

The Captain said, "Easy, Cason supported her in retaliation against Richards and Thompson. Would have been a great motive for her to kill the two, but she's dead. Tells us Cason couldn't quickly get the funds in his account for buying a bond. Cason needs a partner who is a money man. Did he know at the time of the payment, Keisha was also a bidder? I put each of the bidders in the murderer cat bird seat; they all almost fit, but I don't have a perfect motive. If the murders are all connected and one of the bidders is the murderer, he or she would have to be strong enough to murder Darla and then string her up. James, Jay, Brad, John, the Colonel, Albion, and Cason are possible except Albion and Cason were in the hospital when Darla was murdered. Could either of them have escaped the confines of their injuries and from the hospital? No, I think not. Could either of them have hired someone? Absolutely a possibility. Zed Albion has a host of followers who would kill for a pittance, while Abu's groupies would kill to please the master from God. Teisha Abbot could have killed Darla. She has a black belt, was a kick boxer, and generally was known for her athletic prowess. If she had killed Darla, that action could be related to a motive in her death. The question remains, why would she kill Darla? James said his mother really liked Teisha."

Petra piped up. "James is not a parent killer and I don't think he killed Teisha. He was a man suffering when speaking about Teisha's death. I'm telling you, Captain, I would have felt the vibes. He could have been greedy enough to kill the others; but I don't think he'd kill Teisha or Darla. Darla and Teisha's deaths screw up any motive matching to a perp."

Beauregard said, "Are we looking at two killers? Look at the weapons: explosives which require some technical skills and shipping of materials to the lot, auto accident with drugged driver, strangulation to resemble hanging, and where the hell is the autopsy report on Barney? Call Gerrelson. He's dragging his feet."

Petra called the ME. She reported, "Captain, Gerrelson says it's on Millie's desk because you were out. He didn't trust it to be left on your desk because of the last time when it sat there for two weeks under a pile. He says you told him to send it to Millie, but she's been out for twelve days for COVID. She's due back tomorrow."

She stood to leave, causing a disgruntled Captain to say, "Don't leave now, Lieutenant."

"Captain, I'm going to search for the report on Millie's desk. Won't take long. She's a neatnik."

The detectives appeared to be suppressing smiles. Beauregard's desk was not similar to Millie's. In the past they had all searched for reports on his desk. It was a task none liked. A short time later, Petra returned with the report. She'd obviously read it, remarking, "Just like we thought, Captain, murder."

Rudy read the report. It saddened him to think Barney at over ninety years had to die in this manner instead of dying in his sleep. The report including technical terms to support death by suppressing by asphyxiation. A report on fibers was attached showing a pillow at the scene as the weapon. The Captain reasoned, "Perfect weapon for killing a ninety-year-old man. He was safe in his own home. He was ninety which is a good age to die. Normally, it would not have been seriously investigated by us. How did the perp get in? Was the door locked? Did Barney leave his door unlocked regularly?"

Juan said, "Sergeant Barr said in his report the door was opened. He later checked with neighbors who said Barney always left his front door open. He did not hear particularly well and was social enough not to want to miss a caller. Not one of his neighbors remembers anybody calling on Barney during the significant time span of his death."

"What was the possible time for his death on the report, Petra?"

"Captain, it says between nine and twelve in the evening."

"Who the hell is watching his house at night? He was in his chair and at his age probably napping. With a hearing deficit, the perp could have just walked quietly in and smothered him with Barney not knowing what was going on. A perfect scenario for a murder, as good as any I've heard. It wouldn't take much to smother him while he was sleeping."

Petra said, "Captain, the only murder that would take a great deal of physical effort was Darla's. When I think about it, strangling a woman in good health at that age would take strength and total lack of empathy if the murderer had any knowledge about her stand-up lifestyle. This murder is quite coldblooded and speaks to me of a professional hit. Who has the connections for a professional hit? And back to access, how'd he or she get into the home on a quiet city street without being noticed."

"Nice analogy, Lieutenant. It fits, but another option is the sociopath, who is able to turn off empathy if she or he has any − meaning a psychopath. Who fits that description?"

Juan answered, "Easy, Albion maybe, Cason for sure, and Surnani leaving Connault, Conlon, and Richards as needing more background work."

"Go to it, Sergeant," was Beauregard's answer.

17

Hackers at Work

Oliver connected with his old college friend Todd who worked back channels for both liberal and conservative policymakers. Todd had no ideology. Oliver had remembered Todd's conversation with him over coffee in their senior year of college when he questioned Todd's moral agenda. "I am moral, Oliver, and a great believer in good over evil prevailing. I'm no different from your average guy, maybe a salesman selling get rich investments or second-class windows or day-old produce. I access information for the buyer who doesn't know how to access. I give good info with quality references. What is done with the info is not my business. If the buyer leaves out the reference, I don't care. If the buyer changes the language, well unless I'm sued, I don't care. If I am sued, I have back-up and, to be safe, off-site storage."

Todd seemed pleased to hear from his old friend. He said, "You in town, buddy? Decided to return to the biggest little city in the USA?"

Oliver laughed. "Not now, Todd, maybe in the future, but to be honest, I like West Side. It has surprised me. My mission is to ask you to do what you're good at, but of course not telling you directly."

"I'm so good at everything, ladies, best bars in Boston, best restaurants. Try to be more specific, old friend."

"I have a direct interest in backgrounds of some folks for a book I'm writing. One of them may have had help in hiding his life's trail. The others are quasi-public figures. Would any of that present a problem?"

"Nope. I'm assuming you want to know all for your book, right?"

"Yup, all. Remember our language systems we used to use? I'll get you who."

"I remember. I hope you do. I don't want to kvetch for the wrong fellow. Give me a call tomorrow if you get me the folks today. Got to go, I have a deadline. No charge for this and don't ask. You were the best when I needed help. The trip was nice out here and I'm meeting a lady who lives here. Don't ask who, but know you've done me a favor. I've been putting off seeing Devi. Your call to come out here was just the right impetus for me to get off my lazy ass and follow a dream."

Oliver smiled at Todd's remembrance thinking, *I bailed him out of jail on a drunk and disorderly and attempted assault on a police officer. Mom got him an attorney. How did we know we got him the best of the silver-tongued lawyers in town? It all went away without his parents in California hearing about his fall from grace. I know it got him off the booze. Now if I can remember our code.*

It took Oliver over an hour to code the names. He then sent them to the storage dump Todd had always used saying it's almost untraceable. He checked his watch noticing it was well into happy hour time, left a message for his mom informing her she could meet him at the country club for dinner at seven if she was available. He fed Amico, his mother's rescue dog, who Oliver often referred to as the best of all possibilities for a rescue, claiming his mixed breed gave him a loving nature. And with a smile he left the house.

Well into his second beer, Oliver noticed Attorney Norbie Cull had settled into a seat, two stations away from his. He only noticed Norbie because of the loud welcome he received from several of the club members. Oliver told the bartender Norbie's drink was on his account. He waited for Norbie to get the message when the bartender delivered the cocktail. Cull looked at him and said, "You're Oliver, Beryl's son.

Good to see you again and thanks for the drink, but it's an expensive one. Let me pay for it and we'll have a beer some other time."

Oliver laughed. "I knew what it was when I offered. Take this gift from me. I love having famous people owe me."

The two got on discussing world's events, Beryl, Cull's children, and finally the killings in West Side. Cull did not seem surprised at Oliver's knowledge of the bidders or of Barney, and Darla's family. Oliver explained he knew Tim Richards when they were students in Boston years ago. He thought he was an okay guy despite what he heard about the dad. Even then Art Richards caused controversy when he pushed through a land deal in Boston. It was all over the news and those against the building project had very unkind words about Art. It was troublesome for Tim who was a relatively quiet guy.

Cull was about to ask Oliver his thoughts on who killed Darla and why, but Oliver placed a question to him in first. "How did the killer get in and out of Darla's home in midday on a city street with houses on both sides and directly across? Someone, the mailman, neighbor, cruiser, maintenance truck driver, someone must have seen the perp entering. I checked around the back of the house. It has a six-foot fence and backs up to a parking area for a B-n-B. Have the police interviewed neighbors?"

Cull said, "Oliver, this is a Springfield murder. Beauregard would have surveyed the neighborhood and I'm sure Springfield police would also. I don't know what were the results. I'll ask Beauregard what's up. He may or may not tell me. You raise a good point but an obvious one. Don't you think police would be on it?"

"The house has such a position on the street, it invites you to look that way. How did the murderer arrive, by car, or walk, or sneak over the back fence? Someone must have seen him or her."

Cull laughed, saying, "Why don't you develop an environmental assessment form and survey the neighbors? You're an engineer and could be doing it as a project. The neighbors have reported a host of wild animals in the woods and valleys surrounding that area. They'll love to talk about it. You're personable. I suspect they'll tell you their life story."

Oliver smiled. "Norbie, do you always get someone to do your dirty work?"

"Mostly, I pay for investigations. I don't have a paying client here, Oliver."

"What about Barney's murder? Wasn't he a paying client?"

Cull did not respond immediately. Finally, he answered, "You go for the jugular. What do you need for payment, Oliver?"

"I don't want payment. I just wanted to know if you thought this search effort was worthy enough you would pay. You've answered the question and I have a job to do."

Cull left when his take-out dinner for his family was ready. Driving home, he thought, *the kid is as nosy as Beryl. They are both charming and bright. I hope the Springfield police don't get a call about a man soliciting in the neighborhood. Is Oliver smart enough to have developed a foolproof cover? If he has a problem, he'll be calling me. I should have told him to use me as his employer on the wild animal nuisance case. I've one client who asked me to call the police and wildlife control. He's a paying client. Oliver will be okay.*

Dressed in his best plaid shirt, jeans and LL Bean lumber jacket, Oliver canvassed the streets. There was the street on which Darla's home was located and the perpendicular busy street offering entrance to her street. Darla's house was the second house in. He had no success with the neighbors. He drove around looking for work trucks. There were none. He stopped at the convenience store at the corner two blocks away when he saw two cruisers parked while the officers spoke with some teenagers. He could see it was not a confrontation but a get to know the neighborhood kids kind of interaction. It took ten minutes of casual conversation before he could even broach the subject of Darla's murder. His tone was all sympathy, when he wondered why the police weren't able to find out who entered Darla's house that day. The response was, "We waited for the autopsy report when someone got suspicious it may not be a suicide. Makes us a week late. No success, and I know we saw nothing."

Next, Oliver visited the B-n-B. He met the charming owner who was quite willing to entertain him all day. Her name was Leeann Sellers. She invited him in, made him coffee. They sat in the extra-large kitchen furnished with three round tables along with modern appliances couched in nineteenth century charm. She told him she served a full breakfast for her guests. When the seven bedrooms were full, she relied on her guests having varied sleeping schedules. Generally, crowding was prevented, but if necessary she could use her dining room when there was an overload. Leeann shared some history including her childhood in New Hampshire, her later culinary education at Johnson and Wales College in Providence and ten years' experience as a sous-chef and chef in New England, when she decided a shorter work day would be better.

Oliver asked, "How on earth did you end up here in Springfield in a Bed-n-Breakfast centered in residential neighborhood? Do you have family here or did some guy entice you with his golden charms?"

"Nope in both cases and I'm not easily enticed as you call it. Look at you. What brought you to Springfield?"

He laughed."Not a cool answer for you, Leeann. My mama brought me here."

Leeann laughed. "If you were really a Mama's boy, you'd not admit it. I'll wait for your story, but first I'll complete mine. My sister lives in Vermont, just over the border going north. My eleven-year-old niece

Melody had a seizure disorder. The first seizure, a Tonic-Clonic, you'd know it as a Grand Mal seizure, was so frightening because there seemed no end to it. She was aired out by helicopter to Baystate Medical Center, because she had some temporary paralysis and small seizures afterward. I was working in Boston at the time, and when I got here, there was no room available to stay at the Ronald McDonald house nearby. I ended up for two weeks at a downtown hotel, but found it pricey. later, I hatched a plan to develop a B-n-B in the area mainly to cater to families of hospital patients. I charge a reasonable fee including breakfast and a discount for long-term patients' families. It was not an easy task, Oliver. I applied for a variance for use. This is a residential neighborhood. This house is a gem but it needed a major rehab for the kitchen and baths as well as electric, heating and air, a new roof, complete redecorating both inside and outside, new driveway and parking lot. The whole project took three years, but it's where I want to be. I have a life here. I meet people who need kindness and good food. Best of all, I have more time. Time is everything. Please excuse me, I've talked too long and all about myself."

Oliver said, "I think this house is wonderful and you have a lot of guts to go about this project on your own. Is it hard work to clean the rooms daily and cook breakfast? I mean it does tie you down. What if you have a medical appointment and it's in the morning?"

"I have help from two women who come in daily and sometimes can cover for a weekend. As for a couple of weeks' vacation, my sister and her husband take over. He's a great cook and she is the best organizer. My taking on this project required professional services. I had help from bankers, vendors, City Councilors, the Mayor, the hospital administration, my attorney, etc."

Oliver asked Leeann the name of her attorney and was surprised to hear the name Norberto Cull. He redirected himself back to business, asking, "Were you around the day the lady next door was murdered?"

"What did you say your work was? You're not an investigator, are you? I thought you were here to estimate wildlife in the area for neighborhood   problems."

Oliver's thoughts raced, *do I continue to lie or tell her the truth? I don't think I can make her believe my big lie.*

"I confess, Leeann, I'm here under false pretenses. It's just I think the cops are too slow. I knew Tim Richards from college and the Richards' kids have heard nothing. They don't think the cops went door to door. I thought I'd give it a try."

"They are wrong, Oliver. I saw the cops hitting each house a few days ago. They didn't come here because I'm not on Darla's street even though my parking lot backs up to her house. Don't mind me, but you're not cut out for telling fake stories. I like that in you."

"I am embarrassed and you are smart. Can you tell me if you saw anyone around that day?"

"No, I didn't because I was on a small vacation. My sister and her husband covered for me. I can call them and ask them if you wish."

"Please do, if you don't mind. I have to assure myself I've done what I could. She was the nicest lady."

Oliver waited while Leeann made the call, thinking, *I'm still not telling her the whole story. I didn't know Darla, just knew Tim, and I didn't know him that well. I didn't even go to the funeral. The name at the time didn't register. It wasn't until later. If Mom wasn't involved, I wouldn't be here.*

Leeann said, "I'm putting you on speaker phone…Oliver, meet my sister Addie."

Addie listened to and answered Oliver's questions. When she saw a man over by the fence, she ran out the back door to ask him where he was going. In the minute it took for her to get into the parking area, he was gone. No cars were next to the fence and the four cars in the lot she could account for. Her description was not overly helpful. She didn't think he was six feet tall, more likely five foot nine or ten inches. He wore a knitted ski hat and his hair that showed looked brown. She remembered his shoes; they looked like her husband's chukka boots by Skechers with the gray wedge showing on the side. Her one definite statement was 'He looked agile and moved well.' She would know him if she saw him walk. He wore an N95 COVID mask pulled down by his neck letting her see the side of his face. She said, "Maybe I can identify him if I can see the side of his face."

Leeann ended the call asking Addie if she was available to help if the police found a suspect. She was.

Oliver spent the rest of the afternoon chatting with Leeann. She gave him a tour of the unoccupied rooms. He complimented her, saying, "You've taken such time to get the nineteenth century details in place. It's beautiful."

Leeann said, "Come by for breakfast tomorrow; that's where I shine."

His answer: "I'd like that. What time?"

"Whatever suits you, Oliver, between eight and eleven. I look forward to seeing you again."

18
Fortuitous Connections

Sergeant Barr and Stacia Kovac ordered the same chicken club sandwich at the West Side local health food market. They sat in the separate area for diners. Its informality allowed the two to relax. Stacia said, "How is the investigation into the explosion going, Bobby?"

He replied, "You probably know more than we do. What do you hear out there in the news world?"

"Am I being quizzed as a witness?"

"You already have been. Don't you remember your interview. You gave details and they were helpful. I wondered what else you've heard."

"The gossip is Surnani was responsible for the explosion because his world was being pulled away from him. Some think he killed Teisha, but others say no woman was that important to him. Others think Art Richards planned his wife's death before he died, not knowing he was about to be killed. It's all subjective."

19

Beryl Smells a Rat

The Library Board, despite its staid reputation, was ripe with gossip this evening. Beryl's friend Kay, head librarian, whispered, "It's all your doing, Beryl. You brought in the concept of placing mystery novels up in the front lobby, and now the board members feel entitled to discuss all the murders in West Side."

A return whisper said, "I'm not that important, Kay, but thank you for thinking so. Multiple murders in our town, not yet solved, will of course bring on discussion. This is not gossip. They are just trying to figure out the why, just as you and I do."

The Board Chairperson announced an open discussion forum and there was a jumble of words from just about every member causing the Chair to say, "Hold on, one at a time. Please raise your hand if you wish to speak."

Aaron Bloom, normally a quiet man, spoke first. "Our author Jay Bird is investigating these murders on his own. He's questioned everybody connected. I heard they thought his questions were better than those posed by the police. It's been said he is following all the land bidders because he thinks they are the most likely to have a motive to kill Richards and Thompson."

A somewhat nonsense discussion continued. Beryl's face registered disgust, leading her to say, "The police, especially our Captain Beauregard, are the best. Jay Bird lives in the fiction lane. I like Beauregard's manner of investigation. He never pre-determines the outcome. He waits for evidence. Often, he has brilliant insights but doesn't allow them to interfere until he can support them with evidence. The fact they mostly turn out the killer is extraordinary. My bet is on Beauregard over our highly regarded mystery writer."

One board member, Roger Abran, agreed. "Beryl is on target. I know both the Captain and Mr. Bird. I can tell you the Captain is a reliable known quantity. Mr. Bird has lived in this community for a lengthy bit of time. When has he ever participated in community affairs? Beryl's persistence led to his giving our library a lecture, but, before that, he used our library but was not involved. I have dear friends, honest people, who have told me Jay Bird is noted not just as an author, but for his participation in some sleazy business deals."

The members attempted to pursue the conversation, when Kay broke in with a financial report while reminding the members, "Poor public relations is always the consequence from gossip."

Beryl was the first to corner Roger after the meeting. She knew from past meetings Roger rarely said negative words about a book, person, or action. She asked him if he had a few minutes to talk. They settled for a small coffee house restaurant around the corner. After imbibing a tall ginger tea, Roger said, "I don't like to talk about people, Beryl. I know you are not a gossiper, but Jay Bird lives up to the noted blue jay, who robs from other birds' nests. He was the source of an investment in some not-for-profit athletic complex and gained the trust of the investors. When the town in Connecticut did not come through on the proper zoning as their councilors had previously agreed, the deal went flat. Mr. Bird had spent all the investors' monies on what looked to me like bogus vendors to the tune of three and a half million dollars. None of the costs were what are called hard costs, but in areas of architectural drawings and copies, wetland review without a document drawn, environmental impact and traffic studies by students from a local college, and other unprovable expenses. It was a rip off, but despite that, he talked twelve investors into accepting the loss of their retirement funds. He'd hired a lawyer in the beginning of the project. I found out later the attorney told Jay the councilors were reluctant to vote on passage of the project. That was early in the game, but he still took more funds from investors. The lawyer quit, which made my friend antsy. My friend wouldn't invest any more, and Jay told him he could not return his investment as it had been spent. My friend doesn't like notoriety and wouldn't sue."

Beryl questioned, "Jay Bird is independently wealthy. Why would he run a scam? Could it just be a poor business decision and he was out time and money as well?"

"No, Beryl, from what I've heard from others, he always has a project for investors and none of them end up well. Could be his wealth comes from these fake business deals. He is a great sales guy and from his books, which I've read, he has the skills to tell a good story."

"Roger, are you inferring he'd go as far as murder for money?"

"Don't know and hate to accuse him, but I know he is greedy and sleazy and doesn't have a lot of empathy for others. When he informed my friend and the other investors their money was gone, he showed little sympathy and blamed every vendor and the attorney for the problems. I think he's one of those guys you see on television. They're called sociopaths, some of whom murder when they don't get what they want."

Beryl thanked Roger for his wonderful work as a library board trustee. As Beryl drove home she gave some thought to Roger's words. *The Jay I've experienced doesn't look or act sleazy. I did not get that vibe. I do think he's a bit self-important and his behavior borders on narcissism. He tries to control. Did I see him express any empathy? No, I didn't. I have to say I enjoyed his company until he got too nosy. I know I don't like being questioned about personal matters and he did a search on me. I didn't like it, but I searched records on him. I do see he is self-absorbed, a narcissist for sure, but is he a sociopath? When I didn't roll over and give him info he wanted, he could not hold back his annoyance with me. Could he be the murderer? He has motive. He is a writer who researches daily and easily may have put together the explosive murder weapon, but who put the containers in the building? Would he know how not to leave a trail? I wonder if Beauregard has knowledge of the source? He'd not tell me.*

Beryl, determined to get to the source of the explosive material, rushed home. She had set up her own version of a murder board showing the source of her info and the locations in her files of support. Eating a tuna and lettuce sandwich on multi-grained rye bread stuffed with potato chips, Beryl noted the reference to her files on the explosive weapon and pulled out the hard copies consisting of multiple news articles and a one-page summary of her thoughts.

One article stated the front building had storage of gas cylinders thought to be filled with argon, nitrogen, and oxygen. The article referred to the absence of date labeling. The rest was a nasty suggestion the owner of the building would be facing serious fines. In another news article, it stated the fire marshal said the first blast came from those cylinders. The owner's rep said, according to another article, he never authorized storage for anything. Beryl spent the afternoon reviewing online minimum requirements related to storing chemicals and the uses for the particular chemicals mentioned in the fire.

To her surprise, it was not an easy task. She didn't know the size of the cylinders. The papers stated the cylinders were large. She printed a chart on cylinder weights, both when empty and full on each type of gas mentioned. The cylinders, even when empty, were all heavier than she had imagined. She thought, *add another forty pounds and for sure Jay wouldn't lift a whole bunch nor do I see Nate, James, John, or Brad doing dirty work. Well, maybe Nate could but he'd never leave a trace. Someone was hired to deliver these. I think gas delivery vehicles have to have permits. I'll check. Can't be too many.*

Beryl weeded through the boring Massachusetts rules and regulations for transporting compressed gas cylinders. She honed in on the requirement where the transporter must deliver the cylinders to a place where the facility had a license for storing. *I suspect no one was there to receive the cylinders and sign for them. I don't think this avenue of investigation will work out for me. Someone who doesn't worry about obeying the law delivered them. Chancy, but if it paid well, not unusual. The truck could have been stopped by police. The trucker would have to have paperwork for the delivery, but the truck was never stopped. I'll tell Beauregard.*

Beryl entered Beauregard's office accompanied by Detective Shaughnessy. She immediately noticed he was not just a patrolman now and asked him about his role in MCU. He gave her a big smile, saying, "It's a first for a patrolman to be assigned to MCU in West Side, not so in bigger departments. I'll have to take the next sergeant's exam. I can't believe my luck. Take a chair here, ma'am, Captain Beauregard will be here shortly."

Beauregard acted pleasantly, as if he was pleased at her visiting. She apologized by sharing her story on the gas cylinders. He said, "We're on it, Beryl, and like you suggest, it appears someone illegally dumped them, because it would take at least an hour to transfer the cylinders from the truck to the building. The trouble is there is no normal paperwork. There is a trail for particular gas type storage facilities. Also, a difficult task in that we can easily check the storage sites in West Side, but it takes much more work to go into other communities. Thank you for the lead.

"You said you had some questions about Jay Bird relating to land deals. What are they, Beryl?"

"I don't like to put thoughts in your head when my source of info may be based on rumors. I ask you this question, have you heard of Jay being involved in some business swindles? Or better yet, has his background check pointed to business deals where investors later made complaints to the Better Business Bureau or the Attorney General's Office?"

"Come out with a specific and I'll answer you."

"Captain, I heard Jay took a great deal of money from investors in an athletic complex and the project went kaput."

"Where was the project?"

"Not far from us, south, somewhere in Connecticut."

"If it's close to us, I'm surprised I haven't heard about it. If it was reported, I should have heard. Let me call Lieutenant Smith. He'll have the file."

Mason said, "Captain, nothing on social media about him which is surprising if the rumor is true. Most cheated investors rant their problems there. If the investors don't want to be known for their poor choices, they might keep quiet. Aside from Mr. Jay Bird, I remember a few years ago about a project causing a row in Hazardville, which is an older section of Enfield, formerly home of a lot of farmland. I've friends down there. Someone will know if Jay was involved."

Beryl thanked the Captain and Lieutenant. She looked surprised when she got a generous thank you from both. While driving home she gave thought to what she would delve into next. *What did I get from the Captain, that I didn't already know? Mason Smith will discover whether the rumor is true. Just his knowing there was a water project in Hazardville is all the confirmation I need to believe the story about Jay. It's too bad, because at first I rather liked him. If he swindles people, then I don't like him. I know sociopaths can fool anyone and I was almost fooled. Well not really, I know and always knew he was narcissistic. He lied to me about being a bidder so easily, but I caught him in the lie. What did he say? "I was thinking about being a bidder."*

Partial truths are always the best lies. He covered the lie so easily making me think I was too imaginative. But is he a murderer? I don't know. I believe he is a philanderer and a swindler, but murder is a stretch. You'd think his writing murder fiction would leave him cautious about committing murder. If he only knew Captain Beauregard, as I know him, he'd be careful about even thinking of murdering anyone. For now, let me eliminate him as a murderer. I'm left with the two severely injured men. Nope, too chancy, they're out. Who is left but James, Nate, and Brad, John, and Teisha. Nope again, Teisha's out as the main culprit, but she could have been in partnership with him, and was killed because of her knowledge. Lots of work to do and how do I investigate Nate? Been there, done that in the Bleeding Man case. Oliver chased him. I'm going to pull a personal card and not suspect him. I don't want him guilty. I can't be that wrong about a man I let get this close, can I?

Beryl hurried home. She had a date with Nathan.

Beryl and Nate were tucked into a back table toasting the beautiful night, the great bNapoli Restaurant's ambiance, and the joy of a quiet evening together. The waiter interrupted, saying, "There are two gentlemen who would like to send you a drink. Is there something special you'd like?"

Nate's face closed into a grimace, but he answered, "Two more champagnes would be lovely. Please tell them thank you."

Nate then waved to the men who were sitting at the bar. Beryl thought, *normally, Nate would excuse himself and go and thank them. Oops, they're coming to our table. Nate is not too receptive. This should be interesting and fun. I like seeing Nate upset with someone other than me.*

Brad Surnani and John Conlon were full of good cheer acknowledging both Beryl and Nate. "Nice to see good folks enjoying great food. You guys were deep in conversation. What's so serious? If it's personal, tell me. If it's not, please share."

Nate got serious. "Four murders in the area just calls for analysis, and Beryl is the best at figuring things out."

"Nate, since when have you let anyone other than you do any analyses."

"Since I've met the Beryl Kent."

Beryl thought, *words, words, words, all meaningless flattering words uttered by three men. I thought women had the rep for over-speaking. Maybe they're covering up their discomfort. They want to get info from each other and don't know how to start; I can help.*

"Brad, John, I've not had the opportunity to ask either of you what your thoughts are about all these murders. Is it the land deal, and if so, why murder over one deal? Secondly, why on earth would anyone kill Darla?"

Her ploy did not at first work. Brad and John tried to push Nate for answers. They all sparred for a few minutes until Nate insisted Darla's murder must be connected to Art in some fashion. Brad surprised him. "Nope, absolutely not, no one hated Darla and most folks disliked Art. He was overbearing on a good day. I've spent a long time with Art. He could not be trusted. Darla was the most trustworthy person I have ever met. She put other people's needs before hers. She finally pushed Art out of the house. Corinne was not going to live with him. His businesses were suffering from his lack of attention. He was not stupid, but had lost his drive. He was angry Darla wouldn't allow him to just live in the house he bought. Darla was a loss to all of us."

Beryl heard emotion in Brad's voice and noticed the knowledge of his sadness appear on Nate and John's faces. John said, "So why did she need to die. She wasn't connected to his land plans or other deals. She has James to protect her financial interests. She faced no money problems. Did she have a lover?"

Brad did not answer. After a moment John said, "If she did, she kept it under her hat. I hope the hell she did. If anyone knows it would be James Richards and he can be as silent as the Sphinx. Don't be fooled by his happy go lucky manner. He is sly."

Nate asked a question which surprised the two men. "Darla was strangled with what I understand to be a silk cord and then hung to imitate a suicide. The stool was kicked out in a perfect fashion for a suicide. There were no other marks on her body and no threads on her hands. Often when suicides hang themselves, they automatically put their fingers on the cord. I know the CIA has used this method, and the military. Do either of you recall a similar death? You were both military."

Brad questioned, "Is that a statement or request?"

Guessing, Beryl said, "Both."

"How did you know? I was only in for the short haul."

"How I know is not important. John, you also were in the military. I think Nate's question needs answers. How about answering?"

John's answer was slow in coming and at odds with his usual cheery quick answers. "Yes, of course I've heard of the old KGB or CIA elimination styles. Anyone who had any rank in the military knew about these. But to assign this type of methodology to Darla's death boggles my mind. I never thought of connecting this weapon to her death. She was just a nice housewife; why murder her this way?"

Nate said, "Why is a good question. Can you think of any reasons someone would take the time to strangle Darla and hide the evidence with a rope hanging, get in and out of her home without being noticed, and leave no forensic evidence? Sounds like a pro, doesn't it?"

Brad sarcastically answered, "Darla must have been important to national security causing the CIA to get active."

Nate ignored the sarcasm, saying, "I'll go along with her importance. Great analysis, Brad. Leads me right to your knowledge of Art Richards' affairs. He was involved in many military and other government investments. Think if any of those deals could be connected to information that would be dangerous. Could Darla know about dangerous information? I have heard Art trusted Darla. I'm told she was his confidante."

Brad looked stunned. "I never thought about that possibility. It's farfetched, Nate, farfetched. Yes, he trusted her and told her everything. I often thought it was why he didn't divorce her. I mean he spent a long time in an open relationship with Corinne. Why did it take so long for him to leave Darla?"

John piped in, "Darla told him to get out, not the other way around, Brad, and you know it."

Nate asked, "Were any of you ever worried about any questionable investments getting to the public?"

Brad replied, "What do you think we were running, drug operations? We're nationwide and all, I repeat all, our companies have stellar reputations. We've developed software in one of our companies that's used by the Feds and other governmental agencies because we're the best. We develop parts for the latest air technologies. We're into about every aspect of American business outside of food. We never got into agriculture with the exception of equipment and components."

Beryl asked, "Do you own any businesses in West Side or in this side of Massachusetts?"

John said, "Yeah, we're partners in several restaurants, one hotel, many commercial buildings which because of COVID have been a downer, and some more."

She asked, "Did you have problems with any of the local businesses?"

John said, "There were some public bids that created controversy mainly because the public didn't want them. Any detail you'd be interested in would be in the papers."

Brad and John rushed to leave the two diners in peace when their appetizers arrived causing Beryl to comment, "Something we said, Nate. I've never seen two men happier to leave my company - Oops, our company. I did not know Richards was so involved in West Side. It might explain why John Conlon attended the public hearing our women's group held on the audit of DSI Digital Storage, Inc. Remember I told you I never met him but he knew me. I looked for the attendance sheet and he did not sign in. Was he really there?"

20
Commonalities

Beauregard regaled his detectives with a repetition of his favorite mantra in solving cases. "Look for commonalities. Let's start with a review of all the interviews. I'm thinking about Darla's death. It's not ours, but my gut tells me solving her death is important. I got a call from nosy Beryl's son, Oliver. He scoped out the Richards' house and questioned the B&B owner. She said her sister saw a man over by the fence behind the Richards' home near the time of the murder. She looked away for a minute and turned back. She has a description of him. He is about five feet nine or ten inches tall, definitely not six feet. She thought he had brown hair under his knitted ski hat and thought his shoes looked like her husband's chukka boots by Sketchers with the gray wedge showing on the side. He was agile and she thought she could identify him if she saw him walk by his gait."

Sergeant Tagliano remarked, "Not much help unless we get a perp. Captain, Beryl's got her son working the case?"

"I don't like it either, Sergeant, but remember it's not our case. I thanked him for his help. Springfield police don't know this. I wonder why they didn't question the owner."

Petra answered, "She may not have been home. Her B&B is not on Darla's street. It backs up to her house. They missed the possible connection. Happens."

Beauregard mumbled what sounded like, "Shouldn't have. And how did you know about the location of the B&B?"

"Captain, you told us to check the house out and I did. Maybe you didn't directly tell me, but that's what I do."

Sergeant Flores said, "Captain, if this is the guy, then we're in trouble. None of our contenders are shorter than six feet tall. The only one with brown hair is John Conlon and I think it's blondish brown. Maybe Darla's death has nothing to do with the other deaths."

The Captain grumbled, "My gut tells me otherwise. Who else have we interviewed who is under six feet tall?"

Lieutenant Smith answered, "We've got paper on the photographer, the injured minister and biker, James Richards, John Conlon, Nate Connault, Jay Bird, and Cull. James Richards has black hair and is six feet tall. Nate's hair is brownish with a touch of gray and he is tall. Cull is blonde but could match the height. John Conlon is not six feet. He's more like five eleven. Brad has brownish hair but he doesn't look to me like he could climb a fence easily."

Beauregard said, "Enough of this. How tall is the photographer? He had brown hair. Remember, whoever killed Darla must have been strong enough to lift her dead weight and hang her after strangling her with a silk cord. I don't see Stacia doing it."

Sergeant Barr's face reddened. He said, "Stacia is a black belt in karate, but no way would she do this to another woman. She told me Darla was liked by everyone."

Sergeant Tagliano, not one to let a hazing moment pass her by said, "Bobby, be careful of the lady. Black belts are not an attribute you should be looking for in your main squeeze."

The Captain silenced the laughter with a scowl and said, "The photographer as I remember was wiry, but what's the connection? I want more background material. When did each person's history show an intersection with Art Richards or Corinne Thompson, or Teisha Abbott or Darla Richards. Motive must be in the histories. We need motive."

———————

Oliver had received a coded message from his hacker friend asking him to meet him halfway in Worcester. They met not quite halfway but in the liquor store parking lot off the Sturbridge exit on the pike. It was often used by travelers for parking a car to catch a ride to Boston. He laughed when he saw Todd. His ride was a ten-year-old Toyota. Not surprising if some of Oliver's other friends drove it, but Toddy's inclinations ran more to sleek late modeled race cars. He thought, *must be Todd's idea of a cover. And look, he's in old jeans and a fisherman's hat. Todd is not a fisherman. How can he meet a lady looking like this.*

Oliver jumped into Todd's car feeling assured the car had been inspected for all devices. He said, "How's the little lady going to remember you in this outfit?"

"When I called to make a date, she said she was scheduled to fish today and I could join her. She gave me the feeling there was no alternative. I didn't tell you she is an Aquatic Biologist. I want to get out of here right away. Take this flash drive and print it. There are no identifying marks on its content. Destroy the flash drive after you have your info. It could be traced back to me. Okay?"

And the clandestine meeting between two college buddies went totally unnoticed. Oliver returned home and busied himself looking for details in the backgrounds of the witnesses to the explosions. He printed all the materials which numbered over two hundred pages and destroyed the flash drive in the fireplace. Setting about the reviewing process, he was at first overwhelmed. He scanned all the pages first. He thought, *too much data is here. I'll pick categories to check and compare all the potential candidates for a role as a murderer. Physical descriptions, military service and roles therein, business dealings, negative press as well as positive press, education, love life, reports of anger issues, alcohol and drug habits, and auto accidents.*

He was still working filling in data in his worksheet when he heard his mother close the garage door. He immediately closed the file labeled 'rotator variances' happy in the knowledge his mom would not find the file interesting enough to open. He thought, *it's not that I don't trust my darling mom. I do, but once she discovers I was snooping in Darla's neighborhood, she'll be looking for info. Knowing Mom as I do, she'll visiting this computer. Since she sometimes uses my computer for some search engines I have she does not, I can't just change the password. And for certain Beauregard will question her, not Norbie Cull. He can keep a secret, I think.*

Beryl and Oliver ate a light supper. She thanked him for setting a fire, saying, "What motivated you to build a fire, Oliver? I normally have to do it unless we have company."

He denied her charge, saying, "Mom, you don't remember the little things I do around here. It's chilly outside. This fire is nice, don't you think?"

Beryl could not help thinking, *Oliver needs to be pushed to light a fire and it really is not cold outside today. I wonder if he has a problem he's not sharing. I can't solve what I don't know about.*

Beryl said she was in for the night and asked if he wanted to see the new movie on Netflix. He agreed although he thought, *can't work on this project in front of nosy Beryl. I'll have to wait until tomorrow afternoon. I have Zoom meetings in the morning. I'll share when I have some success. She can cover for me with the Captain as to methodology for gaining info. That's if there is good info.*

Amico kept barking right in the middle of the mystery movie Beryl and Oliver were watching. Beryl remarked, "Must be some animals out there. Does he want to go out, Oliver?"

Oliver laughed. "Nice ploy, Mom, to get me to check the yard.

Amico's not a big dog. An electric dog collar does not protect him from animals in our woods. I'll go out with him."

Oliver lit up the spotlights and opened the door. He saw a man running into the woods. Pushing Amico back into the house, he ran after the man but his delay put him at a disadvantage in this foot race. The half mile out of the woods took the man to a small car. Oliver could not see the color or make of the car but knew it was a smaller SUV. Returning to the house, he called the police.

Oliver was impressed the boys in blue took the report seriously. He was brought to his senses when the officer asked for a description, thinking, *I chased him for at least ten minutes or more. His back was in my vision and at times a side view when he looked back at me. He was fast and moved in and around the trees as if he'd been there before. He had good boots on but I couldn't see a brand. They weren't high on the leg, just up to the ankle. He wore a good COVID mask probably one of those N95 ones. The punk is in great shape, able to run faster than me with a mask on. What was he doing in our yard? What has Beryl gotten into this time?*

He gave what little details he could remember to the officer, who said a detective would come with an officer when there was daylight and take a search through the woods. He also claimed there was very little traffic up on the road above but they would contact the neighbors. Beryl said, "Nathan Connault has a good view of the road from his home. Contact him."

———

Detectives came, Captain Beauregard along with Sergeant Bill Border and a uniform. Beryl and Oliver watched from the kitchen. She was going to step out when Oliver stopped her. "Don't you think, Mom, the Captain is here for a reason. He doesn't need you to butt in. You had better have a good story as to the reason some young guy is casing your home, and this was not the first time he was here."

"Oliver, why do I have to have knowledge about this criminal? I don't have the slightest idea why he came here. And what makes you think he's been here before? You're exaggerating the danger and you are scaring me. Stop it."

Oliver quickly said, "I chased him through all the low brush and between trees. He did not stay on the worn path. He never once faltered. He has been here before. It took me a couple of weeks to walk through the jumble before I could do it quickly without tripping. The Captain will ask me what I think and I'm not hiding from the truth. You have to think about why he came here?"

"Robbery must be the motive, Oliver. I do have some pricey jewelry and museum quality art. He's just a thief."

There was a knock on the back door. Oliver opened it finding Beauregard and Border on the large top stepping stone holding a bunch of debris in their hands. He directed them to the oversized plank kitchen table spreading a cloth for the debris. Sergeant Border said, "How'd you know this stuff was important, Oliver?"

Beryl laughed, saying, "My son is quite aware that not even the king of detectives would bring a mess in my home unless it was important. What have you captured from my woods, Captain?"

The items were spread on the table. Beauregard and Border wore gloves, a signal not lost on Beryl and her son to resist touching the items. There were two pieces of paper with notes on them, a bicycle clip for holding pant legs, a wrinkled and wet news article, a piece of what looked like a man's shoe heel, and some blue threads from clothing. Beauregard said, "Problem here is we don't know when these items ended up in the woods. The bike clip is not rusted. The papers are damp but still legible. The man's shoe heel piece could also be from a woman's boot. They were all the stuff we do. We can have the threads analyzed. Oliver, would you show me the trek you and this guy took? I've everything marked where it was found. If it was found on your route, I'm comfortable looking further into the items."

Oliver Joined Sergeant Border for the follow-up of the last evening's trail, while the Captain enjoyed Beryl's excellent latte and muffins. He asked, "Beryl, are you responsible for Oliver's investigating Darla's murder in Springfield?"

The look of astonishment on Beryl's face told Rudy she knew nothing about it. He also saw a bit of anger in her blue eyes. She said, "No, why would you say he was? He doesn't know these people."

"He knows you're interested in all the murders. Beryl, he is your son. Maybe he wants you safe and thinks he can help."

And Beauregard relayed Oliver's story and the description of a potential killer.

"Why did he investigate? Where was there to look we haven't looked?"

Beryl was surprised by Beauregard's detailed answer and thought, *I hadn't thought about double checking in the Darla's home area. I should have. All he's come up with is a shadow figure and general information. The woman's description of the man is vague at best, but if it's true, it eliminates some of the men who were at the explosion. I don't think we can rely on the info. Oliver is not all engineer, is he? Neat! Neat!*

"Captain, do you give any merit to this?"

"I'll tell you what I do think, Beryl. In light of a prowler who has been in your yard, maybe been there several times, I don't know if it's you or Oliver of interest to him. If any neighbor described Oliver, it wouldn't take much to figure him out. He gave his real name. I don't want either of you in jeopardy. On another topic, Brad Surnani's place was vandalized. He doesn't know yet what was taken. Jewelry, art, and technical stuff were not removed. Too close to our investigation, Beryl, you are all too close."

Beryl's face brightened. "Were any of the other spectators at the explosion site houses disturbed?"

Beauregard's answer was, "Not as of yet. Remember, they live in different communities. Only Brad and Nate and James live in West Side. John lives in Springfield."

"Strange, Brad and I were chosen."

"Not so strange, Beryl, I'm beginning to think there was a deal outside the land deal behind this. The land deal itself would never have brought scrutiny to you."

21

Stacia Kovac, Bobby, and Other Lovers

Sergeant Barr received a call from news anchor Stacia Kovac. His face lit up when he said, "I'll be right there."

Some neighbors in the old row houses in the old factory area of West Side were creating havoc in front of one of the houses. Barr thought, *it looks like a domestic, I'm not surprised the police were not called. The folks in this area are mainly Russian immigrants and would never call 'the Policia'. Patrols don't go by here often except for a few hotshots looking for trouble. There's Stacia in front with her photographer.*

"Hey, Stacia, how'd you get here before the police?"

"I called you first and then 911. Before Robbie picked me up for the day's shooting opportunities, he'd gotten a call about some unrest. He didn't know what type of unrest. He knows everyone in town. It must be a repetitive domestic to have drawn such an audience. I have little on my agenda from the station. Robbie always finds something to fill in for the program. He makes me look good."

"You look good to me all the time, Stacia. You don't need Robbie."

Loud yelling and children screaming could be heard from the third floor. The nineteenth century rehabbed brownstones each had a small wrought iron balcony on each floor giving the building a good look far beyond the rental income earned by the HUD subsidization. A man came out on the balcony screaming in Russian and held his little girl out over the balcony. The crowd screamed back in English and Russian vitriolic curses while the child sobbed. The wife took this opportunity to escape with three other children leaving the one girl alone with what appeared to be her drunken daddy. Sergeant Barr hastened to the open door of the apartment block while calling Captain Beauregard. "Captain, husband is holding daughter hostage on third floor balcony screaming in Russian."

Rudy answered, "Try to hold him up until we get an interpreter. Try English first. See if a spectator knows anything. Stay close. If you are able to talk to him, talk him down."

Barr approached the wife. "Do you speak English?"

And Mrs. Lana Belyaev answered, "He's only like this when he's drinking. Don't hurt him. He will not hurt Maryana. She looks afraid, but he won't hurt her."

"Mrs. Belyaev, would your talking to him help?"

"Why you think that? I been talking to him for an hour and this is where he is. He listen to men and police, not wife."

"What is your husband's name?"

"He is Yuri."

Hoping her words were true, Barr raced up to the third floor. Lana had left the door open when she fled. He entered the well-kept apartment less two turned over tables and chairs and headed to the door to the balcony. The noise below hid his footsteps. He was on the balcony within a foot of Barr, but his holding the child with extended arms out beyond the balcony prevented Bobby from pulling Mr. Belyaev back. He waited, scarcely breathing, hoping the man would relax for a moment to get a better grip on the child. And he did, for one moment, lean back with the little girl screaming in his arms. The child was now on the inside of the rail as he adjusted his hold. Bobby Barr prayed as he grabbed both the man's waistband with one hand and the child's leg with the other. His action pushed the drunken man off kilter letting Bobby pull the girl to safety. Yuri was surprised by the move and let go of the child, but reacted with a heavy blow to Barr's cheek. Eleni was now on the floor and Bobby, despite the pain in his face, yelled to the little girl in English to get out, to run to Mommy downstairs. And she did.

Bobby turned in time to avoid another blow to his head. He said loudly, "Yuri, I am Detective Barr from West Side Police. Your family is safe down there. Don't let them see you fighting with the police." Yuri appeared to hear Barr's words, while he prepared to swing again. Bobby thought, *this son-of-a-bitch weighs about two hundred and fifty pounds. I can't take too many direct hits. It's time to remember some self-defense training. I'll go for his legs.*

Bobby took a second punch to the head before in reflex he grabbed Yuri's leg. The resulting force caught the drunken man off balance. He fell and hit his head on the wrought iron railing. Bobby heard a scrunchy sound and it frightened him. Yuri lay at his feet. Bobby checked his neck pulse and breathed a sigh of relief. In minutes EMTs loaded the stretcher. Their look did nothing to reassure Bobby. Uniforms swarmed the apartment building. Almost immediately, Lily and Petra approached him directing him to their car. They allowed him a moment before giving his remembered facts. Clearly shaking, he said, "I was losing the fight. The guy was strong. I went for his legs. He went down hard hitting his head on the railing. Bad, I know he's hurt bad."

Bobby teared up. A flash went off. Robbie, the photographer, caught Bobby with his head bent over in psychic pain. Petra yelled, "I want that, Robbie! Give me the film."

He started to run but tripped over something. Standing up, Robbie faced Stacia who said, "Not this story, Robbie, not today. I won't file it. Do you understand?"

Robbie apologized to Stacia, saying, "It is a really good story, Stacia. A cop saves the kid's life and feels sorry for the punk who tried to hurt the kid. It makes the police look sympathetic."

Stacia answered before Petra could get a word in. "They'll need it for Internal Affairs. You know that. Give it up."

And it was over.

Stacia's knock at Sergeant Bobby Barr's condo brought a delighted look to the face opening the door. "God, you're a sight for sore eyes. I've been sitting here feeling sorry for myself, and look who comes to save me twice in the same day, my angel."

Stacia smiled, saying, "I never realized, Bobby, the dark side of policing. You did such a good job today saving the little girl and then you get the old 'Are you telling us the whole truth' routine. And as to Robbie, don't get mad. We go for the emotional moments pictures. He'd have won something for your photo. It's outstanding emotionally, and it broke my heart for you."

"I don't want to break your heart, Stacia. I want to own it."

He put his arms around the lady and tried to kiss her, but the injuries to his face forced a loud wincing sound. Stacia said, "Not tonight, baby, but soon. I promise."

In a few, the couple left for dinner at a local restaurant noted for its soup. "Stacia, I haven't lost any teeth but I think they're rattling around. He was a strong guy, and thankfully, I just heard from the Captain, he's doing well. I don't want to kill anyone."

The couple discussed over dishes filled with chicken stew and corn bread every aspect of the day's events. Stacia said, "Bobby, you detectives are not such heavy hitters as private eyes. I don't think one of them would pass by kissing a lady just because he had a broken cheekbone. You disappoint."

Despite some pain, Bobby's face transformed into a huge grin. He said, "Just got to be patient with us who follow the rules. You'll regret you pointed my weaknesses out. Same time in two days, Stacia, I'll be at your house in two days."

"There you go again, making me wait an extra day. Have you a good reason? Because I'm an anchor reporter. We don't wait well."

"Yeah, I'm on desk duty for that night. It doesn't allow me to leave the station. Please be patient."

The news on the television facing them from the bar had Bobby's picture posted with a flash description: "Detective saves child and almost dies. Child's mother says he was crying because he hurt her husband."

Further into the story the mother explained, "My husband has a wicked temper. He killed our dog. I thought he would kill Tia, but the detective beat him up. I don't know how. My husband was a boxer and weighs two eighty. Detective Barr looks skinny to me."

Stacia touched Bobby's hand. "This will be a tough road for you, Bobby. There are those who will accuse you of unnecessary brutality. Keep your cool. You know I'm here for you."

Stacia noticed stares from other diners. She scanned the room smiling, saying with her eyes an unspoken thank you. It was as if in her acknowledging their interest, she was saying, 'I know you care.'

A man approached them and told Stacia, "You know I'm the one who called your photographer Robbie. You can thank me. I call him for every iffy situation I see in my neighborhood. I'm glad I called in time for you to get there."

Sergeant Torrington had a large lump of explosion case witness files on his desk. His legendary attention to detail allowed him not to be overwhelmed. Mason walked by his desk and said, "Want some help with those, Bro?"

"Normally I'd say yes, Lieutenant, but I sometimes need to see all the details to figure out who's lying. You know, sound out their language when they mention one or the other witnesses. See if two witnesses' language is the same. With all the news now out, I'm settling in for the day. Just don't interrupt me with a call, please!"

"Ha, you think detail will protect you from going out in bad weather. I'll try, but no guarantees. Do you have all the latest forensics reports in your files?"

A nod told him an affirmative. The noise in the room would appear to a stranger to be too loud to do any real thinking and analysis. Ted had no trouble honing in on his task. Not even an hour later, he'd drawn some conclusions. *I don't feel the Brad Surnani and John Conlon interviews flowed like the truth does. Surnani was known as the velvet glove axe man and yet he appeared to deliberately act defensively, particularly in discussing Corinne and his relationship. With his public relations experience, he could have used one of his typical turn of phrases. No, he got squirrelly. This guy is out of whack. Now, is it because he's the perp or because his whole life has disappeared? He's wealthy enough. It's clear to me Brad is not emotionless. He's practiced a discipline for years to hold back his emotions. The whole interview is a contrast to his noted reputation.*

And John Conlon is just too good to be true. Very likable, but he has an answer to everything. He's cool, but attempted to direct us in specific directions. With his background he should have been smarter than that. It's not a savvy move to tell your interrogator about rumors that can't be substantiated. None of my insights point to these guys as murderers. They just have the usual habit of lying. Although Brad really took offense when questioned about Corinne. And the question about Art's health was raised. I'll check the autopsy report.

The autopsy report spoke about Art Richards' severely charred body. Toxicology reports were limited. There was nothing listed about the condition of the body before death. Ted searched the files for Art's previous medicals. Sure enough, his doctor was listed. A short phone call later confirmed the statement about Art's health. Art Richards suffered from early Alzheimer's Disease. He had few symptoms until a few months before his death. The doctor did not think Art had shared this information with his wife, saying, "I knew Darla. Despite his horrible treatment of her, if she knew he was sick, she would have stayed the course."

Ted said, "I don't know, Doc, it may have been her get out of jail free card. She spent her life catering to his business and public needs. A future life as a caretaker could have been just too much."

Mason walked by with his fourth cup of latte and said, "How's the detail going, Ted?"

Ted shared the new information. Mason said, "Why kill a man when he's on a downward slope? Unless of course the perp didn't know. I assume Corinne knew and Darla knew. I would guess Brad knew unless he's an idiot. If he was showing symptoms of forgetfulness and disorganization, anyone close to him would notice. James would know. And as to a relationship between Corinne and Brad, do more interviews on Corinne and Brad's neighbors. Someone must have seen something."

Ted asked, "Mason, you have some strong financial and banking connections, can you see if Art Richards made some changes financially such as putting some businesses in other names? Anything that would show readiness to meet his negative future with good business decisions."

"Why would his readiness matter? Oh, I get it, if he was moving money around and changing recipients, then Corinne and Brad would know about it and his family and possibly John Conlon. What you really need to see is his will."

"I have a call into his attorney about a will. I'm hoping he'll call back."

"If you don't get one soon, Ted, I'll pay a visit. I'm good with all the legalese."

Ted made some more calls on Brad. He realized Brad lived not far from him in a glamorous condo unit. There were three separate condo buildings with different addresses almost next to each other. He hooked up Brad's condo on the GPS map and realized it was in a building next to Corinne Thompson's building. They had different street addresses. He would never had picked up their closeness without going there. He thought, *added evidence there could be a bond between the two.*

Ted took a ride to Morning Bird Terrace and talked to the condo manager at Corinne's home. He said he was interested in a showing. The manager claimed the police asked them not to show the condo for at least two more weeks. Ted showed him his badge, but said the Captain knew he was looking for space and suggested he take a visit. The manager let him in. Ted thought upon entering the home, *this unit is twenty-eight hundred square feet of usable space. It puts my three thousand square feet house in the garbage in comparison. It's breathtaking with a view of a run-off from the Connecticut River.* He walked through it with the manager who watched his every move.

He opened the closet and was surprised. There was menswear in the closet along with Corinne's dresses. He checked for labels. They were not local and were from high end clothiers. There was only one suit, a tux, and one sports jacket and slacks. There were no shoes. In the third drawer in the dresser, he found some men's briefs. There were initials on the briefs – BS. He expected to find AR, not Brad's initials. He thought, *confirms there was some personal relationship between Brad and Corinne, but there are so few of his things. Must be relatively new. Why is it necessary for his clothes to be here? He lives on the next block.*

Excited by his find, Ted entered Brad Surnani's building and contacted the super. He questioned Corinne's visiting with Brad. The super recognized Corinne's picture, and said, "I think she was going to move in with him once her condo was sold. He had not much else to add except the relationship had been going on and off for six months."

Not more than twenty minutes later, Ted was in Mason's office, saying, "Put your finance hat on, Mason. How much can you find out about Corinne Thompson and Brad Surnani's finances?"

Ted reported his findings, leading Mason to say, "You've got some info. Sounds like a soap opera to me. It would have made the two of them good perps for Art's death, but then Corinne died. I can do a number on Corinne's finances because she's dead, not so easy with Brad. He'd have his attorney on me at the first sign of inquiry. I'll check his bond application for the land deal. I can get that. I thought these two were unemotional. At odds, with what that super thought. They're in love, man. You never know."

22

New Ideas Shine

Oliver and Beryl entertained Nate for the big game. Brady lost. Would he play another season? Oliver, who loved the Pats, still had hoped Brady would again play whether for either Tampa Bay or New England. Oliver didn't care which team, saying, "He's worked so damn hard and come so close. He deserves another try."

Nate agreed but said, "You just don't know what other influences surround any decision he'd make. In the big time, your decisions may not always be your decisions."

Beryl insisted Tom Brady would make his own decisions, thus ending the conversation on Brady. Oliver asked, "Do either of you know if the police have TV coverage on the area around Barney's home during the hours he may have been killed. I mean, Barney lived on a main road. Even if there's not a camera near his home, there would be traffic cameras on the road away from his home."

Nate and Beryl both insisted this thought would not have been missed by the MCU. Beryl remarked, "I'll check with the detectives. Lieutenant Lent is now head of Traffic. He'd know.

Beryl made the call and was surprised Lieutenant Lent invited her to look at camera coverage. When she arrived, Beryl thanked Ash.

Ash said, "I have not even scanned the footage. One of the officers in Traffic did. He saw nothing unusual, but this was before we realized Barney was murdered. I thought why waste time. Together we might see something. It's a lot of time to cover and fast forwarding too quickly often loses the slowness of a car and other details. It takes time, Beryl. I thought we could take turns."

Scrolling through three hours of three separate camera video was boring. Beryl found herself, nodding off and then going back. She realized Ash was looking over her shoulder at the same time. "I thought we were doing it separately?"

"We are. I'm two feet behind you. It's a different view."

At the clocked time of 10:42, a car slowed slightly in front of the third camera. Beryl said, "What do you think, Ash? Where did this car come from? It didn't pass camera two."

Ash pulled down a computer map of the area. "It must have come from this driveway. It's fifty feet after camera two and two hundred feet before camera three."

Beryl said, "That's not a driveway, Ash. It's a road. There's no name attached on the map that I can see. Scroll up. Look, it goes up beyond the house and turns left into a small street. Survey Road is the name and must be the name of this street."

They followed Survey Road and noticed it was parallel to Barney's street, offering another access to the home with no cameras. Beryl said, "Where is this third camera? How come the killer couldn't see it?"

Ash pulled some detail sheets on cameras and laughed. "It was installed three months ago. You know, Beryl, the city has about five pan-tilt zoom cameras. A sixth one was requested because of suspicious activity and drug movement on this backroad. Barney requested it after he notified police in time for them to make several drug arrests. At ninety, he was a good citizen."

"I can't identify the plates on the car, not even its model. It's an older model."

Ash answered, "It's an older SUV and banged up. It looks like a

Rav4."

"Who makes a Rav4, Ash?"

"Toyota, and it's a good car for dependability. Although we can't see the plates, it had to come from somewhere. Unless the perp lives on Survey Road, there should be pictures of the car when it entered Survey Road. I can see two main entrance streets, Almond Street and Terrace Road. I'll get them up."

Beryl and Ash were disappointed. They did find the suspicious car entering from Terrace Road, but the plate was still not visible. Ash thought the first letter on the plate looked like a B to him. Beryl disagreed. She thought she saw a P. Beryl asked, "Why not follow the car through its travel on Terrace Road and before? He or she was probably living not very far or at least close by."

The car was seen entering Terrace Road from a main corridor, Route 20. A Route 20 Italian restaurant showed the car leaving its parking place. They looked for four hours prior but the car did not move, nor was it positioned such for plate reading. Ash was disgusted. Beryl was not. "Why don't we go to more footage. And I could question the staff there?"

Ash answered, "Because you're not police. We'll do it, Beryl. Stay out of it. If the Captain hears you are interfering, he'll go ballistic. I should not have let you see the travel route we found. As to more footage, the camera was out before six p.m. I'll have someone see if there is another camera further out capturing this car, but I wouldn't hold my breath."

Beryl did not hesitate in driving to Barratta's Italian restaurant after leaving the police station, thinking, *no one will know if I've asked a few questions.*

Beryl ordered a delicious lunch of beans, macaroni, and sausages in a hybrid sauce of wine, fresh tomatoes, basil, and garlic. She took the opportunity to share her enchantment with the robust dish. The waiter explained, "We have a new chef and he is awesome. Everyone comes back within a week after eating one of his dishes. They all have a new twist. He calls it the interjection of perfection. We agree."

Beryl said, "I bet you know all your patrons."

He agreed that he did. She went on to ask him about what was going happening at the restaurant on the date of Barney's death. It took a minute for the waiter to recall, but he did. "The place was blazing. We had the raucous country band, 'The Five Silver Dollars'."

Beryl asked about cars parking because she said, "My boyfriend was in the parking lot and his car was hit by a small, older car, maybe it was an SUV. Do you remember someone complaining about the accident?"

"Accidents in this parking lot are a dime a dozen. Look at its arch shape and most of the parking lines are faded. There is a guy with a car matching your description who comes in here often. He parks horizontally down by the arch where there are no lines. I've told him before he's tempting fate, because any of the cars within the lines near him have to back out close to his car to get out."

Beryl asked, "Can you describe him for me?"

"Five-nine or ten, about a hundred and sixty pounds, lean and flexible. Wears athletic shoes or soft construction style boots and dresses casually. He's pretty friendly. Always has a crack to make or a joke. His hair is light in color. Always pays in cash. I remember cash payers because I get my tips right away and he barely tips twenty percent. That's it."

"Do you think you could call me when he comes in again? I won't make a scene. I just want to get his license plate for the accident. There's a twenty in it for you."

The waiter smiled in agreement and Beryl gave him a card.

Zed Albion and Abu Cason were allowed to leave the hospital on the same day and the same hour. They found the alerted press outside when staff wheeled them out in their chairs. Their injuries were mostly covered up. In fact, the two men appeared to be inordinately healthy. The press had burning questions to ask, such as, 'Do you think you were meant to be murdered?' or 'Are you part of a land grab to put a marijuana facility on the Barney property?' Or 'Is this payback, Abu, for what Corinne did to one of your acolytes in killing Teisha's chances for a job promised to her?'"

Abu almost punched the reporter, but Zed held his arm so he could not move forward. Snarling at the reporter who had asked him if the explosion was aimed at him, Abu said, "I'm a minister of God, not a wealthy CEO. Look elsewhere or are you too dense to see."

Zed had all he could do to marshal Abu into their car, saying, "It's not how we fight back, you know that, Abu. Shut your damn mouth. This is not a church audience going along with all your magic. These are reporters who would find fault with Jesus."

Their car sped away forcing two reporters and the photographer to back off. Abu and Zed did not go home. They stopped at the explosion site. Abu said, "I actually went into the front building. It was open. I saw the storage but thought nothing of it. Zed, I smelled aftershave. You know how I like to smell nice. I've tried every aftershave sold and this is my favorite, so don't tell me I don't know it when I smell it. I swear it was 'Obsession for Men' by Calvin Klein. I'd know it anywhere. I didn't think about it then or I would have told that Captain."

Zed said, "Make a call now. We're in no condition to investigate. I know you don't like the police, but Abu, Beauregard is legit."

After some grumbling from Abu and serious debating by Zed, Abu called Beauregard. The conversation was short. Beauregard thanked Abu, saying, "This is something tangible. We'll use the smell test. How much does this stuff cost?"

Abu laughed. "Send me the bill, Captain, and let me know when you've caught the guy. It's a guy. This was not the woman's version of the scent."

Beauregard was surprised by the call. He never expected Minister Abu to give him a piece of evidence and thought, *you never know. Abu said Zed convinced him to call me. Zed remembered my bringing him home instead of arresting him when he was younger. Thank you, God. I get help from all the unauthorized folks, kids, Beryl, Norbie Cull, the elderly, people I've arrested.*

Petra, when told of the smell test, said, "Put me on it, Captain. I have the nose for scents. Keep this news quiet. If it gets out everybody will be wearing Calvin Klein. I'll call all our witnesses back for a quick review of their previous interviews. If we have no luck, Bill Barr and I will visit them. I'll use their bathrooms and see if Obsession is in there. Can't convict on this alone, but it could lead us in the right direction."

———

Beryl was in the process of feeding her dog Amico and arguing with her son Oliver. Both males were testing her mettle. She thought, *love has such strings attached. I must put up with their foolishness. I swear they have the same genes.*

"Oliver, you haven't finished your investigation. I met Lieutenant Aylewood-Locke today and she said they think the perp wears Calvin Klein's 'Obsession' aftershave. Why don't you ask the lady at the B&B if her sister recalls any lingering odor when the man left the yard."

"You're beating a dead horse, Mom. The man was outside. Any odors would be gone in seconds in the open air."

"Oliver, if I have heard anything from the police investigations it is to go back over material many times and ask the stupid questions again. You started this, now finish it. I got the impression you like this gal. Why not call her. You know, make a social call and fit the question into the conversation."

Beryl left the kitchen and Oliver made the call, thinking, *I have Mom thinking she's pulling my strings, but she's right. I was looking for a reason and this time I'll be straight with Leeann.*

He didn't call Leeann in advance. He took his chances and fortune smiled. Leeann was picking up sticks off her lawn left by a ferocious windstorm two days before. He thought, *she looks good even in her gardening clothes. I don't need a reason to visit, do I? I have one, but why do I think I need a reason. I'm a jerk. I'm afraid she isn't interested in me. Well, Oliver, I should keep my ego in check. If she doesn't like me, best to find out now.*

When Leeann saw him, she gave him a huge wave and a smile. *She wants to see me. Maybe she is just lonely and wants to talk. It's a starting point.*

Leeann dropped the bundle of sticks in her hands on the side garden path, saying, "I'm so happy to see you, Oliver. Come on in, I made a lovely pastry for breakfast today. It's good enough for teatime."

Conversation bubbled and flowed. Between bites of pastry Oliver asked her if she could contact her sister again. When he explained the reason, Leeann laughed. "You expect her to remember a scent in the air in the outdoors when she was there seconds after the guy left. I don't know. Addie does like perfume, but it doesn't mean she remembers scents. And how would she know if it was 'Obsession' unless her husband wears it?"

Oliver debated the issue for a few minutes before saying, "It won't hurt to ask."

Addie answered the call. Leeann said, "Oliver has an additional question. I'll let him ask it."

Oliver posed the question carefully. "Did you smell a cologne in the air the day the man disappeared from the parking lot?"

Addie laughed. "I did. It was lovely, but I don't think it was from a man, Oliver. It smelled like a spicy cinnamon."

"Do you think you could go to a cosmetic counter carrying good men's colognes and identify the smell."

"Oliver, I'll try. Better yet, I'll be in Springfield with Leeann next week. Meet us at the Holyoke Mall. I'll sniff for you then. Will that work for you?"

"Thank you. I'll make sure I'm around."

———

Lieutenant Aylewood-Locke and Sergeant Barr were loopy with unused energy from drinking coffee at several witnesses' homes. Petra said, "What a bust. I saw 'Obsession' aftershave in two bathrooms, but placed in the back of the cabinets. John Conlon and James Richards still don't seem likely as murderers. I do not think James would murder his mother; his father maybe, but not Darla."

"Petra, the only use in finding the aftershave is as another supporting evidence piece. Not the first time we've chased a useless idea."

Petra asked, "Has Art Richards' will been read yet?"

Bill looked in his notebook, saying, "It's today at Richards' attorney's office over on Elm Street, West Springfield. His name is Lennie Authier and he's been a stickler about giving us info. Said something about there being several wills he'd have to chase down. He did say he'd let us know when he knew. If he's got the heirs in there today, he knows. Let's book over there."

The police were welcomed into a conference room crowded with family and friends. The crowd included Conlon, Surnani, James Richards, and Jay Bird. Petra whispered to Bill, "How the hell did he get in here? He's not an aide."

"I heard he's writing a 'true crime' novel on Art and Corinne's deaths."

Petra replied, "I'd like to get my hands on it. Probably not enough evidence on him now to get a search warrant; although maybe we do have enough. We'll check later."

Attorney Authier did the usual welcome acknowledging the size of his audience. He droned on about three wills Art made in the last year, which was astonishing to him, because he'd kept his last previous will for fifteen years. The changes in the will mostly reflected business partnerships. He stated in the will he was disappointed in some business deals and personal connections which, "…cause me to adjust my estate in various ways."

Attorney Authier said, "I have written two of the last three wills. The one in between was a holographic will. None of it's relevant since the last will was written by Art and I, Attorney Authier, signed and notarized."

He only read from the current last will. Art left most of his business property in trust to his children. He left the minimal allowable for a spouse under Massachusetts law to his wife Darla. The remaining substantial amount was left to Corinne Thompson. Corinne's estate was complicated. She had no living relatives and her will left her estate to Art Richards. To say some of the people there who did not receive mention was a problem would be an understatement. A quiet roar of dissatisfaction ended when Attorney Authier said Art Richards was in sound mind at the time of the signing and it was videotaped. There was no one accompanying him.

Petra whispered to Bill, "Now there's a question there may not be an answer to: who died first?"

<h1 style="text-align:center">23</h1>

What Next?

Beauregard finished a touchy debate with his good friend Gerard, the medical examiner, looking for some answers. His detectives waited for a response. The call came in during their morning meeting. The Captain took the call and after, said, "He does not think there is enough evidence to determine who died first. He is willing to bring in a specialist in physics to calculate, based on the video, who landed first; which probably would determine who died first. Do any of you remember who landed first?"

Up went the video. Estimates were made concluding the two were ten feet apart and thrown into the air seconds apart. Lilly insisted Corinne landed first. The others were not certain, leaving Beauregard with, "Up to the medical pros now. This is a problem for the lawyers and heirs, but it seems to me it doesn't matter. If Corinne dies first, her estate goes to Art's estate, if she dies second, a good portion of Art's estate goes to her just to be flipped back to Art, if they die simultaneously, there's no change. Interesting this may be, but not important to us."

Sergeant Barr said, "Maybe important, Captain, if one of the heirs knew about the wills. With the two of them dead, there's a pretty big amount when the estates are added together. With Darla dead, her portion goes back into the estate, and the remaining amount goes to the kids. Together, the estates are worth upward to fifteen million. That's not chump change; it could be a motive."

The Captain wondered aloud, "So someone had notice of what each one had for assets and who would be the heirs. That someone also knocked off Darla to eliminate her portion from the estate. What is in Darla's will? Did she leave what she had to her kid or to someone else? How much of their assets were in joint accounts? Tricky process to follow. So, the answer leaves a question as to why kill Barney and Teisha. Wrap them into it and I'll go along. Till then, look for evidence. Get back to the boards. Something is glaring at us."

Mason asked, "Petra and Bobby, did you check that photographer's home for aftershave? He doesn't look the type, but he was at the explosion site and he is a man."

The two detectives groaned. Petra said, "Haven't we wasted enough time on this? And the photographer probably lives in his car."

No one was sympathetic to their needs, leaving the two detectives another interview. Beauregard asked them how they could get into Jay Bird's home? Since no one answered, he said, "Bring him back in here for his second along with his lawyers. Petra, go buy a bottle of 'Obsession' aftershave and smell it. Does your nose remember smells?"

"Sure, Captain. Can I keep the bottle of aftershave for Jim?"

Several comments hit the room mostly using the words 'cheap' and 'stingy.' Beauregard moved the conversation to Corinne Thompson's file. "What do we really know about her, Mason?"

Mason said, "Not much to know, Captain. She has a cat, a condo, some men's clothes in her closet that are not Art Richards', a car, lots of money, few friends. I've gone through her cell phone. It's organized by need. Her attorney is under A for attorney along with seven other lawyers. All doctors are under M for medicine along with pharmacies. She has a F for friends but Art Richards and Brad Surnani are not listed. I did not look under L for lovers for those two."

Beauregard showed impatience at the jesting and Mason continued.

"There are eight friends listed including James Richards, John Conlon, Darla Richards, Colleen Richards, Barney, Poppy Deardon, Lucy Eichen, and Robbie Layden. The last one is a surprise. I mean, what does she have to do with a photographer? She's not noted as having a 'talk to all in a democratic fashion' personality."

The Captain said, "Lilly, you talk with Colleen Richards. Mason, you get Poppy and Lucy in here, and Petra, get Robbie Layden in here again. He never mentioned knowing Corinne in his interview."

Bobby Barr's stomach tightened as he thought, *this isn't good. Why would Robbie not mention being a close friend with Corinne? Why didn't Stacia mention it? I hope I'm not being played. Please God, tell me I'm not being played.*

Bobby called Stacia for a lunch date. She was quick to suggest Calabrese's Market. "There are a few tables there. I have just a short time before meeting Robbie."

Her smiling face reassured Bobby she could not deceive him, then again he remembered being deceived by a beauty. They both ordered 'The Daniele' and laughed at their common interest. Stacia said, "I'm starving, Bobby. I did a load of paperwork I've been avoiding. Nothing builds up hunger pains more than sitting. When I'm busy physically working I never think how hungry I am."

Once mouthing their sandwiches and chips and chugging ice tea, Bobby asked Stacia about Robbie Layden, about what he was like to work with. She asked, "Is this for your investigation or are you interested in what you think is a relationship between us? If it's the latter, there is nothing, not even a friendship. Robbie's difficult to friend because he is so private about his life."

"Actually, I'm glad you brought up his sense of going it alone. It is what's of interest to me. Where does he live? Does he have a girlfriend or boyfriend or kids? What are his interests? For example, does he bowl, or hit the bars, or volunteer his services? Right now, he is an enigma."

"Bobby, I don't think Robbie is capable of murder, but I don't think he's the most honest person. He cheats on his business expenses for the station and gets caught every time because I don't cheat. My boss checks one against the other. Robbie says he picks me up before and lets me off after events, but the city's not big enough to show such miles discrepancies as he lists. He tries to get my boss to give him cash for all his connections who point him in the right direction, but he asked for too much. It was settled for an extra fifty dollars a week. I think he pockets it. He's quite cheap. I buy the coffee and put it on my expense account. Little things, Bobby, make me think he's just a small-time manipulator and thief."

"Did Robbie have a friendship with Corinne Thompson?"

"It's strange you should ask me that question, Bobby. We covered many of Corinne's functions. He always knew when there was going to be a development in a business where she had a vested interest. I asked him about whether he was playing cozy with her, because Corinne had a reputation of being a bit loose when it could get her someplace. He said she just knew what was good for her. He also said Corinne and Jay Bird had common interests, but he wouldn't elaborate. Robbie likes to make himself out as more important than he is. Left me with the idea I could never know if a fact given by him was the truth or an embellishment."

"Why didn't you mention his relationship with Corinne before when I was set to interview him?"

"Why would I, when I still don't know if he had one. I'll ask him if you want me to, Bobby?"

"No, Stacia, please don't do that. He's antsy about being questioned in the first place. You do that and we won't have a witness."

They finished lunch quickly and left with Bobby thinking, *she's okay.*

———

Kay Whiterly called Beryl with something like calamity in her voice. "We may be in trouble, Beryl."

"What are you talking about? What kind of trouble? And why the 'we'? You never do anything wrong. Me, always, so why the plurality?"

"The Government Accountability Office, you know the GAO, is investigating the fund we reviewed. Remember, Beryl, it got no further action from anybody in power. It was just kicked upstairs to the Federal Government. I've been notified our committee members are to be interviewed. You specifically were mentioned. I asked why you, and it's because you signed the Freedom of Information Filing ("FOIF")."

"Not to worry, Kay, they just want to see what we got without their having to file one. Saves them labor. I am not concerned."

"Well, you're the only one. We never reviewed the FOIF."

"That's right. Everything went haywire with the explosion. Do you have it easily available? Is it on digital or hardcopy?"

"Hardcopy."

"Are you available now? I'll come over. It's better for us to see what the GAO thinks is so valuable to include me as a special witness to interrogate. I don't know any more than the rest of our group."

An hour later found the two women looking over the redacted evidence from the FOIF. The redactions centered around the names of the city grant director and staff members who were in charge of authorizing expenditures from the grant. There were an abundance of expenditures of large amounts. Beryl said, "Kay, eighty percent of the funds were disbursed within ten days. Seems awful quick considering the timing was in the middle of COVID 19. Lot of little expenditures to small non-profits, but then we get to the big money. Three of them to the tune of three million dollars each to non-profits not in our city of West Side. DSI grants equal or more than the one given to West Side were given all over the Northeast. Why would West Side give its funds to companies outside our city unless their work was done for the city? Let's check on the three biggies. And why didn't we know any of this at the time of our public meeting?"

The names of the three corporations that received money were not familiar to either of the women. They were all sub-chapter S Corporations. A Google search showed minimal webpages. Corporate structures were not listed and the webpages were first posted in 2018. The corporate mission statements were on point with the grant funds directive for spending. The search for the corporations showed them listed as Commonwealth corporations with the Secretary of State. Beryl noticed that two of the corporations had the same Secretary listed. She googled the corporate addresses. All were based in Worcester, although with different addresses. Most surprising of all was the familiar name popping up as President of Work-Placement, Inc. She thought, *what is a fiction writer doing as president of a work placement firm when he was principal of another firm? What is the connection?*

Kay responded without knowing Beryl's thoughts with, "This is funny stuff. Maybe the GAO knows we brought Jay Bird in to lecture on fictional mystery writing because we're close friends with him. Is that enough to make us complicit? And he was at our speak-out. We didn't know him then."

"No. What is the connection Jay has with a Will Nudham who is secretary to two of the corporations? Those two corporations are different from the one Jay is president. We need to search Nudham's history. Could it be they know each other? Our public meeting set this off. We were successful. I'm thrilled. Don't worry any more, Kay. And look at our list of attendees at the forum, Jay Bird and Robbie Layden. Robbie probably was there with Stacia. I remember press attending although we didn't' even get on the nightly news."

Beryl immediately called Norbie Cull's office after she left Kay.

Sheila, his admin, said he was free at two. Since it was close to that time, Beryl headed over wondering how Sheila could make appointments for Norbie without his knowing. She thought, *you never know who's in charge of a person's calendar.*

Norbie welcomed her, saying, "News on the explosion, I hope?"

"Nope, I need you to represent me before the GAO."

"Beryl, just what are you involved in?"

She reviewed the public committee meeting the women's group held and the letter from the GAO had her research. Norbie frowned. "You're safe and I'll represent you for free except I need a check for a dollar as Perry Mason would say. I want in on their information. Can I have a copy of your FOIF and research? What was Jay Bird doing as president? I have a guy who in a minute will tell me if any of these corporations do legitimate work. I know Will Nudham. He worked for several towns as assistant manager. He never lasted. Not a bad guy, but a bit of a knucklehead. A million dollars would help Jay Bird develop Barney's land. You keep being in the right place at the right time, Beryl. I don't know how you do it, but this time, I think you opened one door."

Beauregard was Norbie's guest for a drink at the country club. Cull's story retold in dramatic fashion brought incredulousness to Rudy's face. "You and that woman, together, give me a headache. But I thank you for this information. I better get Bird in here before the GAO strikes."

"No, you can do that but you can't mention the GAO. You have every right to search the Secretary of State's website for corporate common ownerships and principals. I'm not sure if it does all of that, but he won't know. Ask him why he didn't mention his connection with this company to you. Let him sweat. I wish we could get a trace on his cell to see if he has calls out to Will Nudham. Although he could explain the calls because they both are operating in the same industry. It does let us know if they connect, that Jay Bird may have access to funds from all three corporations' grants proceeds."

"Motive! Motive, Norbie, larceny for over nine million dollars is a prime motive for murder. He could be assured of winning a bid if Corinne and Art were gone. What did he want the land for – to distribute and sell cannabis products? Nine million investment is cheap given the proceeds he would expect. Still, why would he also kill Darla and Teisha?"

"Teisha for jealousy, and maybe he made a play for Darla? Do we know if he knew Darla personally? All we know about Darla are good things. Nobody's completely good."

Rudy replied, "You're a cynic, Norbie, but I will find out. And thank you. Thank Beryl too. She seems to understand this has to be investigated."

"The lady has good instincts."

23

Who Was Where, When?

Sergeant Torrington was busy working a spreadsheet showing the timing of arrival at the site for all explosion site witnesses. The data was not helpful with the exception of excluding the biker and the minister. It was in agreement they would have not been on the premises at that time if they knew the building would be blown up. Arguments toward their being unaware of the width the blast would encompass were rejected. Both wounded victims were considered too smart to make that mistake. The timing of the blast was most likely set remotely. To date, there was no witness showing cars or trucks or walkers entering the building one or two days before the blast. They agreed the igniter would not have been set at the date of the delivery of the chemicals. When it came to Barney's death, Ted thought, *at night when people are sleeping. Who had a housemate or spouse to vouch for them, certainly not James Richards or Surnani or Bird or Connault or Conlon?*

Talking out loud, Ted asked the heavens, "Does that leave calendars to check for Darla and Teisha's deaths. If so, they were all at the explosion site for Darla's death. As to Teisha's, who gave her the drugs in her drink and fiddled with her car? Almost every one of our witnesses have been excluded. Captain, need your input."

Beauregard, holding his second coffee for the morning said, "What do you need now? I just gave you the assignment on timing. You already have questions."

"Nope, Captain, just putting logic skills in the analysis."

Ted went on to explain his thought process. Rudy could find all kinds of exceptions to his logic but agreed most were farfetched. He said, "For the umpteenth time the clues lead to Darla and Teisha and the motive must be there. Motive and opportunity are needed. Darla's death looks more and more like a professional hit. We have Connault, Conlon, Bird, Surnani all having military backgrounds.

"Ted, forget opportunity and go into service records and other experiences for motive. First, though, is Jay Bird. He's waiting in the conference room with his attorney who's from Boston. Be careful how you ask questions. I want him long enough to tire of us, but still stay."

Sergeant Border called this waiting for the prey to come closer 'stand hunting' and compared the conference room to a rush of grass near a tree in the woods. Bird was flipping and flopping like a scared Blue, a name Ted and the other detectives had previously called him. Ted asked, "Jay, how well did you know Darla? We heard you were good friends with her."

"Good friends no, friends yes. I would see her at various business and political and social functions when Art had to bring his wife. She was great at conversation with good political and business acumen. She was interesting enough so I googled her. She has a Master's degree in Philosophy from Georgetown along with her education degrees received locally. Before she married, she worked on several local politicians campaigns. She was smart but had this silly Catholic idea that marriage was for life. Hard for my mind to get around that idea when she was married to a known philanderer. Even the Church doesn't require you to stay where there is no respect. Don't know who would kill Darla. She is one woman I found special. And I don't know why she was forcing him out in the end."

"How often did you see her in the last year? I mean often enough to see if she were depressed?"

"Sergeant, Darla was never depressed. She never complained about how Art treated her. She never bitched about work. Her kids were the one area you had to be careful with in your conversations. Me, I had no interest in her children. They were grown, but she was still protective. Take for instance when I told her James was hitting on Teisha, she questioned me and said, "He's a grown man.""

"I told her the truth about Teisha. She knew about Art causing Teisha's loss of a job and wanted to know if Teisha was righteous in her anger. She used that term 'righteous' like in the Bible. I laughed and said it was politics. She wondered if Teisha wanted James for his money and I laughed and asked her what else. She gave a dissertation on the wonderful traits James had. It was sickening and the only time I ever had a conversation with Darla when I wanted it to just end."

Ted changed the subject. "Tell me about your military experiences? I mean, did you know John Conlon, Nathan Connault, Brad Surnani, or Art Richards when you served?"

"Sergeant, I certainly was not close to them. I also served with Zed Albion. I can tell you this, Zed was a fabulous soldier. If I were in a tight spot I'd listen to him over the others. Connault was CIA or something; always there when there were rumors flying. Never trust undercovers anywhere. I don't care what branch of the service they're in. He made me uncomfortable. Brad and John weren't Army, but I saw them at functions. Business types, even when in a uniform. I never saw Art. Did he serve?"

The interview ended. Jay Bird and his attorney walked out looking quite pleased with themselves. Ted thought, *stupid lawyer, he didn't shut his client up. Although how do you shut up a writer? No soldier would be meeting with or aware of Connault as an agent, unless Connault was looking at him. And this guy was smitten with Darla. He lied. He saw her many times. More work to be done.*

More interviews were conducted, but stories were straight up in agreement with previous interviews. Only one item didn't gel. James Richards did not think Jay Bird knew his mother on a personal level. Ted spoke with the Captain. "Something's fishy here. Why would Jay enlarge on a relationship with Darla? It puts him in the middle. James Richards says one didn't exist. Can we speak with more of her friends, Captain?"

"Yes, and try the only daughter Colleen. Ask her about her about Darla's whereabouts on Tuesdays and Thursdays. Also, call Stellato and request a copy of her calendar, and where her car is garaged."

Ted insisted, "Something doesn't gel here. Darla was one handsome woman who never deviated from the mother of the year description until one day she throws the guy out. Now, it could be she is practical and didn't want to be a caretaker. I can tell you he would have told her he was in trouble. He would have leaned on her. Even if he didn't, she knew her husband well enough to see the changes in his memory. I think she had enough, but I believe Darla needed a support system. She may have found a man."

"We've been over this before, Ted. You go find who it is."

Ted took to the phones and arranged for an interview with Colleen Richards. She had a two-hour opening but he would have to come to her, otherwise he'd have to wait two days. He arrived at her location, in the cafeteria of a private school on the edge of the Massachusetts/Connecticut line. Colleen was a handsome young woman with strikingly light blonde hair. Upon greeting, he said, "Your parents both had black hair. What happened here?"

Colleen laughed. "Even the police know about recessive genes, Sergeant Torrington. My youngest brother has lightish hair also, although not this light. Thank goodness or I would have wondered if I were adopted. Now what is important enough for you to drive way out here. It is a test. You bit and were unwilling to wait two days. I really don't think I know anything with value enough to have enticed you here."

"It's simple, Colleen. We don't have a good profile on your mother's likes and needs. I've heard you were close to her and less so to your father. Seems likely you'd have a reasonable perspective on your parents, particularly your mom."

"Go ahead and ask. I will give honest answers. I realize they were both murdered. It was difficult for me to reconcile us all being victims at first. Then I thought, why not. Crime hits every group. I am still recovering from the impact."

"I can only imagine your devastation at the loss of both your parents."

Colleen cut in, saying, "At the loss of my mom. Dad was not close to any of us with the exception of James and only because James has the business mind my dad valued. My mom was a saint attempting to find her place in the real world after spending twenty-five years as the perfect mom. And I do not say that in jest. Mom was a perfect mom in every way, even to the point where she gave credit to Dad he didn't deserve."

"We have her calendar and notice she blocked out every Tuesday and Thursday from four in the afternoon on. There was no note attached re her location. It goes back about eighteen months, Colleen, and it doesn't seem like her personality to hide a standing appointment. Was she perhaps ill?"

"I can't truthfully answer that. I don't think she was sick. About the time blocks, I was suspicious. Mom never hid anything from me, ever, Sergeant, but it was too large a block of time to successfully keep and not have questions asked. At first she said she was helping out at some church getting clothes for the poor. I let that one go. It was well within her norm. But her dedication was too much. She refused to go with my dad to a fundraiser for the homeless which she initially started fifteen years ago. She made a big issue out of his choice for a Thursday night when he was directing the staff to set the date. She knew Thursdays were big for charity events. That was when I became more inquisitive."

"Did you ever find out where she was going?"

"I followed her three times. She went to Brad Surnani's condo. I thought at the time 'Good for Mom.' Give Dad a taste of his own medicine."

Ted pushed. "And now, what do you think now?"

Colleen looked away as she answered. "I followed her a few more times. And realized on the third try I had been a dunce, Sergeant. I know Brad well. I know his car. Each time his car was not there. I went the fourth time, followed Mom into the main complex. His condo is a double on the first floor. It is quite something. Mom had the keys. By itself, not important, except in walking in I saw her turning on lights in the unit. No one was there but her."

Ted said, "After all of that, she wasn't having an affair, what was she doing?"

"Sergeant, she was having an affair but not with Brad. I went out and waited. I had never done that before. Twenty minutes later a tall handsome man about her age went into the building. On a hunch I followed him in. He knocked on the door and Mom let him in, saying, "You're late, Darling." I didn't stay for more. I don't know who he is, but I know Brad must know."

Beauregard was lunching with his wife Mona which meant crabmeat salad and fruit. As his weight loss guardian, she was the best, but her practice sometimes strained Rudy's patience. He would have much preferred a luscious six-ounce burger with fried onions, catsup and maybe a bit of lettuce. His lunching at home with her today on her teacher's day off was not the norm and she knew it. "Okay, fess up, as you eat my favorite lunch. What's bugging West Side's diligent detective enough for him to bring his problems home?"

Grumbling, Rudy said, "It's a woman's perspective I want to know. I thought I'd ask you before I ask Petra, Lilly, and Millie."

"Go on. I can't wait for what you think we women know more than you men. I could be sarcastic with you, but it's wasted on you, Rudy. You're only interested in what you're focused on, not on general fun."

Rudy explained the situation with Darla and her romance with the good-looking guy, but his real question was, "Why would Brad leave a few selected clothes at Corinne's house when his condo building is next door to hers? And if he did, why would he leave a tux there? Aren't tuxes special use clothes kept safely stored in the best side of a closet? Why would one be squished in with Corinne's blouses?"

"Rudy, there are a million answers to your questions. Do you want to know what I think are the most logical answers or just want me to give a list of possible answers?"

He grimaced. "Mona, don't you think your ace detective husband could come up with a list of possible? I want your best opinion, from your gut."

"I think from what I have heard that Brad was trying to let the public know he and Corinne were having an affair. He left the tux because he doesn't use it every day. He didn't want to go back and forth for his belongings in her closet. It's as simple as that. It's a ruse. It would be one thing, Rudy, if he left some hang around clothes there to change from if he came after work in his suit or whatever. You were right to hone in on the tux. That's the key. And if he's letting Darla use his condo, it's clear he didn't give a hoot about his boss Art Richards."

Rudy thanked Mona, saying, "I knew that, but you gave me the key to understand my gut feelings. Thanks for that, Honey, more than for the seafood salad."

"You may not have loved it but there's none left on your plate."

Back at the station, Rudy asked all the ladies the question put to Mona. They came from different directions but all reached the same conclusion, although some of their reasons why gave him too much personal information. He mused aloud, "Brad was not hiding Darla's relationship with the handsome guy, but not talking about it either. Knowing your boss's wife is playing around is one thing, but assisting her is quite another. All this happens when Art is sick and losing power. Maybe he killed Art and Corinne to go after the land deal. If he murdered those two, why would he murder Teisha and Barney? What's the motive there? And why kill Darla? I think she knew too much. There are other secrets."

Mason arrived timely. Beauregard said, "I want Brad Surnani in here ASAP. Lie to him, tell him we want confirmation on info garnered from our other interviews. That should stir up a storm."

Surnani was amenable to presenting himself within an hour. Lieutenant Mason directed the questioning while Lieutenant Aylewood-Locke seconded. Beauregard watched from behind the glass thinking, *I've got to really watch this guy's body language. I haven't grasped the totality of his resentment toward Art.*

Mason played no games. He asked about the clothes in the closet. Brad responded, "Corinne and I were good friends and colleagues. We spent a lot of time together. I'd sometimes drive her to functions so the press wouldn't see Art and Corinne arriving together all the time. We got along well."

"What's a tux doing in her closet? Dropped it off one night and stayed?"

"I don't remember and I don't like your inference."

"Several witnesses have stated with some certainty that you and Corinne were lovers and after the bidding you were moving in with her."

"They are simply wrong."

Petra questioned after a nod from Mason, "Who's the guy you loaned your condo to on Tuesdays and Thursdays for the last year and a half?"

Surnani's coolness took a hot flash. He was momentarily silent, but answered, "Lots of guys use my condo for business. I don't recall a specific on those days."

"Brad, realize that we know even more. The truth from you now will go a long way in verifying you're not hiding anything."

"I simply don't remember."

Mason said, "Do you remember withdrawals you made to cash for the last fourteen months?"

"Just my spending money which I need for various business items. I'm sure I have a log totaling that amount. Give me a day and I'll have it for you. Wait a sec. You can't access my bank accounts without a warrant. What are you trying to do?"

"Were you having a relationship with Darla on those days, Brad?"

"F--- you. Now you're trying to destroy that woman's name. She was a saint."

Petra said, "We know Darla was at your condo on all those Tuesdays and Thursdays. Who else would she be seeing there, but you?"

Brad said, "This interview is over. I want my attorney."

Brad quickly left the building. Petra asked, "Okay, Mason, just when did you find the monthly payments out of Brad's account and do you think they were for blackmail?"

"I didn't. It was a lucky hunch. I wasn't sure until he made up the weak excuse about his log. He'll be busy tonight developing a log of expenses. It would be okay to do, in review for a few months, but finding receipts he hasn't turned in for payment over fourteen months would be an enormous task. And remember, he knows we will have access to Darla, Art, and Corinne's accounts. We can also check for cash flow in and out on all their accounts."

"Mason, are they all being blackmailed? Or is maybe one the perpetrator?"

"Let's speak with the Captain. He saw the interview. He'll know where to go from here."

Rudy was behind them. "You guys should be careful about speaking outside of a closed room. I heard the whole conversation. Check all the bank records, Mason. It was a good move to use with Brad, and he is involved. I want to know for sure who is the condo visitor. Maybe there was more than one visitor. Someone can give us a better description of the romantic lover."

Petra spent the afternoon talking to all the condo unit owners who were at home and to maintenance. Several had seen the handsome man as a regular visitor. One woman thought he looked familiar, but could not remember where she'd met him. The agreed upon description was for an over six-foot man with dark hair, nattily dressed in tweedy sports jacket with denim shirt showing and who moved like an athlete although not overly built up. The lady said, "Just the right amount of biceps."

The maintenance man said the visitor parked on the second rear row of visitors parking. He had a dark low-slung sedan which could have been a sports car. He offered up digital photos and Petra spent an hour going through the last month of coverage. Earlier coverage was kept off sight, but could be had. Unfortunately, the visitor wore a cap and must have been aware of the coverage, because he never turned full face to the cameras. The car was picked up not at entrance or exit, but in the parking row which did not allow a view of the license. Petra could see the make of the car, an Audi A6.

While Petra was matching cars, Mason was accessing bank

statements. There was no problem getting Corinne's, Art's, and Darla's accounts because all were murder victims, but getting Brad's was more difficult. He thought, *he'd use his personal account for this, not his business account. I can hustle and get it, but better hit Judge Jarrow. He'll go for the blackmail question in two murders and issue a search warrant.*

Two hours later Mason served the bank with the warrant on Surnani's account. An excited Mason spent two hours developing a spreadsheet showing time, date, in inflow or outflow of regular sums over fourteen mouths. The results were telling.s

24

A Fire

Beryl received a visitor. "Well, hello, Jay."

"I hope I'm not disturbing you, but I know you're good friends with Captain Beauregard. I need your help. May I come in:"

And Jay Bird pushed himself into the room and headed for the kitchen. Beryl was put out by his lack of manners and said, "Really, Jay, you could wait for me to show you the way."

"I've been here before, don't you remember. I know the way."

She did not offer him coffee which he clearly noted. In answer he asked for coffee. Beryl did not say 'no' or argue. After a quick brew she placed his cup in front of him not having one herself. Jay said, "I know you're angry with me. I got the feeling the last time we met. Why do you think I haven't called?"

Jay did not wait for a reaction. He continued. "Look, Beryl, you know Beauregard and somehow he has an idea about me. Please speak with him. I know it was Brad Surnani who put it in his brain I was seeing someone. You don't need to know who. Please tell the Captain I'm just a writer. I'm not in the big leagues and couldn't be guilty of what he thinks."

"Jay, I don't know what you're talking about, but I will not go to Rudy to complain about Brad for you. You do it. You sound as if you are plotting a story. Now, I am busy today. I have an article due on the library for the local free paper and I'm short on time."

Jay sneered at her, "I would help you out, Beryl. What kind of friend are you?"

"You had better leave and now!"

Jay left and Beryl fumed, thinking, *he wouldn't tell me who was the problem, just that Brad told Rudy. I'll meet with the intuitive Captain and see what he has to say about Jay.*

Captain Beauregard appeared delighted to see Beryl. He welcomed her with, "What information do you have today, Intrepid Citizen? What is this, your third visit? Tell me the scuttlebutt you heard. Your gossip is often more truthful than what I get from our witnesses."

She laughed. "Thanks, Rudy, for seeing me. I don't have information that is useful, but I want to share a conversation with you. No answers, but it left me with some questions."

Beryl relayed the substance of Jay's visit. She didn't have to explain her question. He immediately framed for her the same question. He said, "Do you know what woman Brad was inferring had a relationship with Jay?"

"I do. What I don't know is how he knew I knew unless Brad told him. And why would Brad tell him about our conversation unless he and Brad are in a situation together, one which Brad denied."

"You're very interesting, Beryl. Your question gave me several answers I didn't get from Brad Surnani. Jay is not as smart as he thinks he is, or he's one very frightened man."

"Rudy, what does he think you think he is guilty of doing?"

"I know he's guilty of something he denied. What else he's guilty of is a question. And no, I can't tell you now. I'm sorry, Beryl, but the information given in this office is a one-way street going in my direction. You know that."

"I do, and still I came to you to help, not to hurt your investigation.

And you have given me information. I'll be thinking on it, Rudy."

———

Rudy was interested in Beryl's conversation with Jay Bird, thinking, *Jay wants Beryl to convince me he's a good guy, but won't tell Beryl enough for her to assess his truthfulness. I think he knows Beryl would come to me. How does that serve me? More revealing is Surnani's telling Jay about our conversation.*

Why would Surnani go to him? Proves Surnani has some sort of a relationship with Jay. What could it be? Is Surnani blackmailing Jay?

I think with the amount we guessed as substantial being drawn from his account and his sensitivity, he is being blackmailed. His going right to Jay means Jay is also being blackmailed. Let's see if Darla is being blackmailed.

Who would be the blackmailer? Corinne could have been. She, even if she wasn't the extortionist, could have figured who was. It could not be Art, no motive. It appears he was in the dark about Darla's lover and any financial outflow on Darla's account. Who else?

Ted loomed over Mason Smith's desk. Mason was the only detective other than himself who had a private office. Although at times of intense collaboration, Sergeant Torrington joined him. Mason, known as the MCU IT guru, liked Ted Torrington. Ted's habits were similar to Mason's, and he had research skills and was noted as mildly OCD. Rudy called them the micro-analysts of the unit. He said, "Mason, I'm sitting here until you get the financials on Corinne, Art, Teisha, Jay, and Brad."

"I have some. Petra's at the bank with the warrants for Jay and Brad. Fortunately, they use the same bank. She's bringing lunch from Red Rose."

Rudy joined them, saying, "Ah, enough for me, I hope. Mona packed me a salad with chicken. Probably has seaweed in it. Let's look at what you have before lunch arrives."

"You're in luck. Red Rose's dishes are oversized and if I know Petra, she's getting a pizza for dessert. Not to worry, Captain, there's enough for you."

Mason thought he heard the Captain whisper, "There better be."

The bank statement searches for Corinne, Darla, and Teisha surprised them. Regular cash withdrawals were made starting fourteen months ago for the first three, and eight months ago for Teisha. The amounts were regular once established, but Corinne and Brad's were for a substantially greater amount than for the other two women. Mason said, "Captain, we have two thousand a month for Corinne and Brad, and a thousand for Darla and Teisha. The blackmailer's made a killing, but is he the killer?"

Beauregard replied, "Don't know, but blackmail is a motive. Thousands of dollars is a nice second job for the blackmailer. I think the blackmailer is small time. Brad and Corinne would have gone for a hundred grand each in one payment if asked. This blackmailer doesn't think in big numbers. Another thing most smart blackmailers know are 'long-term repetitive payments' will surely be discovered by a spouse and are always chancy."

The rustle of bags and the hitting of the doorframe with cardboard announced to Rudy's salivary glands lunch has arrived. Mason said, "Thank goodness for my conference table. Thank goodness I'm neat. We're ready to over imbibe, Petra. And what took you so long?"

"The banker was nosy and tried to hit on me with the "being a detective must let you meet all kinds of people. I bet you'd be an interesting dinner date." To get him off my back I pulled out pictures of my darling baby Carlotta. He lost interest immediately."

Mason remarked, "Still attracting the no-goods, Petra. I hope the banker gave you the info after you let him down so handily."

The bank statements for Brad and Jay lay in front of the three detectives as Petra divided a dinner of chicken parmigiana and one of eggplant rollatini. The pizza was placed on a makeshift table of ledger books giving it height over the litter. Mason griped, "I hate doing this work in my office with all the bacteria from food falling on paper. Ugh. We should have moved this over to one of the larger conference desks."

Petra, not known for worrying about a little rubble, admonished Mason, "Your OCD is sometimes annoying. Try the rollatini and be grateful, Mason."

"What the heck. Were they all being blackmailed? The fact Brad spoke with Jay, makes me comfortable in assuming they both knew about each other as a victim of blackmail. I'm uncertain about the reason Corinne was being blackmailed. After all, she had no role in Brad's apartment being used for Darla's love nest. I previously thought Brad may have been the blackmailer or Corinne, especially since Corinne died, but I don't think by itself the explosion case is the main answer to the blackmailing case. Who is getting the monies? Mason, how long will it take to follow the money?"

"Not long, Captain. Eat your pizza and relax. I'll have the greedy recipient before you finish."

Petra, whose police nickname was 'Bolt' for her proclivity to move too fast leaving everyone else behind, was busy simultaneously stuffing pizza down her throat and scanning monthly bank statements. The speed of her chomping defined her level of happiness with her results. Woe to all, if she put the pizza piece down. They would then have to listen to her frustration. But this time she had results which in 'Bolt' fashion were announced loudly. "Go ahead, feed your faces. I have a recipient of blackmail funds right in my hands."

Mason answered, "Not hard to guess which one is the blackmailer."

Petra said, "Who is it, smarty pants?"

Mason laughed. "Brad of course. Jay was a victim and the one who would not want to be publicly identified as sleeping with 'Saint' Darla."

Petra said, "I do like your deductive powers, Lieutenant. He has received a regular payment totaling the amount of the others payments. Why did Brad not try to hide the payments made to him?"

Mason answered, "First of all, we're making an assumption here. The deposits into his account are large and are made in cash. Does not allow for searching a source. Because the extortionist didn't expect their accounts to be audited, he thought he knew his mark. Did Brad deliberately plan a blackmail scheme in advance before offering his apartment to Darla? Hardcore if he did. Jay must have figured out who was blackmailing him. It wouldn't take a genius."

The Captain said, "Did he pay taxes on the moneys received? Brad knows better than to screw IRS. Although he is known for his dislike of the government, is he arrogant enough to think he'd not be found out. You'd think a high-class financier would have covered all the bases; not so smart. Was the money given to Brad by mail or direct deposit?"

Mason answered, "Not too bright, or fearless. The moneys went directly to Brad's checking account as cash deposits. I don't think we can quickly discover if he paid taxes. I mean discover it through normal channels. I do have a friend who can answer the question for us before we inform the Feds. That way we don't look stupid if they did pay taxes."

There was no answer from the Captain which to Mason meant do what you want and he intended to do so. Beauregard headed for the murder room to sit and stew as he viewed the boards, thinking, *what am I missing? Blackmail over Darla's sleeping around is not quite enough. Why would Corinne care who Darla's sleeping with unless she orchestrated the affair so Art would live with her. Problem is it looks as if Corinne wanted nothing to do with Art and his progressing illness. So why would she not just laugh at the blackmailer.*

Teisha wouldn't care if it was known Darla was sleeping around. She'd be happy if it was known. She didn't like Jay's attention when it focused on her and she hated Art. If Brad was going to leave his business relationship with Art soon, why would he care if Art found out he put the wife and Jay together?

Wait a minute, could Brad be blackmailed and he resultantly blackmailed the others. Could there be multiple motives for the blackmail? Could Brad, as the receiver of the blackmail funds, use different reasons to blackmail each one? Are there other payments made in larger amounts from Brad's account we have not seen?"

Rudy called his three detectives back into a free conference room and said, "Are there any other regular payments from or to Brad or any of the other accounts showing regular payments of a different amount? The withdrawals do not have to match the amounts of the other payments as long as they are a consistent amount, and they could be over a longer or shorter period?"

Mason said, "What are you thinking, Captain? You thinking Brad was being blackmailed by someone else and developed this scheme to pay for the blackmail?"

"Could be, could be, Mason. What I do know is this blackmail is connected to murder and I think the motive or motives are convoluted. Too much power, money, and love affairs to suit me. They are all motives for murder, or at least potential motives for murder. We need to develop the path of the motives to find which path leads to the murderer. I want Brad and Jay's history under the microscope. I'm uncomfortable with Teisha in this game of blackmail. Why would she care if Darla was playing around? And Barney's death has to be related to the land sale. We may have one or two murderers playing a game and one or two blackmailers."

Petra considered aloud, "Captain, you have made it all more difficult. Most people being extorted do not murder the blackmailer. They would seek help from the police. You've left us with too many people having a role as a victim and therefore a role as a potential murderer. You've expanded the field not lessened the field of potential perpetrators. Help us out here, Captain."

"I know. I know. And I've not done a complete search on Nate Connault or the photographer or Stacia. I'll rule out Stacia for now and we can't go after Connault because I think he's working this case for the Feds. Why the Feds have interest eludes me, but I've been told they have. Beryl and Connault have some kind of special relationship. I'll have a chat with her."

A meet with Beryl was easily made. She agreed to come to the station, saying, "I know you have a busy schedule, while today is a do-nothing day for me. I'll be there in ten minutes."

Rudy met with her in his office and quickly asked her about Nate's interest in the explosion murder case. She tried to feel Rudy's intentions out, but did not make any headway. Distressed at Rudy's continued interest in Nate, she said, "He did tell me in the beginning to be careful in exploring or investigating the explosion. I shut him down, so I have nothing to tell you, Rudy."

He asked, "Just from his statement, would you conclude his government work was related?"

Beryl smiled. "I don't easily conclude, Rudy, but I doubt he'd say something to me if he didn't feel some threat. Knowing there may be a risk that could put his work in jeopardy, and like you in your policing, it would be confidential."

"I think we're on the same wavelength here. I know several of the witnesses to the explosion were in the military as was Connault. Has he explored their backgrounds with you?"

"Haven't you searched their military experience, Captain? Why don't you ask Nate what he thinks about their personas?"

"Touché! There is your advantage, Beryl, one which I do not have. Nate would discuss personalities with you and he would not with me. It would be on the record if he spoke with me."

"Now I'm just an information conduit."

"Only if you are interested."

"What about John Connolly? You have not mentioned him."

"Beryl, I didn't mention any of the witnesses by name. I'm interested in them all."

Rudy's cell beeped. He took the short call and said, "I'll be there. Text the address."

Rudy apologized for leaving so quickly, claiming an emergency. Beryl thought, *something's up. I can't follow him. I'll call Oliver and tell him to listen to the police scanner.*

Oliver called back and directed her to 1243 Acorn Drive. "Mom, there is a major fire over there. The police and fire are all over. It's a warehouse for explosives. I'll meet you there."

Despite her repeated negatives about his joining her, Oliver arrived at the fire before her. The blaze was enormous with dark smoke. The area was already cordoned off. The news people had arrived before Beryl. She saw Stacia, now her friend, and her photographer partner. They had zero visibility from where they were allowed to stand. The rumor was there were no victims. Beryl asked Stacia when the police pushed the press back to where Beryl was standing, "Stacia, I hope no one's been hurt."

"We were here first, but not before the police. No, it is Holy Week and the owner had his crew at his house for a luncheon. He does this every year."

Stacia's partner photographer took Beryl's photo and she questioned him as to why. "I always take the street scenes for fires. You never know if it's a set fire. Fire starters often like to stay and see their work."

Beryl said, "I've met Stacia before but I don't think we've been introduced. I'm Beryl Kent."

"Hi, Beryl. I've seen you at several events in town. I'm Robbie Layden."

Robbie shook her hand and gave her a big smile. Beryl listened while Stacia and Robbie discussed the situation. Stacia suggested a better view for her statement stream to the station where she would be backed up by the most vivid flames. Robbie said, "I gotta hand it to you, Stacia, you're a stage setter if ever I've met one. Great eye."

The two moved over to Beryl's left and did their work leaving Beryl thinking, *those two have a great working partnership. Two other news crews have arrived. How come they took so long? Stacia, Robbie, and Oliver all arrived before me. Oliver's over near the police car. I'll ask the officer to question Stacia how she got here so quickly. Were they here before Oliver?*

Oliver was happy to relay the latest from his viewpoint. "There is talk, Mom, that a body is inside. A neighbor saw a man in work clothes enter the building shortly before the fire broke out. The owner insists it's not one of his employees. They were all with him at some kind of Easter/Passover luncheon. The firefighters can't get in the building yet. They said it will be at least an hour before the fire dies down and they don't know if the rear of the building will collapse. Right now, the fire's all up front. It's going to fall; you want to bet on it?"

"Nope. I lose in all those bets."

Beryl asked Oliver if he knew Robbie, the photographer and was surprised that he did. They'd met at a local bar one evening when they were catching a beer and a sandwich and talked for an hour. Beryl asked, "What's your spin on him?"

"Nosy as anyone I've ever met except for you, Mom. Everyone in the bar that night knew him. I guess he's all right, but he is pushy."

Beryl asked him if he could be pushy and find out who told him about the fire. She said, "Oliver, were Robbie and Stacia here before you?"

"Yes, and they got really good video of the police and fire arriving. I see where you're coming from, Mom. How could they get here so quickly? They were maybe in the neighborhood."

She watched as Oliver ambled over and renewed his relationship with Robbie. She noticed Robbie looking at her twice while Oliver questioned him. Beryl waited at the scene and when Captain Beauregard saw her, he joined her. "Heck of a mess here, and there may be a body. I hate fires. This one looks like it was set, at least the Fire Chief thinks so. If it is arson and a body is found, we have to decide whether the dead person set the fire or is a victim. Did I say I hate fires? The bodies in a fire don't leave much for forensics to work with. I see Robbie and Stacia were here almost at the start. They were here before I got here. Amazing skill that guy has."

Beryl answered, "You are being quite open with information, Rudy. Unusual for you isn't it?"

An enormous noise caused the crowd to shudder as the rest of the building collapsed. Beryl waited another hour until her feet told her to leave and combined with the aching in her legs encouraged her to go home. As she let Oliver know she was leaving, Robbie walked over to say goodbye. Stacia then followed. Beryl could not get Oliver alone amidst all the small talk. She said her goodbyes and left.

25
Motives, Motives

Oliver did not come home until much later. Eating dinner alone did not bother Beryl. What bothered her was he didn't answer his phone. That was until she realized he'd left his phone on the hall table. Beryl uttered, "Ugh! He never does that. Today he does."

Her supper of leftovers satisfied her hunger as did a glass of Rieslings. For a moment she was content until her antenna went up. *Oliver must have answers to my questions. Every night he's in the kitchen rustling up something. He must be hungry. I'll bet he's at The Flying Boar Irish Bar all set for the night. I have to wait for my info. Ok, Beryl, stop your griping. You just like having your own way. Why didn't I wait for him?*

The front door opened and Oliver entered. "I have lots of thoughts for you, my dear mom, who looks like you did when I would come home at three in the morning when I was a teenager. Put your dissatisfaction away."

"Give it up, Oliver. What have you learned? Can I fix you some dinner?"

"Now you're nicey-nicey. No. I had dinner with Stacia, Robbie, and Nate at The Flying Boar. The place was packed. You should have been there. The talk was all about the fire."

"You should have told me you were going."

Oliver had asked Robbie and Stacia both about how they got to the site so fast. Stacia was quick to answer, "Robbie got one of his calls about suspicious activity in a closed building. He's the best, Oliver. He has contacts everywhere."

Oliver asked Robbie who the caller was. Robbie didn't know and said, "You hear a voice on the phone and you can't place it with a particular person. I just act. It happens all the time, because I talk to everyone and everyone talks to me."

Beryl coaxed Oliver for more information. "How did you run into Nate? Was he at the fire and I missed him? Is there a dead man in the building?"

"Slow down, Beryl, we have time. Nate says hello to you. He saw you at the fire but could not get your attention. The police moved him back at the scene. He got there later than us."

"How did he know about the fire? The building's not on a busy street."

"I asked that same question. He gets police calls in his car. Bet you didn't know that. Bet he uses another car to take you out to dinner."

"You investigated him once, Oliver, and you didn't know he had a police scanner."

"Touché, Mom. There is a body in there. On our way out of The Flying Boar Pub, he got a call. The body is so badly burned the police couldn't find anything to identify him. Beauregard will be investigating again. You and I watched the building burn. We may be under suspicion!"

"Oliver, do not raise my blood pressure with your sarcasm. Did Robbie or Stacia have comments?"

"Yeah, and I wonder about it as possible evidence in the explosion case. Stacia told me the owner of this building had been contacted by the police about their storage cylinders possibly having been used in the explosion case. He was vigilant about inventory. The Fire Department was scheduled to come in next week delving into whether the registered cylinders were shipped from there to the explosion site. He had one of his men working half a day to follow shipping and receiving registers. The job was to check the manual paperwork and not the digital sheets. Shipping and receiving was too busy to use computer input. It took too much time. Instead the workers would check off cylinder registrations numbers and amounts on dates received or dates of shipping. The owner didn't have the paperwork yet, but his employee told him over the phone there were discrepancies."

"I don't understand. I know the police were tracking cylinders' source locations. Didn't they check this place?"

"Yup, but they initially took the word of the manager who looked through the computerized list and it looked good. No inventory was done. Their just catching up to that question is the reason there was a visit scheduled. Someone knew this and burned the place down. Must be a worker or the owner covering their tracks. Pretty costly for the owner who now has to build a new building and get all the permits if he can. The neighbors don't like the facility located near them. After the explosion and fire messes, do you blame them?"

Beryl asked, "Oliver, I'm glad you were there today. Two brains are better than one and I love your logical brain. Given the compliment I just gave you, what do you think about this photographer Robbie? He does get everyplace before any other news media."

"From a guy's point of view, I wouldn't trust my girlfriend with him. He's the kind of guy who is always on the prowl but doesn't look like what the ladies call 'a hunk.' He's strong. One of those guys who never build showy beach muscles but is strong and moves fast. I think he's done karate or some other martial arts. He is quick. I'm amazed he hasn't scored with Stacia."

Beryl answered, "He is not bad looking, but dresses in those khaki vests with umpteen pockets as if he were a war correspondent on location at a battle scene."

"He is, Mom. He's at every fire, domestic abuse scene, bar fight, you name it. Stacia's success is fueled by him. The camera loves her, but where would she get the news if he wasn't her partner? Funny thing is Stacia told me he partnered with a couple of women before her and they both left the job. Must be a coincidence. Whatever, it's now a winning news team."

———

Norbie Cull was holding court at the country club bar with several defense attorneys. They would meet casually on the same Thursday evening once a month claiming it was an ad hoc kind of thing. Cull was saying, "To say West Side was having fire problems would be an understatement. There was the Masterson Cylinder, Inc. company fire and three more commercial fires during the next two days. Two were on Easter. Screwed up my holiday in the midst of dinner. Two of the company owners are my clients. I think these were set fires. Looks to me like a serial arsonist."

Hack Denney answered, "I have the Alarm Security Company as a client and Jim Balfour the owner is loving this. He has crews on half the companies in West Side that have good size inventories. No one was hurt or killed in the cylinder fire except for the unknown body. The fire chief told me he thought the man was homeless or the arsonist. Then said, it couldn't be the arsonist, because they truly thought the fire was set remotely. My problem is finding enough workers to staff the various locations."

Rocky Marsone, most known for defending clients in their altercations with the police, insisted, "Hack, you'd make money off any catastrophe and still complain about worker shortages."

Cull listened. Conversations continued focusing on the fires when the bar television announced a summary of recent fires in town. He noticed all the fire locations were on main roads. All were around or during the holiday weekend. All were remotely set. Neighbors saw nothing before the fires. One dog was seen running away from one of the fires. He thought, *strange. Someone hates Easter. Could be the fire starter hates Passover. It's the same weekend. The perp is knowledgeable. Knows remote starts. News says there were gas cylinders in all the sites.*

Guy must have known. Narrows the possibilities down. When there is a person of interest, background in gases for business may be the nail in the coffin. Perp lights fires where traffic brings the city right by the sites. He wants attention. Sign of a dedicated serial arsonist.

Upon leaving the bar, Cull ran into Stacia Kovac and Sergeant Bobby Barr. Feeling an opportunity, he asked to join them. After settling in, he directed the conversation to the multiple fires over the weekend. Stacia said, "It was to be my first holiday weekend, but as life would have it, the other newscaster had COVID. My mom was not too happy."

Sergeant Barr grimaced, saying, "Neither was I, Stacia."

Norbie said, "So you were at all those fires. Tell me about them. Who was your team photographer?"

"Why Robbie of course. He eats, sleeps, and dreams events. There is another photographer on staff. He tends to do graduations and Chamber of Commerce events; those happenings with lower public grab."

"Stacia, did Robbie get his usual call about the fires?"

"Yes, for two of them, but we just seemed to find the third by accident just as the flames hit the building. The fire trucks were a minute behind us."

Bobbie who was listening intently said, "Wait a minute, Stacia, you didn't tell me you got to one early. Which fire was it?"

"It was the one on the old factory row. Robbie was as surprised as I was to find it accidently."

Cull asked, "He didn't get a call! Was he touching his phone and maybe accidently silenced it?"

"He keeps his phone clipped on his vest and often touches it, but Robbie doesn't often make mistakes, Mr. Cull."

"What is he like, Stacia? I mean you've partnered with him for a while. You must have heard about his social life."

"Everyone asks me that same question. He is quite talkative about world affairs and I must say knowledgeable, but then again we are news people and incredibly interested in world happenings. I notice he likes the ladies. I settled that question with him earlier when he tried to hit on me. He backed off easily. We work well together. He's not shy about questioning bystanders at events. It's where he gets all his contacts. I think he promises them publicity if their information gives dividends. I don't know for sure, but I do believe it.

"He is interested in politicians and business people's personal lives. He has all the scoop on who is cheating on wives or husbands, or who has sticky hands, and all the old hates that broke up businesses and relationships. He gives me a load of background which I of course check out. I've only found him wrong once. He was shocked that I check his gossip."

Bobby asked, "Who was the maligned person, the one he was wrong about, Stacia?"

"He thought Darla had something going on with someone. He didn't know the name, just that the gossip was out there."

Captain Beauregard was in full uniform at the Chamber's luncheon honoring West Side Police. He was called at the last minute by Chief Coyne who was sick with the flu. Rudy thought, *it's a weeknight and Mona is here with me. The restaurant has great food. It's a change from Mona feeding me salads with fish or chicken. She looks good over there and happy to talk with different folks. She does have the gift of saying all the right things.*

"Rudy, I'm happy to see you here. I thought you always got out of these public displays of the Blue and yet tonight you're the main speaker. Good to see you looking so spiffy."

"Beryl, how do you find yourself at all these socials? I thought you'd be out dining with Nate."

"I am. He's here with me. I understand you'll be sharing the dais with the Fire Chief meaning there will be lots of talk about the fires. I'm all ears."

"Beryl, I don't know if there will be new information for you unless the audience gives up some, but I would like to explore some ideas with you."

"I'm all ears to hear what you think I could offer."

The Captain winced at her not so subtle sting. He said, "Let's try a hypothetical. If a man was getting on in years and facing a negative medical journey, knew his business partners were all trying to screw him, and discovered his long-suffering wife was not going to be there for him and was maybe no longer suffering alone, would he act out? Would he attempt to get revenge?"

"I think Art would want revenge. When a man is used to great power and has abused that power over many years, I believe the loss could bring out the very worst. Certainly, he had motive for all the killings, but unfortunately he died before all the killings. He'd have been number one for suspects except he died. You hint at Darla having someone. Even if she didn't he'd be furious when she turned him out of his home. One of two things happen when you face debilitating disease. You could turn to the heavens and try to repair any damage you've caused in life. I don't see Art going there, but you never know. The other way is to get revenge."

"Could Art have been suicidal when he realized the extent of his illness and as he saw his memory and balance go?"

"Captain, you know the answer to the question. Why are you asking me? Are you exploring the merit of Art having orchestrated Darla's death before killing himself? It is an interesting idea."

Beauregard was called to the mic. Both Rudy and Beryl appeared annoyed by the interruption. Beryl was not alone for long when Mona Beauregard quickly sat next to her. "You don't mind, Beryl? I'd rather sit with you. This is going to be at least an hour-long session. Look at the press. They're ready to jump down Rudy's neck. And the crowd is not the usual one fifty. I'll bet it's double."

"I'm happy you sat down. One of the library board ladies was headed toward me. She's nice, but she would try to hold a discussion on book locations while the speakers are talking. Has Rudy spoken to you at all about the explosion and murders? I know I shouldn't ask, but I am nosy."

"Not to worry, Beryl, he's interested in a woman's point of view on motive. He's afraid he's missed something. I told him he was sexist to think we wouldn't have similar judgements coming from our brains. He is right, however, I didn't tell him he was. We see motives from slights more often than men. They look for big causes for motives."

"I'm right with you, Mona. Especially when you consider the fragility of some egos in high functioning men and women. They get used to being a star in their own world and when they are dissed or ignored, they fret and fume. The problem Rudy has is finding a common motive for one murderer. If there are two murderers independently working, it gets messy. There could be two murderers murdering in concert with different motives. And is there a suicide involved? With all the actions taken by the killer or killers, I don't think there is a whole lot more information to be garnered from physical evidence or backgrounds."

Mona agreed. She added, "Darla's murder and Teisha's murders complicate picking one motive."

"Just leaves us, Mona, with the deadly sins of greed, lust, envy, pride, and wrath which are my choices. I am beginning to believe pride and wrath lead the way."

Mona said, "Over lust and envy and greed? Why so?"

"I suppose my thoughts are running to the suspects or witnesses, who are all heavy hitters; well to do, easily able to find partners, and have enough ego to believe no one is better than themselves."

Mona answered, "Greed and lust and envy can all be overpowering. If a person is greedy having money, no matter how much, is not enough. I think envy is similar. I remember the story my mom told me about the little girl who lived in a hovel but had a beautiful Easter lily growing in her scrappy yard. A rich lady going by was so taken with it, she stole it. In the story which Mother made mystical, the lily grew back ensuring the concept that envy could never be satisfied. Lust is no different."

"You are quite philosophical tonight, Mona, and also quite right. Shh, the program has started."

Beryl thought, *Mona is right on, but I have to choose motives most fitting with these murders. The problem is I think there is more I don't understand. Why Darla?*

She whispered to Mona, "But why Darla? Could she have been involved in a romance?"

Mona answered, "Supposedly."

"Do you know who was the lover? Was it one of the witnesses like John, or Surnani?"

"I thought you would know. I don't know if I should tell you if you don't already know."

"Mona, I don't want to compromise you. Was it Rudy who told you? If not, I think you would not be giving out info improperly."

Mona was about to whisper, when Nate crossed in front of her to sit next to Beryl. Mona then motioned a pushing hand meaning to Beryl, I'll tell you later. She was not to be deterred. She turned to Nate, said a hello and asked, "Who was Darla's lover? And don't tell me you don't know. All the cops know. I think I know."

Nate said, "And how do you know, smarty pants?"

"Easy. If Darla were going to cheat with one of the witnesses we think are suspects it wouldn't be with ones she knew for years. He would have to be new and exciting. Exciting enough for her to look when she was ready to look."

Nate said, "So, who?"

"The stud author, Jay Bird, is my guess. Darla was not out clubbing every night. She would not have developed defenses against his type."

Nate said, "So you don't know who, you are guessing. Why would he have dated Teisha if he was having an affair with Darla?"

"Well, guessing again, I'd say he was checking her out for Darla or for himself. He'd go with more than one lady at a time. She would want to know if Teisha really liked her son. Maybe she wasn't interested in Jay. Darla may have walked on water but she was smart enough to have Art Richards' total confidence. I'm told Art went to her for advice. I assume he thought she gave good advice. She could have cooked up a deal with Jay to test our Teisha's worth, and was satisfied for I'm told Darla approved of Teisha for James."

"Could have, would have."

Beryl said, "I know I'm on the right track, Nate, because you haven't told me I'm nuts. You know but can't share privileged info with me. By your subtlety you have assured me I'm on the right track."

"What difference did this affair make?"

"I'm looking for motives. I find motive here."

"What motive, Beryl? James killed them both because he didn't want his mother running around with an educated bounder like Jay? Unlikely! Or maybe he made hay with Teisha and everyone has it wrong, so James kills them both. Or ????"

"Nate, there has to be multiple motives. There has to be multiple motives. We know the land deal could be one motive. Perhaps more were scheduled to die in the explosion based on greed. I've heard the killer sent invitations at a certain time for each one, but each time was only a few minutes different from the next. Perhaps more should have died. He did not think potential buyers would be there so early and perhaps didn't believe some would be late since the one letter for the explosion time had the bidder arrive late."

Nate laughed. "Kind of sloppy to trust the bidders would all arrive timely. Following your thinking, any bidder scheduled before the blow-up time was marked for death. Stunning idea, Ms. Marple."

"Stop laughing at me, Nate. It is possible, and certainly worth investigating."

The speakers were now getting interesting because some of the audience, normally used to sitting in their seats and listening attentively, were now raising a hand for recognition to be heard, and even speaking aloud without asking. A serial murderer and serial arsonist all working their same poison on beautiful West Side seemed more than unfortunate. Questions on the serialist's identity revolved around the two serial artists being the same man. The discussion soon got crazy. Was it a plot to upset the political control of the city, to the secular ways the city's citizenry instigated evil. Rudy took the helm at the mic and suggested quiet. He suggested they do what good citizens had a duty to do: inform the police on unusual activity, to not confront any suspicious person in their neighborhood, keep a light on at night at their homes, drive carefully, etc. When asked what those measures could do, the Captain's answer was, "Leave our workforce of police more time and energy to get these murderers off the street."

In some ways it was a masterful move as it brought those in attendance back to a normal mode of reason. Beauregard went on explaining the tedious police procedures that had been followed and were bringing the department towards an end to these horrors. He thanked Chief Coyne and the Mayor for their direction. The meeting went on without a hitch.

Ignoring the successor speakers, Beryl said, "We will never know for certain if Art and Corinne and Teisha were planned victims, because we don't have their bidder letters. Were Brad, John, James and you given bidding letters?"

"James' letter gave a time after the explosion time, as did mine. I don't know Brad and John's times. If I don't know, Rudy doesn't know. As to Corinne and Art, the police did not find the letters in their condos and wouldn't have. It is normal to take your invitation to the site on the date of the visit when you sign in. We'll never get them. What remained of their cars was searched. No letters."

"How do you know police evidence found or not found, Nate?"

"Easy, I have connections."

"Well, are you or I going to get busy and search for Brad and Teisha's times?"

Nate said, "We know Teisha's time, Beryl. It was at 10:30. Your theory would eliminate her as a possible victim."

Perhaps in spite of Nate's little put down, Beryl made a call to Brad Surnani, who answered immediately. She asked the question.

Brad said without hesitation, "I got there late. I was scheduled for 9:45. I am never late but I had an early morning emergency. Believe me, Beryl, I have worried since then that I was the target. I can't understand who would hate me enough to kill me. Art and Corinne both had abrasive attitudes when dealing with tough business situations. I am much smoother. It was my forte, only to be beat out by John Conlon. Look, Beryl, I have to go. One of my neighbors is having a problem."

Beryl thanked him, saying, "Captain Beauregard will want the letter, Brad."

"He has it or must. I gave it to the Desk Sergeant the day after the explosion."

Nate, who had listened to the call, said, "You are one up. Brad could have been a target."

"Where does it leave us? Three targets and success on two of them. What do the three have in common. Would John Conlon plan to kill them? I mean he had access to all their business dealings and could easily take hold of most of their clients.

"I don't get the killer vibe from John, Nate. He has access already and according to him has closed more deals in the last couple of years than the three of them together. I also think there was no romantic relationship between Brad and Corinne. He shows no emotions over her death. He'd have to be a great actor to hide his feelings consistently. Nope, no romance there."

Later in the day Beryl called Captain Beauregard and gave him Brad's reported bidder appointment time for the explosion. She told him to look on his desk for the bidder letter.

Rudy grumbled, "You don't think the Desk Sergeant lost it, Beryl, but you easily believe it's sitting in a mess on my desk?"

"Yup, Rudy, as my father would say, "You have history, Buddy."

26
Who's on First?

Sergeant Lily Tagliano entered the squad room looking like she'd been beaten up. Lily faced difficult situations with the bravado of a street kid. Today there was no bravado. She sat down with great effort. Her pretty face showed scrapes and scratches. Her ripped clothing exposed a shapely leg and torso compromised by blood on her back. But her mouth took away most sympathy as she said, "I hate fighting with women. They don't shoot so easily, but they sure as hell scratch, bite, kick, rip and anything to inflict pain. These are a hundred-and-fifty-dollar pair of jeans. She deserves the fight I gave back. She's a husband and child abuser. Five people in that house are petrified of her; her mother, husband, and three kids. Do you think Juan is afraid of me? How did she get the power. Ooh, I hurt."

Petra said, "Why didn't they send you to the hospital at the scene? You're truly a mess. If your Juan sees you like this he'll go for blood. You're pregnant, Lily, what the hell were you thinking to engage like that?"

"She went at me with a knife before Bobbie could get to her. He was over trying to contain the family. We both thought I'd be better with a woman, but this lady is no lady."

"Where was the domestic? I wasn't here for the call. Was it over in the Flats area?"

"Nope, not where you'd ever expect. It was over in the condos where

Brad Surnani lives."

"Which condo? We scoured them for gossip. I met some owners."

"Number 210. Beautiful place to live doesn't make crazy people happy. Wacked out or evil explains her actions. Child services took the kids. Her mother and husband were left there. They won't make a complaint, but the kids are smart. They don't want the mother back. The oldest boy who looked so sad said, 'My mom is nuts. Gramma and Dad think they can make it okay. They can't. She needs help. I saw a woman act like that on a televisions show. The psychiatrist insisted professionals need to deal with it. My sister won't come home from school until we call her for supper and my little brother just games. We need help, but please let us stay with Dad and Gramma. They love us and would never hurt us. Just keep her away.'"

Petra asked, "How old is this kid?"

"I think he is thirteen. By the way, it was Brad Surnani who called it in as a domestic. The kid went over to thank him. The boy cried and said, get this, 'I won't be able to keep watch over your place.'"

Petra said, "I want to speak with the boy. What's his name? If he were watching the place he can tell us if anyone else was looking at the condo while Darla was there. We don't know If Darla had another suitor."

"It'd be a problem talking to the kid. The Captain would have to notify the agency for permission."

"I'm sorry, Lily. I'm such a jerk going on about a case when you are in such trouble. I'm driving you home before Juan checks in. We'll clean you up. If I see more than superficial stuff, you're going to the hospital. I don't know how you evaded going when transport came."

Lily said, "Let's leave now. Juan will be here. You are right. He can't see me like this."

The two left for Lily's house only to end up in the hospital an hour later after Petra inspected Lily's backside and found two knife wounds. She said, "Lily, don't you feel a problem there?" as she touched one of the injured spots.

"Only when you touch it. Come on, we better go."

By the time the two reached the hospital, they were met by the Captain and Sergeant Torres. The scene between the two newly married detectives presented to observers appeared to be one of tears of regret.

Petra thought, *anyone looking on these two might think it was the reunion of the abuser and abused for a new start. I've seen it over and over in domestics. The gal all beaten up and the guy crying over her, only to do it again next week. The picture at first glance always gives the appearance of a romantic mess, when it's anything but romantic.*

Who would believe, this lady is a cop who was damaged by another's abuser who was not her partner in life? There will be ramifications from this episode. Beauregard will take Lily off the streets until this baby is born. Too bad, there's no better warrior than petite tough talking Lily on the streets. And she hates paperwork. I hope she and the baby are okay.

Beauregard was tight lipped while waiting for the doctor. Fortunately, they had let Juan into the emergency bed area. What was disturbing was the lady who was in the altercation with Lily was stationed two curtained-off beds away guarded by one of West Side's finest. Juan, fortunately, was not aware of this fact.

An hour later Juan and the ER Attending Physician entered the waiting area with updates on Lily's condition. Lilly's damage included two cracked ribs, two knife wounds that required suturing, and multiple abrasions. Since Lily reported a headache, a brain scan was done. She and the baby would be fine.

Juan responded with, "Captain, I want her off the streets until this baby is born. Please?"

"Not now, Sergeant. Later!"

The doctor pulled Rudy aside, saying, "Captain, I've taken a look at the other woman and she'll be okay. No knife wounds, but your sergeant pounded her pretty good and the woman is quite robust. This woman has two modes of behavior, both of which I've seen today. Rough lady."

Rudy suggested he and Petra get back to the station with the news and said, "Sergeant Flores, stay here with your wife. Don't go near the other woman and don't be asking questions. I've asked Mason to nosy around here. Not you. Understand?"

Petra smiled thinking, *when the Captain uses a full title he means business. Good thing in this case. Juan is not happy not being able to avenge this nasty business on his wife. Freakin human nature exists, cop or not.*

During the drive back, Petra checked the local news. Lily's picture was titled, "Cop Gets Beaten by Husband Abuser."

The story read close to the truth but did not mention the two stab wounds. She was about to click off her phone when she caught a glimpse of Robbie Layden's jacket. She thought, *must be his. I didn't see him at the scene. These photos aren't the best and must have been taken by one of the people outside the condo unit. Robbie still got there and pretty fast.*

She said, "Captain, you don't like coincidences and neither do I. Sometimes coincidences are a sign from above to point us in a different direction?"

"Petra, if God was going to do our work, he or she would do a hell of a superior job than we. He or she would do it faster and have preconceived knowledge. Give up this nonsense because I do think sometimes we get divine insight, but I hope you're not waiting for some. What's on your mind?"

Petra said, "I know it sounds stupid, but two facts hit me. First is, I heard the kid Lily rescued used to watch Brad Surnani's condo for him. I was going to follow up on it. And I will, but it seems odd to me now when I searched the condos before for info and didn't see him.

I suppose I wasn't looking for a kid. Secondly, when I looked on the local news, the picture was taken by an onlooker, but I see part of the news photographer's weird jacket in it. He got there pretty fast. He was at the other Russian husband stand-off when Bobby Barr got all that notoriety. He's been at every catastrophe. If he's always around, maybe the little kid saw him at these condos before."

"Maybe, Lieutenant, and maybe it's time for you to find out. What are you thinking? We were supposed to get more background on him. I've not seen it. I'll call Mason."

———

Lily and Juan watched the complete news from the overhead television at the hospital. There were two short videos given. Juan said, "Good thing the film was shot by an amateur. Most people would not recognize you. You look beaten down, Lilly. For God's sake, can't you remember you're pregnant?"

"Juan, look at the second video."

The video had finished before Juan could catch it. Not to be stopped, Lily took a few minutes before getting the videos off You Tube. She said, "In the second video Robbie Layden is there without his camera. He must have been called by some friend in the area, but why not with his camera? Seems strange."

"The guy's allowed some off time, Lily. You and I don't wear our weapons on vacation."

"You maybe don't, but I always carry."

"Didn't do you much good today, honey. I'll tell the Captain about your brilliant insight. Now, try resting."

———

James Richards cursed aloud, "Mom, I thought I'd finished all your financials for the accountant. Your joint tax return with Dad said I got it all and now deep in your lingerie drawer I find bank statements for another account in another bank."

His frustration deepened as he reviewed the bank statements thinking, *what the hell is this – In your name alone, Mom? There are only one deposit and one withdrawal from the account monthly for the last year of statements. You leave a balance of just five-hundred-dollars in the account. What is this money for? The deposits are from your checking account while the withdrawals are cash. What are the tax consequences of not reporting this account? If I show the accountant, he'd assume it was for vanity issues like spa type things although you are known for ignoring that pleasure. I'd better include it.*

James called the accountant Leonard Selden to explain the account and its singularity of matching deposits and withdrawals. He was taken back at his reply. "Was Darla being blackmailed, James?"

James said, "I'm shocked. I never considered such a thing, Lennie. You knew my mom. Who would blackmail her?"

"James, you knew your dad, he was a miserable bounder of a man. Could be she had a special friend and someone thought keeping the fact quiet was worth some dough?"

"Mom, have a guy friend! I hope the hell she did. I'll ask Colleen. It would explain some changes in her attitude to my dad. I found nothing in her things to suggest a guy. You think she was being blackmailed? Would she care if it were known? I suppose she'd still want to protect my dad. Why keep it a secret? They were getting a divorce. Do you think my dad knew?"

"Ask your dad's attorney, James. The will was read and from what I heard there were no changes, so he wasn't excluding her in any way. Darla's will was made at the same time and there weren't any codicils unless you know of one, or another will. My guess is your dad didn't know."

"Lennie, where'd my mom get the money to pay blackmail?"

"Look, don't get ahead of yourself. I didn't mean to start a big uproar. She could have had a regular expenditure she didn't want Art to know. Besides, it would be stupid for a blackmailer to continue demanding payments from a woman who was leaving her husband. You noticed she didn't pay the last two months. Either she didn't need to or she wasn't going to."

"You have raised serious questions. Who blackmailed her, did she know who it was, and did the extortionist kill her?"

The two talked for a few minutes longer with Lennie trying his best to slow James's considerations down.

James called his sister Colleen, disturbing her at work. "What the hell is so important, James? I'm at work. You know I can't just skip in and out like you do."

"Silly sister, I wouldn't call if it could wait. Query your sneaky little brain on Mom's date life, okay?"

"What makes you ask that question now? Why wait until she's dead before asking about her personal life? Note, James, I say her personal life."

"Colleen, Mom's been paying money out of a second checking account for the past year or so. I wonder if she's been blackmailed about some relationship. It's the only thing that makes sense to me. She's not getting plastic surgery. She looked good, but there were wrinkles. She didn't have a side business I know."

Colleen answered, "She has been tense the last two months. I'll answer your question, but don't take it the wrong way. Mom needed someone. Who'd she have for twenty-five years, just Dad. Remember those Tuesdays and Thursdays when she would never schedule any dinners with us. It was not like her to not put her plans aside for us, but she didn't. Mom met a man, a good-looking stud every Tuesday and Thursday at Brad's condo. She had a key. I don't know who the guy is but he's better looking than Dad."

"Do you think he was playing her for money or was somebody else blackmailing her? Or was the extortionist also getting money from the guy? Describe him, Colleen. He may be someone I know."

Colleen's description was not helpful. The two discussed the issue until Colleen insisted she had to get back to work. James made a call to Captain Beauregard.

Beauregard put his hands to his head thinking, *now we know for certain, Darla was having an affair. Darla and a whole bunch were being blackmailed. Brad figured out who the blackmailer was and blackmailed back. If the blackmailer is the murderer, why didn't he kill Brad as well? The payments stopped from Darla's account but not from the others' accounts and then Darla dies. Who hired the killer? Every witness has an alibi. They were all at the explosion. None match the description Oliver's friend gave. Is it a hired gun, and who did the hiring? No known creep from out of the area was spotted in town for a small job at that time. Brad kept paying. Was he paying himself?*

The Captain got a call. There was evidence of a body from the fire, but the body did not give up its secrets. The ME was certain it was a man and got some DNA but no matches were found on the system. Rudy showed his total frustration, yelling, "I need a break! It could be years before we identify the body unless some local guy doesn't come home for a few days and we get a call. What was he doing in there? It's now a compulsory investigation. It was a hot fire. How can the Chief be certain? He can't see if it was a remote start. It also could be just an accident. Either way it's my job to answer the question."

Juan said, "Got some new info, Captain."

"Yeah, give it up, Juan."

"Petra met with the kid whose mom is the cuckoo bird who slashed Lily. She showed him pictures of our witnesses. This is the kid who was watching the condo for Brad. The kid identified Jay Bird as the visitor on Tuesdays and Thursdays, but we already know that fact. He also knew Robbie's picture. Says he was always parking outside Brad's building watching who was going in and out. A couple of times the guy would walk over to the big lion standing near the front entrance and check its open mouth. The kid went over one time on the next day but couldn't reach the statue's mouth. He thought there were drug deals going on."

The Captain said, "Drugs are everywhere, even at a high-end condo group. I'm not surprised but think it's more likely extortion moneys."

"Captain, we don't have much on Robbie. His work portfolio is light."

"Get Lieutenant Smith in here."

Mason, standing not far behind the Captain, said, "At your command, Captain, and I know what you want."

"I want everything on this photographer Robbie Layden, everything."

"It's not possible. His everything is pretty limited. Before coming to West Side, Robbie had service background and then news stints in Austin, Lubbock, Columbus, and Albany as a photographer. He left each one after a few years. I called every employer. They all reported he was better at getting to surprise events than the news person. They all said, he'd hit on the women news anchors until they'd complain, but no one wanted him to leave. He would suddenly quit. The woman news director in Columbus said it was damn inconvenient when he left in the middle of a serial arsonist investigation."

"Let me see the paper on him."

"The paperwork contains raves about Robbie's performance, but every employer made the same complaints with some calling him 'antisocial.' He was honorably discharged from the Army. It was there he became a news photographer. I found no record of marriages. He has a criminal record in Albany. He assaulted another man in a barroom fight. They were both booked. The Magistrate dismissed the case. The other guy recanted on his first story.

"His reporting is par excellent. Looks as if he's been at every fire site and sometimes gets there before the fire squad gets there. He does have connections, but contrary to what Stacia told us, he pays no one. His home is a two-bedroom condo unit in a decent building. He's on the first floor. I looked in the windows. There were no curtains on the windows and the place looked shabby on the inside. He's originally from Delaware but went to high school in Columbus, Ohio."

Rudy said, "Nothing stands out here other than a profile of a loner who unsuccessfully hits on girls, has no known relations in his world, and is the early arriver at every fire in town. Mason, check all the other cities he worked in for set serial fires with an unknown setter."

"Captain, you think Layden is a Firestarter?"

"Anything is possible. He loves attention. What your background check has not helped with is experience with fire and explosives. The report explains his career in photography, but nothing else. The Army trains, but I don't see his immediate placement in photography. He'd have been in some other training before such as security, weapons, kitchen, etc. It's not in the report."

Mason said, "He was in security, but nothing else was mentioned."

"That helps, that helps. Security training is open after a candidate passes some psychological testing. To you and me, Robbie looks like a smart ass. I think his ego makes him want to achieve. Still he got by those tests. Who fools psychological profiling tests? You know who, Mason, sociopaths. Don't know if he fits the category, but my gut tells me to be careful."

———

Later, a visitor asked to speak with the Captain claiming she had information on Corinne Thompson's death. Rudy greeted her in his office and was taken with her appearance and speech. He thought, *we don't get this type of glamor and refinement all in one package every day.*

Evelyn Heffernan explained she was a dress designer and consultant to several major department stores in Atlanta and Dallas. She'd met Corinne at a spa in New York state and they became good friends. She'd not heard from Corinne and decided to surprise visit her. The surprise was hers when the condo manager explained Corinne had been murdered. "Captain, no one would murder Corinne. She had no man friends other than Art and he was killed with her. If he'd lived I would choose him as her murderer. Unless it was a suicide pact, I don't see it. Besides, Corinne liked her luxurious life and business dealings too much to leave this earth early. She was getting rid of Art. She claimed he'd gotten old for his age and became lazy about business."

Rudy said, "Ms. Heffernan, you were not listed among Corinne's friends in her journal. Do you know why?"

"You mean I'm not under 'F' for friends. Look under 'S' for special. I'm there."

"What is it you know about Corinne's death?"

"I spoke loosely, Captain. I could not have known about her death since I didn't know she had died. What I do know is someone has been blackmailing Corinne for over a year. I'd asked her what the blackmailer had on her. I couldn't understand what it could be because although she was a shark in business, I've seen worse. She said she and her friend Brad were both being extorted for a goodly sum, but not one she couldn't afford to pay, so she paid it. I think you should speak to Brad Surnani.

Corinne thought there were others being extorted. When I asked why, she closed up like a clam. From your reaction, Captain, it appears you know all I know and my visit here was a waste of time. No, I take it back, if I hadn't come, I wouldn't know she had died."

Evelyn sat opposite Rudy with tears dripping down her cheeks leaving a Rudy at wits end. He'd explained to Mona many times that tears reduced his sensible reactions. Bungling in trying to calm her, Rudy asked, "Was Corinne happy with her life?"

Evelyn took a moment before answering. She said, "Corinne was a practical woman who rose from some difficult experiences. For all her sophistication and self-assuredness viewed by others, she could not come out of the closet. I know because I was her lover. She secretly reviled Art, but until recently could not leave the situation. I left our relationship. She called me a few months ago to tell me it was over with Art. I was thrilled until I found out it wasn't completely over because he was sick. She thought it best she not leave him until he was ensconced in his own home. I told her I wasn't going to watch this breakup messiness and to call me when it was really over. I think she was being blackmailed for her choices.

"It's not surprising at all. With me she could share her weaknesses. Why she thought in today's world loving me was a weakness to be kept from others was something I could no longer endure. Captain, I think someone knew she was a lesbian and was blackmailing her. She went bonkers arguing with me that she was doing everything to get out of West Side. She also said she was being watched. It's all she told me."

———

Attorney Cull and Sheila, his Administrative Assistant, were going through Barney's house before the auction company arrived. They had allocated five hours to save any legal documents. Normally one of

Norbie's law associates would purge the home of important papers, but Norbie was still saddened by Barney's surprising death. He thought he owed him. Barney was not a saver with the exception of paper. Norbie told Sheila, "Quite normal with action men. Despite being over ninety-years-old, Barney was spry and went about his various businesses which he had sold but saved a minority interest. He insisted being in the game kept him mentally facile."

Norbie had explained to Barney there may be difficulties in getting real value from a minority share of a business after his death. His answers were consistent. "You'll know the value of my judgment then, Norbie. If they try to screw with you, use all my money to tangle them up in lawsuits. If they're good, give them extra value."

Under Barney's desk was a large box. The two noted with laughter the box had a dress store emblem for a store that went out of business twenty-years before. Inside were photos covering much of Barney's lifetime years. The two spread the photos out group by group on the large trestle table. They drank their coffee while perusing the photos. Barney's childhood pictures gave Norbie such pleasure. Later pictures incorporated his wife, children, and brothers. There were letters written recently and all by hand. There was not a typewriter nor computer in the house, but there were four bookshelves of books. Rudy and Sheila began skimming the letters for legal detail. Sheila spoke first. "Norbie, this one is threatening Barney."

The gist of the correspondence was tremendous anger toward Barney over a supposed agreement. It surprised Norbie because in the past any altercation was brought to him to handle. This one was not known to him. It read, "You SOB. The deal was I would know your choice first. I've done you many favors sharing all the political and business buzz. I got your brother Jake and son Stefan out of trouble by letting you know the problem before the police found them. Some gratitude. You attack me and accuse me of what? Don't go there. You promised me and then I heard you're talking to everybody. You'll learn and so will they. Shut up or else."

There was no date but the letter did not look old. They read some more. Three were from three bidders. All three letters were worded professionally and the tone was friendly. A final cache was a letter written by Brad Surnani, saying, "Barney, do not be fooled by those proposing 'use' for soccer camps and fields. All the bidders including me want the land for its best economic and socially needed cannabis use. There are many other sites in the city more conducive for sports than this site. The others are trying to play you. Let's talk."

A final envelope's content was a handwritten codicil to his will dated a week before Barney's death. The signature was Barney's but the will was written by another's hand. The witness was Corinne Thompson. Norbie seemed annoyed and when pressured by Sheila he said, "More work, Sheila. I will have to verify the codicil. And do you see who is getting half of the value of the land?"

Sheila did and asked, "Why would he throw that money at Darla Richards? I wasn't aware he even knew Darla. He trusted Corinne too.

"Norbie, you didn't know all about his life. The land deal brought you close, but he hadn't been in the office before this land deal for a number of years. You wouldn't know about his recent life. Why didn't he tell you about the nasty note or the codicil? I don't believe it's real. How did he know Darla?"

"Sheila, a motive for Corinne's death is revealed. Brad must have known about Barney's trust in Corinne, unless the codicil is phony and Corinne was not a witness. Call Dec Archer, Sheila. He's a handwriting analyst and the best in New England. Get his opinion in writing."

"How will it help you, Dec doesn't have examples of their signatures."

"Call Beauregard. Perhaps the file will be on his desk. I can only hope."

"Fruit from the poisonous tree, Norbie. You know better."

"Won't matter. It'll never be introduced in court, but will let me know if it's her and Barney's signatures. Who wrote this codicil and why? Who benefits – Darla – and if she dies, the kids? Darla, after Barney's death, becomes the control in the land. Freakin' convoluted, I say. If this codicil is real, it's a reason for Darla's death. She'd never give the land for cannabis use."

Norbie made a call to Beauregard, relayed the news and asked, "Will you see if there is a connection among these three, Barney, Darla, and Corinne? For the life of me I don't get it. When does a man Barney's age associate with two ladies?"

Beauregard laughed. "Barney got around. He knew everybody, Norbie. I'm surprised you would question."

27
Words Again

On a sun lit Sunday morning, Beryl and Oliver were sipping lattes, eating brioche with sour cherry jam from Poland and doing crossword puzzles. Each had a copy of the New York Times and were solving the puzzle in ink with the idea that one could beat the other. Oliver said, "Mom, I'm going to have to fall in love and get a personal life. I'd never tell my friends what I do on a weekend morning."

"It's not that unusual. I've been invited by Kay Whiterly's son to join a crossword puzzles group. They make puzzles and submit them to the local newspapers and other publications. I heard they're quite good."

"Name a publication. I've not heard of them and I get around."

"I think they do all the puzzles included weekly in our free newspaper. Whoever was the lead on a puzzle gets credit for it. They don't sell their puzzles, they give them away. I suppose the free papers can't afford to buy from a computerized crossword service."

She searched the latest free West Side Local for the puzzle of the week. Oliver noticed Beryl's eyes squinch up. He said, "What's up? Really poor stuff! Haven't you done one before?"

"Yes, I do puzzles between reading books to keep the fuzzies away, but this puzzle author is a shock."

She showed him the puzzle and the name attached. It said, "Composed by Robert Layden of the WM Puzzles Group."

"Can it be the photographer? I didn't think words were his strength."

Oliver said, "They aren't. Try having a conversation with him. He's not good at it, which probably explains why he's not too successful with the ladies."

"He may express himself better in written words. I wonder if he and Jay Bird know each other. I had a conversation with Jay where he was defining the use of some words when they were used as a different particle of speech. I'll call Rudy. He might know if they are friends. He'll think I'm nuts but words are important."

The Captain was quite interested in Beryl's comments despite her Sunday morning call. He asked her to detail Jay's comments about words. She did and he said, "Connection, Beryl, you may have helped me with a connection." He said goodbye quickly.

Beryl said to Oliver, "My information rang a bell for Rudy. I think for some reason, he was interested in a connection between Bird and Layden. I never looked for one. I think it unusual; Robbie having interests in words when visuals appear to be his livelihood was surprising to me. Oliver, Robbie was at our speak-out on the Funds Audit. So wasn't Jay. We drew a lot of attention when we rarely have more that twenty-five people witnessing our work."

———

Ted Torrington got the assignment from the Captain. His first call was to his wife Charlotte who was the sister of Mayor Coyne. "Baby, you're in the know. Do you know anything about some crossword puzzle group called Build Crossword Puzzles for Fun that gives them free to organizations?"

"And just why are they on your agenda, darling? Are they a group of serial killers?"

"Not that I know of, but it's weird. There are crossword puzzle digital programs. Why do it when getting a program would be easier?"

Charlotte laughed, saying, "Why mow the lawn with that old time rotary when you could have a ride-em one?"

"That's different. Nothing mows the lawn so perfectly as a rotary. Do you know who the members are? It's important."

"I know two of them. Judy next door and Jay Bird, the author. Call one of them for info. Must I keep quiet about this?"

"Absolutely. Charlotte, it is police business."

He knew those magic works would silence his gregarious wife. His next call was to his neighbor because he didn't want to call Jay Bird. She answered the call and was flattered he trusted her. It was a good call. Judy was secretary to the group and she faxed over a list of names, confirming Robbie Layden was a member. He questioned whether Robbie and Jay were friends. Surprisingly, Robbie brought Jay into the group. With Jay's vocabulary, he immediately became a star.

Minutes later, Ted shared the news with the Captain who said, "A connection I would never have known and a very unlikely connection."

Rudy thought, *new information and most of it undermines our thinking about motive. Scorned lover, greed for a business deal, extortion, serial fires, unknown histories, illegal tapping of federal monies through non-profits, and whatever. Everyone seems interconnected. Who is the lead bad guy now? Surnani is angry with Barney for promises not kept. What promises? Jay and Layden work with words and either could be connected to the cryptic words we received in the mail. Were the messages an invitation to tell us who to look at, or a challenge? They came first before the explosion. Who does that? Maybe it was to warn us about someone, but the writer didn't want to reveal his identity or the writer wanted to laugh at us ahead of time.*

Jay fits one profile and Robbie fits the other. Corinne is a lesbian coming out of the closet at the same time as Darla is enjoying mid-life love. One is Art's girlfriend and one is his wife. Brad Surnani's condo is used for Darla's love affair with Jay, but Corinne keeps Brad's clothes in her closet. Why kill Art now when he is on his way out? Is convenience involved? And what about the damn non-profit thefts with Jay's corporations a recipient along with others. This graft calls attention to the legitimacy of a national federal grant program. Who would be most hurt by the publicity? I've only eliminated John and Nate from my focus. Teisha is in love with James Richards. She has spurned Jay Bird and others. She could be have been a competitive bidder. Barney liked her, and James would have the money from his parents' estate. Getting rid of her may remove her as competition for the land. And the damn extortion plot confounds me. Too many players.

Rudy's ruminations were interrupted by a call from Petra who had visited the lion's mouth at Brad's condo. She said, "Nothing's there. Another resident saw me and laughed at me. He said, 'You're late. Are you police? A man took a package out of there a week ago. There's been no action since. What's going on, drugs or love letters?'

"I scanned photos on my phone for him. He recognized Brad as the man looking in the statue."

The Captain answered, "I'm not surprised, Lieutenant, but I still have no answer."

Rudy made a quick call for a Unit meeting. He laid out his thoughts. After an hour of opinions blasted, the pregnant Lily remarked, "We can't find our way in this maze working in groups. Captain, you insist we go over material many times over a couple of days to take away the drama and our expectations. I need that time. And don't tell me it's because I'm with child."

Juan Flores said, "Lily's right. The answer is before us or not. Give us time, Captain, unless you know the answer."

Beauregard answered, "Unfortunately, this time, I'm right with you. I suspect but don't know and what I suspect doesn't seem plausible."

Norbie Cull running on the treadmill was a sight to behold. Not a tall man but well-built, his energy appeared to move the treadmill. Sergeant Bobby Barr yelled from his resting position after loading weights, "What's the matter, Attorney, one of your clients is charged with murder or some other unspeakable thing?"

"Nah, trying to solve what you guys haven't. If I do, they'll make me detective without being a cop."

And the jabbing continued, forcing them to leave their workouts and sit after grabbing one of the variety of health waters offered. Sipping from their bottles, Cull said, "This stuff is supposed to keep us hydrated. Next year, the FDA will find it's poisonous."

"You are in a pleasant mood today. The treadmill will have to be repaired after your workout."

"Bobby, has your illustrious Captain figured out the motive or motives for this bevy of killings?"

"Yeah, he has about ten motives listed and at least three likely perps, but says we can't use his ideas because there is no certainty. We received all these notes listing synonyms for words like murder. We thought it was a college kid's prank and then all the murders started."

"Whoa, is it a sign of a serial murderer who's making a statement. Serial murderers don't normally send messages until after a first murder. Interesting."

Norbie spent a half hour with Bobby hoping to glean some more privileged info from him, never going too far with his questions which would signal an immediate shutoff of the flow.

Later he thought about the conversation and wondered, *how does this tidbit fit in? Kill for money! Kill from rejection! Kill for greed! Kill from fear of being discovered in an extortion plot! Were the words cut out on paper sent to the police a warning by the killer or by someone who knows the killer?*

News of fires and explosion continued to prevail. Newscasters connected all the fires and despite no confirmation from the police wrote a tale of a serial fire setter. A local clinical psychologist developed a profile for the supposed perpetrator. The public response was interesting. Most thought the description of the perp was too vague. Some added attributes that seemed sensible. The discussions ran over to an acceleration of calls to West Side Fire and Police Departments.

Sergeant Barr, perhaps goaded by his interest in Stacia Kovac, called Robbie Layden's alma mater, South High School. He spoke with a guidance counselor who explained there were two teachers who were still working and were there during Robbie's attendance timeframe. One was still in the building at the time and Bobbie was switched over to his room. Irwin Glasser said he would call back on his cell and in two minutes he was giving a fuller story on Robbie Layden.

"Sergeant, I expected this call twenty years ago. Robbie was a troubled boy. He was smart, but that's not enough. I taught him chemistry. He could have been a chemical engineer. I shouldn't say too much, not what I heard, but only what I witnessed. He couldn't leave a girl alone once he honed in on her. He was a stalker although we didn't use that term then. One gal left chemistry class and I heard later it was to get away from him. He started a small explosion in lab. I thought it was an error. Later a student revealed he did it on purpose. He had absent parents. I know because I called several times and no one returned my calls. He loved attention. I tried to give him a lot of it. It was easy because he was so gifted in chemistry. He didn't want my attention."

"Mr. Glasser, what had you heard but have not told me?"

"It was just a rumor. Columbus had a series of four deliberately set fires at that time, and the students said Robbie set them. I'm pretty certain they were just reacting to the lab explosion."

"Did the police ever find the fire starter?"

"Well no, but the fires stopped."

"Do you know, Mr. Glasser, in what year were the fires set?"

"During spring when Robbie was a senior and had set the lab explosion."

Sergeant Barr asked, "What did Robbie do after high school?"

"The family moved the next day. I know because he was to receive a Best in Chemistry prize at graduation. He did not show. I decided to deliver it to his house and a neighbor said the family had moved. It was not a nice house, Sergeant."

Bobby Barr made notes to himself. In them he wrote, "He's the fire starter and the explosives starter for sure. If I'm right, his motives are to get attention and dispel the loneliness of rejection. The question is what other evil does he have? Greed is a big one in the murder cases."

He yelled over to Bill Border, "Bill, what do we know about Layden's financials? Who was doing that, Ted or Mason?"

"Mason, he's got an in on money matters through his buddy's banking group. They're all from the hood and take financial resources seriously."

A skip away to Lieutenant Smith's office found the IT guru growling at his screen. Wisely, Bobby waited till Mason looked up. "What's up?"

"I'm on this photographer and he is good for a couple of motives. I know nothing about his financials. Didn't come through as did with all the other witnesses. Can you help?"

"Go grab a coffee, Sergeant. This won't take long."

Mason typed away impressing Bobby who thought, *he's a little old to be a gamer. Most of those older guys type with two or four fingers.*

"Lieutenant, where'd you learn to type so fast?"

"My mother decided when I was twelve to put me in a typing class over the summer. It killed my plans and made me look like a sissy in those times. I lied to my friends. Said she had me working to help my Gramma. I am mighty grateful now. This guy Robbie has a nice amount in his checking account. He owns a low-life condo, has a farm in Vermont purchased reasonably, files tax returns as a single man, shows high interest and dividends on his return, and is worth more than a million dollars. For a single guy his age, that's not over the top, but does show he doesn't spend wildly. Given the way inflation's going, he'll be way down in a few years like the rest of us."

"How'd you get all that sensitive information so fast?"

"I have my ways. Now don't you be tellin' the boss."

The Captain was most interested in Robbie's history and didn't question sources. The two discussed motives against Robbie's attributes and both decided greed may not be a motive. Beauregard said, "A sociopath for sure with his history of loneliness and intelligence, and need for unrelenting respect. He needs security also. Why else would a single man who likes attention not spend a little on clothes and parties to attract a woman. Why would someone who wants to be noticed work in a job where he will always be overlooked in comparison to the news anchor unless he wins prizes for his photos.

"Bobby, check how many photos he submitted for the annual news photo awards for the last couple of years. See if they have a record of the photos."

Rudy answered his cell, surprised to hear Beryl's soft voice say, "I think the photographer killed Barney. I don't know why. Remember he is the only one who matches the description of Darla's killer. I can't figure him as going after the land unless he had a deal with someone. Did he know Darla, other than talking to her at events? I've been with Robbie on a few occasions and, Rudy, he can be charming at first. He gets cloying like an overwhelming perfume. It's happened to me before. I get hooked on a perfume smell in the air at a store's cosmetics department. I buy it and can't wear it. The odor is too much. He's just like that. Charming and even witty at first but a half-hour later, I wanted anyone's conversation but his."

"Doesn't make him a killer, Beryl. Tell me what you think about Brad. He's not Corinne's love interest. She was renewing her relationship with a girlfriend. He figures in the blackmail scam. Money is important to him. He knows Darla. How did Darla know Barney?"

"Barney knew everyone according to my friend Kay Whiterly. She said he loved the attention of ladies. Darla was a sweetheart who had more soft charm for politics and business than her husband. I can see her letting both Barney and Robbie into her circle.

"Barney's an old man and lonely. He would have loved her charm. Robbie seems to me a lonely guy, Rudy. Darla couldn't understand how easily Robbie could feel rejection. Have you noticed, Rudy, there are no women connected left? Corinne and Teisha and Darla are all dead."

"What about Brad and Darla?"

"Captain, I don't know. Brad was Art's second in business deals over many years. I don't know why I didn't think of this. You were way ahead of me. Brad may have befriended Darla and it came to more. Do we know anything about his love interests going back to his childhood? Profiling is always about history, isn't it?"

Lieutenant Aylewood-Locke pulled her car next to the news anchor's van. She stepped out and waited for Stacia to finish her interview of Mayor Fischler at his home. Stacia continued to speak with the Mayor as Robbie brought his equipment back to his vehicle affording Petra an opportunity to speak. "Robbie, I was speaking with a young man who would watch Brad's apartment for him. He said you were there about a week ago and picked up an envelope from the lion's statue's mouth. He said you always did that."

Petra had hoped her little insertion of the word 'always' was the truth. Robbie asked, "Why haven't you brought me in for questioning, Petra? You throwing this query out on the fly?"

"Nope, I know what part you played in extorting the others. Not new. Not important except as a motive for murder. You can't hide. I now have a witness who saw you take packages from the lion's mouth. If you have nothing to say, I'll bring you in on blackmail. We have financial records as well to prove our case."

Petra thought, *I did this on a hunch. The Captain will kill me if I'm forced to arrest him now. It's why I'm called 'Bolt.' I like action. We need action here and now. Please, God, make him talk.*

"Lieutenant Petra, nice name, so I picked up an envelope for someone. Why do you care? You'll never get me for blackmail, never. I blackmailed no one."

"What was in the envelope, Robbie?"

"You know what was in it or you wouldn't ask. Money. Cash. Moola."

"Did the moneys in those envelopes belong to you?"

"You might say that."

Petra suggested Robbie come to the station for an interview, or "Instead I'll put you under arrest now. You choose."

Robbie agreed to the interview. Petra insisted he ride with her. Robbie was noticeably upset by this, saying, "Stacia, here are the keys. Get some lunch for me. Pick me up at the station in an hour, ok?"

Petra's entrance to the squad room with Robbie and a uniform officer in tow raised detectives' eyebrows. They headed for Conference Room One. Petra settled the two men in place and headed toward the Captain's office. She was met halfway there. Rudy said, "What's going on here, Lieutenant?"

"I bolted, Captain, and too soon, but I got him to admit he took money from the lion's mouth."

"Maybe you did. You know better. It's not on tape. What were you thinking?"

Rudy called Bill Border over and asked him to be the lead after explaining the surprise visitor. "Question him. When he mentions taking money from the lion's head, read him his rights."

Robbie did not appear under duress when questioned. "Yes, I took money out of the lion's mouth. No, it was not for me. I was a messenger."

He was asked who and why he was a messenger. He said Corinne asked him. He would place these envelopes about once a month. He kept the last one on the 29th because Corinne was dead. "Who received the other envelopes from you and what did you get out of this relationship?"

"Corinne was special. She was a friend. I'd have honored any of her requests. She would help me if I needed it. Her murder confounds the hell out of me. I can't fathom why a person would hurt Corinne."

"And who got the money, Robbie?"

"I think Corinne. Good for her. Probably building up a nest egg to leave the bastard."

"Robbie, where did the money come from? Who would drop it off?"

"I don't know. How the hell would I know?"

"Our witness wrote in his notebook the days and times you watched outside of Brad's condo. You're telling me, you never saw a pickup at the lion's head before? What were the dates of your drops?"

"Corinne asked me to put an envelope in the lion's head on the 27th of the month. I caught Brad putting money in it. I never caught anyone else."

Stacia parked in the visitor's parking lot at the police station. It was a sunny day and she had the windows down enjoying the warm sun. Looking around she thought, *damn, Robbie, this car is a mess. I know we're busy, but this pigsty needs a wash.*

Stacia felt compelled to move some of the boxes and bags in the back seat to find room for her stuff. Robbie's technical photographic and video stuff was in the back of the van. As she started putting folders and packages in order, one flap opened. The box contained electronics. Each item was in plastic and one said igniter. She didn't know what the other labels meant. She realized the box was not original packaging. The items inside had been bagged and relabeled. She continued her work and found boxes with coiled wire. Other boxes contained chemicals without labels. Stacia thought, *it's not him. Please let it not be him. There's an explanation for this. He is into fixing old radios. I think he told me so. I often tune Robbie out when he gets on a technical roll. I don't like this. My job could be on the line.*

Stacia took the keys and locked the van. Across the street from the station was a small convenience store and restaurant. She bought a coffee which was surprisingly good and called Bobby Barr. She insisted he leave what he was doing, saying, "It's police business, Bobby. I hope I'm wrong. Come now."

Sergeant Barr, happily ready to greet his lady, slowed down when he realized there were tears in Stacia's eyes. Before he said hello, Stacia said, "I might be in big trouble, Bobby."

Stacia told him her suspicions and said, "Tell me I'm nuts. Please tell me I'm overwrought. He doesn't always have a mess in the van. It's happened only two or three times. I told him once he better not store personal stuff because the news van could be used by others if their cars aren't available. He said I wasn't to worry. The station would never know about a few personal trips during work hours and that I was an old fuddy-duddy. He'd picked up a few things on the way to work and would unload them at the end of the day. It's scary electric stuff. There is no paperwork attached to any of the boxes both in the back seat and the back of the van. If he'd just bought them, there'd be paperwork, don't you think?"

"Look, Stacia, you don't know what this stuff is and we're not in Jerusalem with bombs going off in the market square. I'll take a look inside and I hope it's a case of an active imagination. You are pretty creative, sweetie."

She said, "He might be leave the station and catch you. I don't want to have to explain anything to him. I think I'm frightened. He's always been a little squirrely, but I assumed it was caused by his discomfort with women."

Bobby called the Captain and requested he keep Mr. Layden busy for another hour. He was told it was no problem.

The two explored the contents of the news van. Bobby said, "Stacia, give me the keys. I don't know what the Captain will decide, but I say you're not crazy. Take my car and go directly home. You are sick, you get me? I'll tell him you called when you didn't know how to get hold of him. You are not crazy and this stuff requires an explanation. I don't want you speaking with him. Can you put a message on your phone so when it answers the caller you say you have COVID?"

Stacia said, "Please don't let him suspect me of colluding with the police. He has loyalty and trust issues. I think he'd get even."

Bobby called Rudy from the conference room and relayed his story. "Captain, you have to protect Stacia from him. I parked the car in the handicapped spot in the visitor's section. There's no handicap plate or hanger. Normally police wouldn't ticket or tow a news van, but it's one way to give us some time."

"No, better would be to go to the owner of the vehicle who is not Robbie Layden. Get the station manager on the phone."

Herb Smith was at the station in less than ten minutes and met the Captain and Bobby at the car. He filled the paperwork as the owner and allowed the search.

The car was impounded and removed from the site. The manager asked, "Please don't find him connected to these fires, but if you do, call me."

Rudy returned to the conference room and motioned for Petra to leave. She terminated the conference but said she would return shortly.

An anxious Robbie was left with the uniform and Bill Border. He said, "Look, Sergeant, your captain and the lieutenant might be able to fudge around, but my news anchor is waiting for me. What more do you want from me?"

When told to Rudy, he said, "Take him into protective custody as a witness. He'll argue. He'll say he has to get the van back and speak with Stacia. Tell him his station manager has come for the car because Stacia has gone home sick. She thinks it's COVID."

"Captain, we're on shaky grounds. He looks good for the fires as a perp, not a witness."

"Yup, but he's a witness in the blackmail scheme and one of those involved is the murderer."

28

Logic Emerges

If excitement could be visualized, then the West Side Police Station would shine like the Christmas star. Petra and Lily, both proponents of moving forward and moving fast, appreciated the shaky arrest of Robbie Layden. Forensics were going through all his boxes from the news station van. Mason awaited results before he could move for a search warrant of Robbie's condo. Bingo, a call from forensics. "Captain, he's a master as far as remote starts and various chemicals. His stuff is consistent with what were used in the fires. Tell Lieutenant Mason he can pick up a copy of the similarities. It should be enough for a warrant. The guy should have joined the fire department. He could light the fires and then watch his work without questions from the police. That's how you got him, right, from pictures of the spectators?"

"Nope, should have. Discovery process took longer."

The Captain asked Petra, "Has he lawyered up yet, Petra?"

"He tried getting Cull. No go, and then he called a few others. He'll likely go out of town for one."

"Get him back in for an interview. He's shaky now. Read him his rights again, and give it a go. Go long and slow. Tell a story. He's like you, Petra. He'll want to hurry the process. Don't let him. Talk a long time about blackmail, and then about fires. He'll get excited. By that time, we'll have searched his crib. Can you go slow?"

"Yup, I will."

"Also ask him about his relationships with all the women killed."

Rudy asked Ted and Juan to join him in his office. The conversation focused on how to connect what was known to the murders. He said, "If Corinne involved him in the blackmail, why would he have killed her? Did he know she'd be there with Art on the bidding day? He does not appear to be interested in money. He doesn't like Jay and Brad. Help me out, guys. Where is this story going?"

Juan said, "I'm a slow goer, Captain, but Bobby's bringing the car in has moved us forward in a big jump for the first time. Let it out there we've made an arrest and then bring in Jay and Brad for questioning. See what happens."

Ted said, "I agree, but first delve into the ladies' relationships with him. I don't think he can take your inferring they dumped him. They probably didn't think they were dumping him. They didn't know he existed as a potential boyfriend. And he does match the description for being around Darla's house before the murder. Make him alibi up. We don't have one on record. Inch by inch is how we'll get there."

Beauregard nodded and smiled.

The authorized court search covered Robbie's condo and personal car. The car was not garaged. Mason's team work tirelessly, excited by instant rewards. The condo was a three-bedroom, not seen so much in modern condos. The building had to be forty years old. The third bedroom was a treasure trove for discovery. Walls were loaded with photos of women. Darla and Teisha photos dominated. What confused Mason were the various stages of the ladies' undress caught by the camera. He noticed the view for the photos was not from inside the room, but through glass. He thought, *the guy's a voyeur. He must have stood outside their windows. Don't most ladies have window coverings on their bedroom windows? Could these be second story windows. There's a couple of Beryl in her kitchen, and one almost nude picture of Corinne in her condo with Art. She looks bored.*

Mason found dozens of photos of other women he could not identify. Two large file drawer cabinets stored photos of fires all labeled by date and time and city. His car was unexpectedly clean and held only one box filled with paper documents. Included were threatening notes to each of the blackmail subjects. What was missing was a copy of notes to bidders. Mason thought, *it's too much to hope. I thought we'd tie up all the incidents, but the explosion can't be connected. Still, we have the type of stuff similar to what was used in the explosion. That and the fact remote starters were used may be enough.*

The bathroom search showed a bottle of aftershave, 'Obsession for Men.'

Beauregard, now informed of the precious loot found at Robbie's place was excited. He waited for progress from Petra's grilling of Robbie. An hour later Robbie's attorney arrived. Boston defense attorney John Skakel shut down further conversation. His client was arrested for arson and murder for the unidentified man in the first of the fires set.

Beauregard consulted with the county's District Attorney who immediately scheduled a news briefing outside the West Side Police Station for the next morning. Rudy advised, "Listen, I can't connect him to the first explosion and resultant deaths. There's enough to consider him as a person of interest, but I don't have motive for the deaths of Art, Corinne, Keisha, or Darla. There is the scent 'Obsession for Men' found in his bathroom. The scent was named by a witness who saw someone near Darla Richards' home. It could put Robbie at the scene on the date and time of her murder."

The District Attorney was sending his Chief ADA over to review the evidence, saying, "She'll take a look. If there's enough for an arrest she'll tell you. An arrest for the other murders will give you time, if you think he's the perpetrator, although I suspect many men use that scent. You make the call. Think about it, Rudy, we don't want a bogus arrest."

Rudy called Oliver Kent and asked him if Leeann could bring Addie in from Vermont for a photo ID. They were in luck, Addie was visiting Leeann for her birthday. The Captain said, "Please ask her to come in for a lineup."

Oliver insisted he be included, saying, "Your presence without me may frighten these women. My presence will be able to assure them."

Rudy then called Lieutenant Stellato in Springfield's MCU. He asked if he could accompany Addie, Leeann, and Oliver to West Side Police, saying, "I can do a lineup and get rid of this identity question."

"Rudy, you do it. I'm busy up to my neck with two killers in three drive-bys. One killed a baby as an extra. If you get an ID, call me. I'll be over for any announcement. You'll hold off on the publicity, right?"

"Absolutely."

Rudy thought, *there won't be enough publicity on Darla's case in Stellato's mind unless the whole world is present. She is a quasi-public figure if not in herself, but in her status as a wife. I know the rules.*

Beryl, when she heard about the lineup from Oliver, marched herself over to the station. Her presence annoyed Beauregard as noticed by Oliver. He said, "Mom, I would tell you everything later. Why did you come?"

"Oliver, I have an interest in these cases preceding your interest."

Oliver questioned no more. The lineup was well done. The Captain asked the men to don the style mask Addie had said was worn by the killer. Addie identified Robbie immediately. Robbie's attorney said, "With the masks on, how do you differentiate? Captain, this identification will not hold up in court."

Beauregard gave instructions for the men to move a certain way as the perp had on the afternoon of Darla's murder. Once more, Addie took seconds to choose Robbie's number. Robbie was quickly read his rights for the new charge for the murder of Darla Richards.

Robbie's attorney insisted there was a problem with the search. Rudy told him, "The court will tell us if so."

Beauregard again called Stellato who quickly agreed to join in the press conference.

———

Beryl Kent did not get to discuss the murder charges against Robbie with the Captain. She hoped he wasn't trying to charge him with Keisha's, Art's, and Corinne's murders. She called Nate and asked if he could meet her for lunch. He already knew about Robbie. "How did you know? I was there. You were not."

Nate insisted she wait until he could explain.

Beryl met Nate at The Crepes Café, knowing they could have a good latte and stuffed crepes, along with the ability to linger. She thought, *there is no motive. Petra told me about the pictures at Robbie's condo. He was covert and clearly invaded the women's spaces. He's a pervert. Nowhere do I see his interest in money. The explosion case is about money and power and perhaps deep resentment against Art and Corinne. That's not Robbie. Keisha's death could be for the same reasons, or not.*

Her first sip of latte quieted the impetuous Beryl. Her questions were not pointed zinger ones. Nate noticed her control, saying, "You want me to explain how I knew about Robbie. I've been working on a string of fires in different states. The authorities in those states asked for help. If a fire starter is not a local wedded to his geographical area, it's difficult for local authorities to catch the culprit. There are multiple current cases of a geographical moving fire starter. West Side's first explosion brought my interest at first, although I quickly realized the perp didn't fit my profile.

"I was then told to explore the fund your audit worked on. Richards was, at first, my interest, because one of his businesses in Virginia got some money from the same fund. Different state but same fund. Everything you touch, Beryl, seems to bring my interest. By the way, I'm retiring in a month. It's time for you and I to discuss our future."

Startled she was, but her second reaction was true Beryl. "How can you bring romance into a serious discussion. I need to put romance off for a few days. You always surprise me. I don't like surprises. I've had too many startling surprises in my life. I'm overwhelmed."

"It's okay to be overwhelmed as long as you're not saying 'no.' Let's talk business."

Beryl sighed, tears fell and yet she laughed. "You do get to me, Nate."

"Well, you insisted in the past that my retirement was a necessary precursor to a life together."

"I am happy, Nate, to eliminate the precursor. The rest comes later. I am happy."

Beryl then said, "Now, to my mixed motives problem. Brad was the orchestrator of the blackmailing of Teisha, Corinne, Darla, himself, and Jay Bird. He included himself in the blackmailing scheme to prove to the others he was also a victim. What I don't know is why Teisha was being blackmailed."

Nate said, "According to Rudy, Abu stated he would partner with anyone who had an edge on the land. We know Teisha and Barney were friendly, enough maybe to give her an edge on the bidding."

"Stop there, Nate. I just remembered something I didn't know enough at the time to question. I spoke with Jay Bird about his status as a bidder. He, at first, denied any status. He said he'd spoken to Cronin about bids. According to Jay, Cronin said the bidding and showing were the next day. That's a lie. Cronin did not know there was a showing the day of the explosion. Why would Jay lie?"

"Beryl, Jay is also mixed up in the fund financial thefts. He is greedy and smart enough to carry out the financial plots. Could he set up the explosion? What is his background?"

"Nate, I don't know but I've read five of his later novels. In two of them the perpetrator murders by use of an incendiary device he remotely sets off. It sounded as if he knew what he was saying. He told me at one point his military experience taught him to sit back and be quiet."

"Strange, I would have said that about myself. I forget what his experience was. Wait a minute, he was in Explosive Ordnance Disposal. Why didn't I remember?"

Beryl said, "It still doesn't help us. Jay and Brad were at the explosion site."

He answered, "You forget, the explosion was set remotely. He could have stood next to you and set it off. You wouldn't know."

Beryl asked, "Why can't I hustle Brad. I'll tell him I know why each one was being blackmailed. And then why he was being blackmailed and it wasn't because he was afraid of Art."

"Okay, Beryl, stop right here. Assign a motive to each. Darla and Jay and Brad, their motives we know. For Corinne, it's to keep silent about her lifestyle. Keisha was being blackmailed about her relationship with Jay before she took up with James. Remember, the payments all started over a year ago. Brad could have blackmailed Keisha because she had something going with Jay before James came into the picture, and she didn't want it known. Notice Brad did not kill her job; Corinne did which was odd behavior. Brad was the nominal death knell on political matters, but he would have known about Keisha and Jay. He knew about everyone. He probably set Jay up with Darla by talking nice about him. You women love a good reference."

Beryl said, "Where are your references, big guy. No one has come forward on your behalf. Jay may be the killer here, but how do we prove it?"

The Captain slammed his fist on the conference room table and said, "I hated algebra when there were more than two variables. X and Y were okay but add a Z and I'd get lost. My math teacher had me do a hundred problems with three variables for me to get it. I've got the Z now. Nate and Beryl and some of you insist Jay is the killer. Of whom? Neither he nor Robbie have a motive for killing Art and Corinne. Jay lies and manipulates for money but I don't see him killing for money. I do see emotional anger in him.

"I see Robbie for the murders of Darla and Barney. I can't connect him to killing Keisha. The motive for killing Art and Corinne still rests in my mind as the land deal. I think the killer blew it up too early. Brad needed to die to get a full benefit from their deaths. He was supposed to be there at the same time as Art and Corinne. He was late. He was meant to die. Now who would benefit from all three deaths? Only one person."

Ted said, "John, the nice guy. How? What's in his background?"

Beauregard said, "You tell me."

Lily answered, "John's business is in fasteners and includes liquid fasteners, Captain. He must have a technical background. If all three were killed in the explosion, he'd be heir apparent for both political acumen and money. But what I don't understand is why John would kill when he is independently wealthy on his own."

Bill answered quickly. "Enough is never enough. He'd be a rock star taking over all of Brad, Art, and Corinne's business. How do we prove it?"

"Bring him in and now. We'll make a start."

Petra said, "Who did Keisha? I don't see Robbie doing it. I don't see John doing it. Who's left?"

"Beryl said Jay does not like being turned down. He has to be the star. I'm thinking about his year-long affair with Darla. Who knew about it? Just about everyone but James and Art. He'd tried to make it with Keisha who is younger and more flamboyant than Darla. She threw him over for James Richards. To top it off, Darla stops paying blackmail money. Why? She found out he was involved. Jay can't take any rejection. My gut tells me I'm right but I can't prove it."

Petra replied, "Captain, get Surnani in here. Remember he said something about he could be next. Play on that fear. He'll fess up about his and Corinne's relationships."

———

Jay and John both appeared for an interview with their attorneys, while Robbie was arraigned in the murder of both Darla and Barney. The video of the now identified SUV owned by Robbie was a major piece of circumstantial evidence. Included in evidence, although not certain, was Jay's knowledge about the land showing and his lying about who told him. Keisha may have told him.

The separated interviews with Jay and John, both of whom considered themselves witnesses, went fairly well for the first half hour.

When Jay was questioned about how Cronin could have given him the date of the bidding when Cronin was not around, he attacked Sergeant Flores, saying, "You don't know where he was. He spoke to me. Now leave that alone.

"You should be looking at that smooth piece of you know what, John Conlon, who wants everything, every dollar. Underneath that handsome friendly façade is a guy who goes for the jugular to get what he wants. He resents me and my relationships with Darla and Keisha. He didn't like my being at Corinne's condo discussing issues. She was an avid reader. His viewpoints are ultra-conservative. Corinne hated him. He took much of her business and as a lesbian, she resented a handsome white guy taking her clients."

Juan asked, "How'd you know Corinne was a lesbian?"

"Anyone with gay radar would know."

"What about your fling with Darla?"

"What about it, Sergeant? It was a fling. It only lasted six months."

Flores asked, "Then why did you and she pay blackmail for longer than that?"

"The blackmailer knew about my relationship with Keisha. Keisha was being blackmailed too, because Abu had a thing for her. She needed him for business. She was a player. Abu didn't like her relationship with me either. Keisha always hid who she was sleeping with from Abu. Then Darla and I got involved. As to Darla, you think I was the only lover. Take my word for it, she's some woman."

"Why did Darla stop paying blackmail while you continued?"

"Robbie told Corrine about my affair with Teisha and in turn she killed Teisha's job. Keisha was out for revenge after that. She found out I was seeing Darla. Corinne knew Brad had a thing for Darla. Fat chance he'd have with her."

"Jay, did that make you hate Keisha so much you'd plan her accident?"

A different Jay appeared. He said, "You can't pin this on me. She was a bimbo. Why would I kill her? I'm famous. Why would I jeopardize my reputation. You have no evidence."

Flores said, "I do. You were identified as the man she had drinks with at the bar before she died."

At first Jay looked shocked but said, "That doesn't make me the killer. Did the bartender see me put something in her drink? No, he didn't because I did not do that. Why would I kill that trash? I'm an author, and she read public relations and gospel books."

Jay was read his rights and taken in as a material witness to Keisha's death. Beauregard cautioned, "Juan, get a search warrant for his home. I'm hoping he kept the drug used on Keisha and check his history with ladies. Get the Feds in here on this. They'll muddy the waters on his participation in the Fund fraud. And have Ted leak Jay's drinking with Teisha before the accident. If Jay doctored Teisha's drink, I'm thinking he did it before. The ladies will come out of the woodwork for this if they were victims."

———

Beauregard asked Petra and Ted to interview John, saying, "I know he murdered Art and Corinne and thought Brad would be there at the same time. He must have ignited the explosion just as he got there. He wanted all they had, Art, Brad, and Corinne."

Petra showed a report from Mason on John. "It's here, Captain. His company uses chemicals for some fasteners. That's proof of understanding. He was in the Army. It's a start. If he killed two of them, then he must be angry Brad is still alive. I'll tell him Darla is Brad's love interest and although he'll get most of Art and Corinne's business, he's really devastated by Darla's death. He'll throw dirt, Captain. I'll close in. I'll do it fast."

"Petra, remember he's murdered two colleagues and shows no guilt. I think he's cool under pressure, but he wants money and status. Get it in the conversation that the land deal is being delayed for several years by Norbie Cull. John thinks he can move right in now that Barney's dead and Art's family will want nothing to do with bidding for the land. They'll stop James from bidding. Use what we know and get him angry. He'll make a mistake. Give me something, enough for a search warrant."

The Captain asked Juan to bring Brad in first for a conversation. Surnani came in quickly. He had heard the rumor that Jay met with Teisha in the bar before the accident. He told Sergeant Flores, "I can't believe that blow-up of an author conned her."

Beauregard joined Petra in the interview with Brad and told a story about blackmail. Petra gave details naming Brad as the original blackmailer including Corinne's and Robbie's involvement. Brad's back went up. "I did not originate it. John Conlon did. He was going to tell everyone about Darla and me and Darla and Jay and about Corinne. At first I didn't know John was the instigator. Imagine in this day and age Corrinne wanted to hide her sexual preference. I always knew. I was her confidante. The extortionist told her she was to put an empty envelope in the lion's mouth at my condo building. She thought I was the extortionist. She asked Robbie to place the envelope. He was her friend or so she thought. She finally told me it was John. She'd figured it out on her own and waited outside for a pickup. It took four days when she saw John's car at my building. He was carrying one of her envelopes. She assumed he was the guy. I decided to blackmail him for the total amount he was getting. He paid."

"Did you repay anyone?"

"Darla. That's why she stopped paying."

"Why her? She was a bit old for you, wasn't she?"

"She threatened to tell everyone. She agreed to shut up if I stopped. I wasn't the blackmailer. I just blackmailed the blackmailer."

"And John, did he know you were blackmailing him?"

"Not that I know. He asked me if I had a problem lately, that I looked stressed. I said I had a money problem, but Art was going to fix it by turning his clients over to me in the next month. He couldn't hide his disgust."

"Brad, you were there a few minutes before John arrived at the explosion. What did he say to you?"

"He seemed surprised. Probably didn't know I was a bidder. He asked if I had gotten a letter. I showed it to him. That's all."

MCU was awash with lawyers waiting to speak with the Captain. He was busy directing traffic to the court for a search warrant on John Conlon's home. Items mentioned related to his checking account, a typewriter to match with the letters sent to the bidders, chemicals and related items, and correspondence with Corrinne and Brad. Three hours later, John Conlon was arrested for the murders of Art and Corinne and the attempted murder of Brad Surnani. He was also charged with blackmail.

That night a small group met at the country club for a toast to Beauregard in absentia. Beryl said, "Beauregard saw through the maze of confusion with three killers, three different primary motives, three sociopaths and five murders. May this never happen again."

Cull toasted his absent friend, saying, "Rudy strips emotion and goes for facts. He has a devious brain. John Conlon was the image of a perfect man. He is a sociopath as are the other two murderers. Jay threw away a prestigious life because of jealousy, anger and resentment. Robbie, well, he may have killed before. Enough of this. I need to go home to my family."

As Nate looked at Oliver and Beryl, he said, "I need to make one."

Care to Review My Book?
(or "Honest Reviews Don't Kill")

Now that you've read the story to the end, I'd love to know what you think of it – and read your honest review about the book on Amazon, Goodreads or other major online book retailers where it is featured.

https://kbpellegrino.com/review-beryl-kent-mixed-motives

Review some of my other books:

https://kbpellegrino.com/review-sunnyside-road
https://kbpellegrino.com/review-mary-lou
https://kbpellegrino.com/review-brothers-from-another-mother
https://kbpellegrino.com/review-him-me-paulie
https://kbpellegrino.com/review-a-predatory-cabal
https://kbpellegrino.com/review-killing-the venerable
https://kbpellegrino.com/review-beryl-kent-bleeding-man

Thank you for your interest in my books!
K.B. Pellegrino

More Books by K.B. Pellegrino

Evil Exists in West Side Trilogy

—Sunnyside Road: Paradise Dissembling

(Livres-Ici Publishing) 2021, (Liferich Publishing) 2018

—Mary Lou: Oh! What Did She Do?

(Livres-Ici Publishing) 2021, (Liferich Publishing) 2018

—Brothers of Another Mother: All for One! Always?

(Livres-Ici Publishing) 2021, (Liferich Publishing) 2019

Other Books in the Captain Beauregard Mystery Series

—Him, Me and Paulie: Drugs, Murder and Undercover

(Livres-Ici Publishing) 2019

—A Predatory Cabal: Worm in the Apple

(Livres-Ici Publishing) 2020

—Killing the Venerable: It's Their Time!

(Livres-Ici Publishing) 2020

—Beryl Kent and the Bleeding Man

(Livres-Ici Publishing) 2021

You can find K. B. Pellegrino's books on all major online Book Stores, such as Amazon, Barnes & Noble, kobo, and iBooks.

Bonuses, Giveaways, and Freebies

Free Chapters

Sunnyside Road: Paradise Dissembling

www.kbpellegrino.com/sunnyside-road/FreeChapter

Mary Lou: Oh! What Did She Do?

www.kbpellegrino.com/mary-lou-free

Brothers of Another Mother: All for One! Always?

www.kbpellegrino.com/brothers/FreeChapter

Him, Me and Paulie: Drugs, Murder and Undercover

www.kbpellegrino.com/him-me-paulie/FreeChapter

A Predatory Cabal: Worm in the Apple

www.kbpellegrino.com/predatory-cabal/FreeChapter

Killing the Venerable: It's Their Time!

www.kbpellegrino.com/killing-the-venerable/FreeChapter

Beryl Kent and the Bleeding Man

https://kbpellegrino.com/beryl-kent-bleeding-man/FreeChapter

Beryl Kent and Mixed Motives

www.kbpellegrino.com/beryl-kent-mixed-motives/FreeChapter

To access more freebies, visit: www.kbpellegrino.com/bonus

Follow K. B. Pellegrino

On her website:
www.kbpellegrino.com

On GoodReads:
https://www.goodreads.com/author/K.B.Pellegrino

On Facebook:
https://www.facebook.com/kbpellegrino

On Instagram:
https://www.instagram.com/kbpellegrino_author/

On Twitter:
https://twitter.com/kbpellegrino

Join My Private Email List

To receive updates about books, new releases, upcoming events, or
to simply keep in touch with me, join my private email list.
We do not release your information to any other vendors.

www.kbpellegrino.com/join-list